Other Titles by Cheryl Brooks

Echoes From the Deep
Dreams From the Deep
Justice From the Deep
Cowboy Delight
Cowboy Heaven
Must Love Cowboys
Unbridled: Unlikely Lovers Book 1
Uninhibited: Unlikely Lovers Book 2
Undeniable: Unlikely Lovers Book 3
Unrivaled: Unlikely Lovers Book 4
The Cat Star Chronicles: Rebel
The Cat Star Chronicles: Wildcat
The Cat Star Chronicles: Stud
The Cat Star Chronicles: Virgin
The Cat Star Chronicles: Hero
The Cat Star Chronicles: Fugitive
The Cat Star Chronicles: Outcast
The Cat Star Chronicles: Rogue
The Cat Star Chronicles: Warrior
The Cat Star Chronicles: Slave
The Cat Star Chronicles Bundle: Slave, Warrior & Rogue
Sharing (Sextet Anthology)
Entanglements (Sextet Anthology)
Occupational Hazards (Sextet Anthology)
Mistletoe & Ménage (Sextet Anthology)
Dirty Dancing (Sextet Anthology)
Small, Medium, & Large (Sextet Presents)
The Lady Takes a Pair (Sextet Presents)
A Tale of Two Knights (Sextet Presents)
Midnight in Reno
If You Could Read My Mind (writing as Samantha R. Michaels

Soul Survivors Book 2

Dreams From the Deep

CHERYL BROOKS

DERRYMANE PRESS

Derrymane
Press

Dreams From the Deep
Soul Survivors Book 2
by Cheryl Brooks
Published by Derrymane Press
Copyright © 2017 Cheryl Brooks.
Cover design by Dragonfly Press Design
Cover image by Adobe Stock
ISBN-13: 978-0-9864274-5-9

www.cherylbrooksonline.com

For the wonderful people of County Kerry

ACKNOWLEDGEMENTS

My heartfelt thanks go out to:

My terrific critique partners, Nan Reinhardt, T.C. Winters, and Sandy James.

My keen-eyed beta reader, Mellanie Szereto.

My buddies in IRWA for their support and encouragement.

My friends and family for their love and understanding.

The wonderful people I met in County Kerry.

And Google Earth for helping me find my way around Ireland.

I couldn't have done this without you!

She alone carries the secret of life's preservation.

Chapter 1

CLEONA MAHONEY STEPPED OUT FROM BENEATH THE ANCIENT TREES and gazed up at a sky shrouded with clouds of quilted gray. Despite the chilly wind, Ireland was a lovely, peaceful country—the perfect cure for the horrors she'd recently endured. If nothing else, her complexion had softened in the days since her arrival. Was the soap responsible or was it the water? Perhaps it was simply the climate, but whatever the reason, she felt more comfortable in her own skin than she had in many years.

If only she could say the same for her mind.

The strange dreams began in Sneem, although there was nothing remotely strange about the charming coastal town. Nothing more sinister than a leprechaun should have lurked in the tiny patch of Irish wilderness on the hill near the hotel. The dark hollow in the mossy tree stretching its roots across the path wasn't home to anything more frightening than squirrels or rabbits. Tumbled stone fences, also blanketed with moss, lay hidden in the shadows created by the dense canopy above—shadows that should have seemed ominous, but somehow weren't. Trailing ivy carpeted the ground as well as the trees, the occasional violet blooming from between the leaves. Nothing strange about that at all.

Leaving the woods behind, she strolled down the hill into town to meet her cousin, Sinead Mahoney, for breakfast. Tourists had arrived by the busload in the town's triangular center, most of them licking ice cream cones and conversing in German or French. Funny how they all *looked* so foreign—and she rarely saw a smile among them. She'd passed a similar group on her way to the round fort at Staigue; none of them had been smiling then either.

"Dour folk," Sinead had muttered in an aside.

Her cousin had been begging her to visit Ireland for so long, Cleona had lost count of how many times she'd had to say no. The last time she'd asked—four months ago, now—Sinead was understandably incredulous.

"D'you really mean it this time? No joking?"

"No joking," Cleona had said. "I'm really coming. It took some doing, but I got my vacation approved for the last two weeks in May."

She would undoubtedly pay for those two weeks with a month of total chaos at the office, but she had deemed it worthwhile. She was finally going to visit the home of her forefathers, although until now, Cleona's name was the only thing about her that hinted at her Irish ancestry. Her accent was as American as apple pie with a touch of western twang, courtesy of her mother's east Texas heritage. Even so, she'd caught herself picking up a slight brogue after only a few days on Irish soil.

"Must come naturally," Sinead had said when she first noticed the change of inflection. "You'll be sounding like a true Irishwoman by the time you leave."

By the time I leave...

Cleona didn't want to go home. The flight from Newark had been miserable—and that was even before the doomed 747 had taken a dive into the North Atlantic. She'd never been able to sleep on a plane, and that flight—the longest she'd ever been on—was no exception. She'd somehow managed to block the horrific ending from her memory, yet tiny images kept popping into her thoughts. Flying had never frightened her before, but having experienced a plane crash firsthand had changed her perceptions, making her want to remain in Ireland forever, never again setting foot inside any contraption with wings.

Unfortunately, her chances of staying put were pretty slim. Her job was in Dallas, not Ireland, and although she'd been issued temporary documents and could depart as scheduled, everything she'd brought with her had gone down with that plane, everything except her life—and the lives of two others.

A total of four, if you count the dog.

All three of the humans were American women in their late twenties: flight attendant Susan Maxwell and two passengers, Jillian Dulaine and Cleona. The three women had endured a bit of celebrity in the wake of the disaster—along with the questions as to how they'd managed to survive when no one else had.

Cleona still had a hard time replying to those queries.

The last thing she remembered was a tray flying up in her face. After that, holding her breath must have been instinctive because after a lung-bursting eternity, her head finally broke through the surface. Inexplicably, she was wearing a life jacket. The coast of Ireland was visible in the distance, and a small flotilla of fishing boats had sailed directly to the crash site as though they'd anticipated the event. Jillian had released a dog from its cage—a cage that had somehow become entangled with another life preserver, making it buoyant enough to float out of the hold. Jillian said she'd been sitting next to the dog's owner and had seen pictures. She even knew the dog's name.

Something in Jillian's expression and Cleona's own peculiar feelings ever since suggested there might be more to it than that. Jillian had shouted the dog's name with such certainty. The dog had even seemed to know her.

Cleona arrived in Sneem a day later than she'd planned, having been issued a clean bill of health by the astonished staff of a Galway hospital, save for a mild concussion and a strange buzzing sound in her ears. Once settled at the hotel, she'd begun having flashbacks of the crash almost immediately. Not of her own experiences, but some that had to have been those of other passengers. Prior to that, she could only assume she'd been too dazed—or sedated—to notice the eerie images. The persistent buzz had since devolved into a cacophony of voices, each attempting to express different thoughts, haunting her like ghosts from within her own mind.

She'd done her best to force those ghosts back into the depths of her psyche without mentioning them to anyone. But the expressions on the faces of the two other survivors also haunted her, making her wonder whether they might also have collected the spirits of those who had perished.

Something Susan had said stuck with her. *That was no accident.* The flight attendant's baby-soft voice had seemed incongruous with her brusque statement, and she spoke, not as though making a guess, but rather as a statement of fact. How could she possibly know for certain unless the dead had been speaking to her?

Cleona had quashed the notion as quickly as it had surfaced, refusing to admit to that level of insanity. Any bizarre imaginings were surely the result of post-traumatic stress—or perhaps survivor's guilt. Even her dreams had been invaded. Sinead must have known sleep wouldn't come easily in the wake of such a tragedy, and she seemed to have been actively trying to wear her out—and her cousin didn't even know the weirdest part.

The dream was always the same. According to his tag, the dog's name was McKnight. Thin and tall with a long tail, he looked like a greyhound and wore a saddle, of all things—a tiny saddle that was small enough to have been a toy, yet appeared to be authentic. Beneath the saddle were festering sores, and a small box labeled "Do not remove" was embedded in his right flank. His collar was embossed with the symbol of a castle with Baja, California written beneath it. What did it mean? Where did he come from and why? In the dream, she'd given the dog a bath and treated his sores.

Then she woke up.

If she'd had nightmares about the crash, she could've understood. But this particular dream made no sense whatsoever. Still, if any country could heal her soul and free her of her troubling dreams, Ireland was perfect for the task. The pace in the west country was gentle, although she doubted that Dublin would have the same relaxed feel.

So much to see, so little time.

Sinead had taken her to places on roads she never would've ventured down on her own, and she'd fallen into bed exhausted each night. But now, she simply wanted to *be* for a while. No rushing about, no obligations, and certainly no travel. Staying put had more appeal than ever before.

Today she and Sinead would set out for the family's farm near Kenmare. Cleona had finally figured out how everything worked in the modern hotel—even the taps and electrical outlets seemed odd at first, and operating the washer and dryer combo was an exercise in futility. Now they would be living in a farmhouse that had been in the family for so long, no one could even say when it was first built. She welcomed the new learning experience as yet another means of diverting her attention from her disturbing thoughts. She longed to focus on more mundane activities, such as how to use an electric tea kettle, which was one of the handier appliances she had yet to run across.

They'd spent some time in Dingle during their sight-seeing travels, having lunch and exploring the shops. Dingle might have been larger than Sneem, but Cleona could still stroll from one end of town to the other—something she'd certainly never done in Dallas—and she enjoyed the small town atmosphere.

Sinead had accompanied her on those outings, but today, she must've sensed that Cleona needed some time alone, having gone ahead to order breakfast, leaving Cleona to catch up after walking the cobwebs from her mind.

The restaurant's neat stone storefront welcomed her with its green and gold sign, charming her with its petunia-stuffed flower pots. The sweet scent followed her inside, mingling briefly with the aroma of sausages and baking bread before being overwhelmed as the door closed behind her.

"I ordered you the full Irish breakfast," Sinead announced.

Cleona took her seat, the chair legs screeching across the floor as she scooted up to the lacquered wooden table. "Can't quite get used to having black pudding with my eggs and bacon, but if you insist..."

"I do." Sinead flipped out her napkin. "All the good Irish meals you've been served have yet to put the roses back in your cheeks. Of course, you actually have to *eat* that food to gain any benefit from it."

"I've eaten plenty," Cleona protested. "Maybe not as much as you, but then, I wasn't blessed with your constitution."

Tall, slender, and blond, Sinead could put away meals that, inside a month, would have rendered Cleona the size of a young whale. If that was indeed her cousin's intention, she had a long way to go. The amount of weight Cleona had lost since the crash would have delighted any desperate dieter, leaving her as thin and pale as the ghosts whispering admonitions to her. That is, if they'd bothered to materialize. So far, all they'd done was talk, and their constant babble had ruined her appetite.

See what you've done to me?

As if shamed into silence, they allowed her a moment's respite before resuming their persistent din. There might have only been a handful of other patrons enjoying their breakfasts in the sunny room, but the noise in her mind was like a sports bar during the World Cup finals.

A waitress with warm brown eyes and softly curling hair brought their plates. Cleona picked up her fork, focusing on the tines before squeezing her eyes closed.

Shut up!

Thinking she might have spoken aloud, she cast an apologetic glance at her cousin. "Sorry."

"For saying I'm a bit piggish?"

Cleona frowned. "Is that what I said?"

"Not exactly," Sinead replied. "But no worries either way."

No worries? Although Cleona envied her cousin's attitude, she had yet to reach that level of complaisance. About the best she could say was that the peculiar voices had diminished over the past few days—in number if not in volume. Was that evidence of her recovery? Perhaps. The doctor had warned her that she might experience headaches and dizziness in addition to her memory loss. Thus far, dizziness had only been a problem once, and though she'd had several headaches, none had lingered long enough for her to take even the mild pain reliever he'd recommended. Of course, he'd never mentioned the possibility that the buzz in her ears might turn out to be voices.

Sinead cleared her throat. "If you're not going to eat that, we should head back to the hotel and check out."

Cleona glanced up from her practically untouched meal, noting that Sinead had already finished her breakfast and was sipping her tea, no doubt anxious to get back to her home. The frequent phone conversations with her boyfriend during the past week proved how much Sinead missed him.

"Sorry." Quickly downing the rest of her egg, she took a bite or two of the bacon and sausage, unable to face even the tiniest taste of the pudding before the waitress brought the bill.

Sinead smiled at her efforts. "Is there anything you want to do here in town before we leave?"

"I just need to mail a postcard, and I'd like to stop at a bookstore."

In addition to the occasional phone call, Cleona had been writing to her family almost daily, reassuring them that she was still alive and well. Something about writing a note and putting a stamp on a letter made her feel more alive.

"I still think you need more clothes," Sinead said with an admonitory wag of her head.

"Are you kidding me? We've already been to every shop in Sneem and most of the stores in Dingle. Trust me, I have plenty to wear. Right now, all I need are some books."

The fact that the entirety of Cleona's belongings fit into one small suitcase was irrelevant anyway. If mere clothing could have erased the residual chill of the North Atlantic, her Aran sweater would have done it with ease. No, what she needed was a good book to silence the voices in her head—something to read at bedtime to keep the memories at bay long enough for her to fall asleep. She only wished she'd hit on that notion sooner. In the wake of the crash, sleep had been hard to come by.

The Irish countryside had helped soothe her during the drive from Connemara to Galway, but the effect had only been temporary. Memories somehow managed to slip past the barriers she'd erected to protect her sanity—creeping thoughts, complete with sights and smells and other sensations that brought it all back. The wake from fishing boats rocking the life raft, simultaneously evoking nausea and hope. The firm grasp of the fisherman's strong, calloused hands as he hoisted her onto his vessel. The scratch of a rough woolen blanket that smelled faintly of fish, but provided more comforting warmth than the softest goose down quilt. The pleasing aroma of freshly brewed tea, mixed with milk and sugar before being thrust into her trembling hands by one of the men. The voices, the clamor, the shocked expressions on the faces of those gathered at the dock at Inisheer.

Then came the cameras, the questions, the officials—concerned but nameless—assuring her that everything would be taken care of and any costs or losses paid for by the airline. She'd certainly had nothing to declare in Customs. Even the clothes she'd been wearing were gone, left behind in an Inisheer hotel room. Only the rings on her fingers and her watch remained—a testament to the water resistance of that particular brand.

The de-Americanization of Cleona had begun. She smiled to herself, wondering how she would handle the culture shock upon her return to Dallas—sprawling, bustling, and hot.

The time spent at the farm would be the vacation from the vacation, and she was looking forward to it far more than touring the rest of County Kerry.

"No problem," Sinead said with a sunny smile. "We can stop at the post office on the way, and there's a bookshop in Kenmare. It won't take long to get there. Thirty minutes, tops."

Cleona rose from her chair, biting back a laugh as she went to pay the bill. She'd already discovered that what appeared to be a short distance on a map took far longer to reach than anyone would expect—that is, anyone who'd never traveled the roads that twisted through the mountains and waterways of Ireland. Even excluding the visit to Bunratty Castle and lunch at Durty Nelly's, the drive from Galway to Sneem would have taken more than three hours. Tours of the Ring of Kerry and the Dingle Peninsula had each taken a full day, stopping at various towns and points of interest along the way.

She and Sinead strolled back to the hotel, chatting about this and that while at the same time drinking in the flavor of the town. Cleona had never seen such beautiful scenery in her life, but even the view from Geokaun Mountain on Valencia Island hadn't silenced the racket in her head. In such a lonely, lofty spot, even ghosts should have had the decency to leave a person alone with her thoughts. She had certainly felt small standing up there—or rather, the world had seemed bigger. Either way, she hadn't been as alone as she'd hoped.

The Fogher Cliffs had reminded her too much of the Cliffs of Moher, which had been the only land visible from the sea where the plane went down. Although she'd been in a life raft at the time and the sight of land should've been encouraging, the mere thought of those cliffs evoked images of lifeless bodies being pounded into nothingness by the constant motion of the sea. Peering down at the churning waves had made her dizzy, and she'd had to lean against the stone abutment until her head cleared.

In those moments, the timeless nature of the rocky island seemed to seep into her bones. Ireland was so steeped in history; the culture, the traditions, and even the language seemed rooted in the distant past. There were plenty of historic sites in Texas, some dating back to the earliest inhabitants. But not even the Alamo had affected her in quite the same manner.

A plaque at the Fogher Cliffs told how the women of Dohilla had traversed a path over Geokaun Mountain to harvest peat. During the space of time it took her to read it, the voices in her head were momentarily silenced as though they also stood in awe of that nearly forgotten time. Those women were gone now, even their path eroded by the sea.

Afterward, she'd had to remind herself she'd actually read that account, and that it hadn't originated with some other source. Even so, the mere mention of peat evoked a long-buried memory of the scent of smoke rising from those fires, a memory that couldn't have come from simply reading about them.

Her thoughts returned to the present as they entered the hotel lobby with its high ceilings, fresh flowers, and stone fireplace. A glimpse of the bar and the elegant dining room through the open doorway reminded Cleona of the dinner they'd enjoyed there the night before. Freshly caught fish and crab in a creamy Parmesan sauce had tempted her appetite better than anything she'd eaten thus far. Even so, she would've done just as well to have ordered a child's portion.

Sinead paid the hotel bill, promising to settle up with Cleona later.

"It's easier this way," she explained.

Cleona doubted that, but for the moment, she let it pass, being preoccupied with matters far more important than mere money. Thus far, she hadn't heard a word from her fellow survivors. Perhaps they felt as strange as she did—apart from the world, somehow changed forever.

She hoped time spent on a peaceful farm would eradicate that feeling.

But she certainly wasn't counting on it.

Chapter 2

CLEONA'S RESPONSE MAY HAVE SOUNDED LIKE A POLITE REJOINDER, but she spoke the truth.

The world should never have been deprived of Kevan MacFinnin.

She was even envious of the breeze that sifted through the dark, curly locks that brushed his shoulders. With full, sensuous lips, a straight nose, and a firm chin, even the rough scarring on his left cheek couldn't diminish his appeal. He was handsome, yes, but there was something else…something about his eyes. She rarely made eye contact with men—especially strangers—tending to let her gaze drift slightly past them. Set beneath brows as thick and dark as his hair, Kevan's brooding eyes compelled her to meet them head on, daring her to glance away.

The touch of his hand had an unexpected effect, silencing the noise in her head. She didn't even realize what had happened until afterward, when the hum of voices resumed.

Great. All she had to do was hold his hand for the rest of her life to find peace—which wasn't a bad thing, actually, although somewhat impractical and difficult to explain. Then again, if simply shaking hands with him could do that, what would happen if she ever made love with him? Would the voices go away for good or would they only be quiet for the duration? Regardless of the outcome, sex with Kevan would be a worthwhile experiment.

For the first time in what seemed like an eternity, genuine laughter bubbled up inside her. Cleona had never been one to make suggestive remarks, but this situation seemed to call for one. Something along the lines of: "Please, Kevan! Make love to me and stop the voices buzzing around in my head forever!"

Yeah, right. Like I would ever actually say something like that.

If it hadn't been for the rather forward and persistent fellow who'd sat beside her in freshman statistics class, Cleona would probably still be a virgin. As it was, her relationship with Billy Everest hadn't lasted more than a month. The sex wasn't bad. She just hadn't cared much for Billy.

Her "haven't met the right guy yet" justification for celibacy had served her well ever since, despite the efforts of well-meaning friends to fix her up with someone new. She suspected Sinead of similar motives, but she honestly couldn't recall that her cousin had ever referred to Kevan as anything other than a friend and neighbor in the many letters and emails they'd exchanged since childhood— certainly not as a potential love interest—although she *had* told Cleona about the tragic incident that left him severely burned while claiming the lives of his parents and several others.

"We're just on our way to the farm," Sinead said, filling the ensuing silence before it had a chance to become awkward. "Come to dinner tonight? I'm sure Mum and Dad would be pleased to see you."

The wording of Sinead's invitation made Cleona wonder how long it had been since anyone aside from his sheep had enjoyed the pleasure of Kevan's company, although his reticence was easy enough to explain. In the past few days, she hadn't had much interest in socializing either. Meeting Kevan changed that, making her anxious to see him again and perhaps discover whether the hum of voices would once again vanish with his touch.

Her breath caught as she waited for his reply.

Expecting a refusal, she was as surprised by his brief nod as she was pleased.

The scene before her shifted, and she lay nestled in his embrace, her sun-warmed skin cooled by a gentle, lilac-scented breeze. Lilting birdsong contrasted with the creaking protest of aged wood as the porch swing upon which they sat swayed to and fro. The touch of his hand comforting her even as the press of his lips sent thrills racing toward her heart.

The sky's brilliant blue made her blink an instant before scudding clouds blocked the sun. All around her, gorse bloomed and sheep bleated. There were birds, yes, but no lilacs anywhere. None in bloom anyway, their early springtime glory having faded as summer approached.

That was weird.

After everything she'd endured recently, nothing should have seemed unusual, and yet it *was* strange. Very strange indeed.

"Great," Sinead said. "We'll see you at six then?"

"I'll be there." With a nod at Cleona, he added, "Nice to meet you."

"Same here."

Still trying to make sense of that peculiar encounter, Cleona trailed along in Sinead's wake as she led the way back to the car. The man intrigued her, and yet she'd practically ignored him while indulging in romantic daydreams. Porch swings and lilacs? Only a loveseat beneath a rose arbor could top that.

Perhaps it was simply her reaction to meeting a handsome Irishman—a *wounded* handsome Irishman. He had Mr. Rochester written all over him. Not the man who fell for his ward's quiet governess, but the man he became after the fire that left him blinded and maimed and longing for Jane Eyre to return to him.

Oh, crap.

Had she seen one of the movies or read the book?

"Both," a chorus of voices replied.

Neither, her own memory insisted.

"You've gotten awfully quiet," Sinead remarked as she fastened her seat belt. "Did the scars bother you?"

Cleona gaped at her cousin for a long moment before arriving at the most logical explanation. "I think it was the blood more than the scars."

"I'm so sorry." She gave Cleona's hand a squeeze. "I should have realized that. Poor Kevan. He's had such a tough time of it, what with everything else that's happened in his life, and now this. The guards are as baffled as the rest of us."

Glancing over her shoulder, Cleona could see Kevan as he crested a low rise near the foot of the hill. He made quite a picture with his dusky curls tossing in the wind and the black and white dog trotting alongside him. She stared at the dog. Long-haired and relatively small, it looked more like the border collie one would expect a sheep farmer to have than the greyhound of her dream, but still, she had to ask: "What's the dog's name?"

If Sinead thought the question was strange, her expression didn't betray her. "Kevan calls him Mac, but his full name is McKnight."

Cleona didn't know whether to laugh or cry.

I should have known...

"Odd name for a dog," Cleona observed once she had her emotions under control.

Sinead shrugged. "Better than Cupcake or Pumpkin, don't you think?"

"I suppose so." Cleona gazed out the window as the car pulled away from the verge. Black peaks loomed in the distance as they rounded the bend. "How far are we from the Black Valley?"

"Not far, as the crow flies."

This time, Cleona truly did laugh. "But miles out of our way by car?"

"A bit," Sinead replied. "We'll take a run through there another day. D'you want to drive on to the bookstore in Kenmare, or stop off home first?"

A tour of the Black Valley could wait. Finding a book couldn't. Hopefully, reading would quiet her mind more effectively than hot showers and relaxation techniques. Watching television hadn't helped at all, and chamomile tea and antihistamines had been as worthless as counting sheep. Given her recent head injury, no conscientious doctor would prescribe anything stronger, and she'd been warned to avoid alcohol. Illicit drugs might have been an option if she knew any drug dealers, but she didn't—not even in Dallas, and certainly not in County Kerry.

Then again, she *was* in Ireland. If reading didn't help, the local pubs would happily provide her with beer and whiskey. She wouldn't be breaking any laws, nor would she need a prescription. All she needed was the gumption to ignore perfectly sound medical advice.

"Let's do the bookstore first."

If that didn't work there was bound to be at least one pub in Kenmare.

Chapter 3

THE HIGHWAY THAT SKIRTED THE LENGTH OF KENMARE BAY provided an excellent view of the rugged coastline and sparkling waters, as well as the misty mountains looming above the opposite shore. Sinead had taken a different route when traveling from Galway to Sneem, but they could have driven down that very same road and Cleona doubted she would have recognized anything now. Still reeling from the effects of the crash, she hadn't been able to appreciate the scenery then and barely remembered the tour of Bunratty Castle and the surrounding park. She vaguely recalled stopping at Moll's Gap, and then there was only a stretch of road that left no room for mistakes, surrounded by mountains, barren and forbidding, until they reached Sneem. The view of those mountains had surely been worth recording, and though the phone she'd been given had a camera, she hadn't had the presence of mind to use it.

"Is there any part of Ireland that doesn't belong on a postcard?"

Sinead chuckled as she dodged a lorry taking a wide turn. "Depends on what sort of pictures you like. Most of Ireland is green and beautiful, but it isn't all sheep pastures and ancient castles, you know."

Recalling the macabre scene of Kevan's butchered sheep, Cleona grimaced. "I suppose that's true of any country." She returned her attention to the mountains and hillsides beyond the bay—rocky outcroppings interspersed with a patchwork of meticulously kept fields. "Funny how a land can be so intensely cultivated and yet still seem so…wild."

"That's because there are some places that can't be tamed and never will be. Parts of the Black Valley are like that—like something out of a dark fantasy. Eerie at times, but breathtaking just the same."

Breathtaking views were everywhere it seemed, many of them bringing back that odd ache near Cleona's right temple. Was it due to the bright light or was it the result of an actual injury? Her head had been x-rayed enough to rule out any fractures. Perhaps this was one of those neck injuries that didn't show up right away, perhaps even causing referred pain. She should probably consult a doctor, but she'd had enough of that in Galway. For the time being, she was willing to blame everything on the concussion that had already been diagnosed.

The bookshop in Kenmare was situated on the main road next to an imposing building that could have passed for a small church, although there was no sign to identify it. The bookshop itself was neat as a pin inside and out, its gold-lettered sign, square windows, and granite gray exterior Irish enough to please the most discriminating reader, whether local or tourist. Determined to avoid mysteries and thrillers—she'd had enough drama in recent days to satisfy any craving she might have had for years to come—Cleona asked for and was directed to the romance section by the pleasant, elderly shopkeeper.

What she needed was a good Regency romance with no violence or murders whatsoever, the only mysteries revolving around what the heroine should wear to the ball and whether the hero would ask her for one dance or a scandalous two. She had chosen three such novels before other items drew her attention, not the least of which a local newspaper that was still reporting the plane crash. Despite not wanting to know what, if anything, had been discovered, Cleona found herself staring at the headline.

Sinead tugged at her hand. "Might be best not to look at that."

Nodding, Cleona drifted into the non-fiction section, hoping nothing more exciting than crossword puzzles would catch her eye. She wanted to put it all behind her, both the parts she remembered and those she didn't, beginning with the first hint of disaster and ending with the gasp of breath that brought with it the acrid fumes of jet fuel mixed with seawater and death.

She paused by a rack of books on local history. Would the crash of Oceana Airways Flight 2324 make it into the history books or would it be swallowed up by time, fading into obscurity like most sensational news of the day? Considering the enormous loss of life, she doubted it would be forgotten anytime soon, and perhaps a lesson would be learned from it. What that lesson might be, she had no idea, but she prayed it would have a positive effect on mankind.

No. People never learn. They kept right on killing each other, and usually did it for stupid reasons or no reason at all. She was sick of it. Surely at some point, everyone would figure out that getting along and working together was in everyone's best interest.

Watching the news horrified her. The vast majority of movies and television shows were just as bad. She wanted to scream at the entire world for finding such carnage entertaining.

What was *wrong* with people? Had the whole world gone mad? Someone certainly had—the person flying that jet for one. Would his motive ever be discovered? She'd heard that several terrorist groups had claimed responsibility for the crash, but no real reason was given, perhaps because terror was a motive in itself.

She was about to scream her frustration when something else caught her eye. There. On the spine of a book. The word *Solar.*

Why that should attract her attention was a mystery. One of the voices in her head—one she actually recognized—spoke clearly and calmly.

"Pick it up, Cleona."

Her hand trembled as she took the volume from the shelf. *The Green Solar Earth* by Jacob D. Emhart.

The title seemed oddly familiar, and yet she was positive she'd never read or even heard of it before. She waited half a beat for the voices to chime in. For once, they were silent.

Except for the one.

"Open it to the back flap."

She obeyed without question, her gaze immediately drawn to the author's photo. His eyes connected with hers in a manner as riveting as meeting Kevan had been, but with an entirely different emotional impact. Time itself screeched to a halt as facts and symbols she couldn't even begin to understand bombarded her jumbled mind.

"What is it?"

Cleona looked up at her cousin's anxious face, only then realizing she'd been staring at the photograph long enough to cause concern. Her hand was numb from the death grip she held on the hard cover, the upper corner biting into her palm.

"I know this man."

"Really?" Sinead's response was normal enough, but she sounded cautious, as though humoring a lunatic. "Who is he?"

Cleona's gaze returned to the smiling bespectacled man with the receding hairline and neatly trimmed beard. "I sat beside him on the plane. I remember now, he's the one who gave me the life jacket. He–he'd leaned forward to get it and got trapped by falling luggage even before the plane hit the water." She shuddered as the memories came flooding back, similar to the way seawater had cascaded into the mangled fuselage. 'He gave me his life jacket, then grasped my hand." She paused, her heart skidding to a sudden—and thankfully brief—halt as realization struck her. "I must've been holding his hand when he died."

"Oh, my." Sinead sounded slightly choked, as though she'd spoken around a huge lump in her throat. "And you're only just remembering this now?"

Cleona nodded. 'Seeing his picture must've triggered the memory." A horrifying memory she could easily have done without. *Thanks a lot, Jacob.*

"Yes, but why on earth would you have picked up that book in the first place?"

Cleona couldn't answer that question without appearing to be even more insane than Sinead already suspected. "I have no idea. My memory is still kinda patchy." That much, at least, was true. "I don't remember actually putting the life jacket on." A short, mirthless laugh escaped her. "That safety instruction spiel must have made more of an impression on me than I thought."

She frowned as yet another detail surfaced. "A flight attendant told us what to do, but her voice was so firm and calm. Nothing like any sane person should have sounded when the whole world was going to hell."

"And no one else heard her?" Not surprisingly, Cleona detected a hint of doubt in her cousin's tone.

"I guess not. Too much screaming, too much noise... Then the plane hit the water. I—I still can't believe I survived. I could almost feel the life being forced from my body. Everything was quieter afterward." She didn't bother to say why that was. Anyone could have concluded that the impact had already killed or rendered everyone else unconscious by the time the interior began filling with water. "I must have unbuckled my seatbelt after that—or maybe it broke. I'm not sure. The next thing I knew, I was floating in the open sea gasping for breath. All I could see were the cliffs and the clouds."

Sinead gripped Cleona's arm, her eyes wide with shock. "How horrible! I mean, I'm so glad you survived, but—" She gestured toward the book. "I still don't see how—" After blurting out those words, she appeared to stop long enough to question her own reaction before adding, "He told you his name?"

Cleona shook her head. "I don't think so. That is, I don't recognize the name, but I do remember the face."

"Read a lot of books on solar energy, do you?" This time, Sinead sounded more skeptical than shocked, her arched brow completing the picture. Cleona couldn't blame her and wouldn't have been a bit surprised if her cousin had taken a step back to avoid a sudden burst of violent, irrational behavior.

Sinead took a deep breath before continuing in a more moderate tone. "What I mean is, his picture is on the *inside* of the book. How could you possibly know he'd written it?"

"I didn't. I just—" She couldn't tell Sinead that a voice inside her head told her to pick up the book, so she settled for the next best thing: a bewildered shrug. "No clue."

"That sounds even weirder," the voice said. *"You can do better than that."*

She thought for a moment. "Well…maybe he *did* tell me his name and I only remember it subconsciously."

Was that her idea or someone else's?

In the end, it didn't matter because it worked; Sinead's doubtful expression vanished. "Seems reasonable. After all, your brains *did* get a bit rattled."

"True." Relieved, she attempted a reassuring smile, for her own benefit as much as her cousin's. "Guess I can expect lots of weird stuff for a while. You'll just have to bear with me."

Sinead returned her smile and patted Cleona's shoulder. "Sorry. My bad. But you look so–so *normal.* I keep forgetting all you've been through."

"Wish I could do the same."

"You will in time," Sinead said wisely. "It heals all wounds, they say."

"Too bad no one can ever tell you how *much* time."

"Ah well, there must be some mysteries in this life." Sinead nodded toward the book. "Are you going to buy that?"

Cleona turned it over, studying the blurb on the back.

"The world doesn't have to end as a barren, global desert. We have the technology and the resources. What we lack is the courage and determination to succeed where others have failed."

Like a voice-over in a movie, a man's voice read the words. Words that Jacob Emhart had written himself. Words that only she could hear.

At least now she knew whose voice that was. If only the others could be identified as easily—although she doubted they were all authors whose books graced the bookstore shelves.

For now, though, they were quiet, the silence even louder than the babble of voices. Perhaps Jacob had them under control somehow—the ringleader of the ghostly band that haunted her. Or perhaps he was waiting for her answer.

"Yeah… I think I should. He saved my life. Buying his book is the very least I can do for his family—I assume they would receive the royalties now."

Did he even have a family? Or was there a foundation of sorts that the sale of his books would fund? She had the genuine article somewhere in her brain. All she had to do was ask him.

"It isn't that simple."

No. Of course not. Nothing ever was.

She bought the book, not batting an eyelash at the thirty-five-euro price tag. The other books were considerably less expensive and would divert her thoughts with no trouble at all.

What Jacob's book had to offer remained to be seen.

* * * *

After leaving the bookshop, they spent a few hours in Kenmare, exploring the shops and enjoying the scenery. Sinead seemed determined to make Cleona's time in Ireland more memorable than the horrors that preceded it, and slowly but surely, she was succeeding. Although the intermittent pain near her temple persisted, the constant hum continued to diminish, and restoring the gaps in her memory had helped more than she ever would have dreamed. The memories might have been terrifying, but at least they were back where they belonged.

Cleona bought a lavender scarf and several pairs of Irish Cottage socks—so called because, like an Irish cottage, they kept one's feet warm in winter and cool in summer. Lunch was a bowl of hot soup and brown bread served at a pub with a battered wooden bar that looked as though it had been in service since the Restoration. She ate as much as she could hold—an amount Sinead had deemed paltry—satisfying both her hunger and a peculiar craving of which she hadn't previously been aware.

They arrived at the Mahoney's farm in late afternoon, just as the setting sun began to work its magic on the landscape, enhancing the colors while diminishing the depth of the shadows. Built in the same style as so many of the older homes Cleona had seen in Ireland, the house was a plain, two-story cottage with chimneys sprouting from either end of its gabled roof. The windows were set deeply in the walls, their frames painted a bright blue with boxes of flowers beneath the sills. Given the age of the building, she wouldn't have been surprised to find the roof still thatched. It wasn't, of course, but though some family forebear had seen fit to update to shingles, the lower maintenance roof didn't detract from the home's inherent charm. Fuchsias crowded the doorway, their bobbing pink and purple blossoms in vivid contrast to the austere white of the stuccoed walls.

Sinead's mother greeted them on the steps with a sweet smile and a motherly hug that quieted the hum in Cleona's head for a moment, although it was more of a collective *"Awww…"* than actual silence.

She's my only aunt, people. Get over it.

Although neither as tall nor as slim as her daughter, Ita Mahoney had the same blond hair, albeit shorter and liberally streaked with gray. Her khaki trousers were slightly rumpled and the sleeves of her plaid flannel shirt were rolled up, exposing the ruddy skin of her muscled forearms and work-roughened hands.

"I heard you drive up," Ita said. "Come on in here, pet. Let me get a look at you."

Cleona's light-sensitivity theory was put to the test as she entered the house. Despite the dim lighting, crossing the threshold triggered yet another twinge of pain. She set her suitcase on a wooden floor worn smooth and shiny with age. The scent of peat smoke permeated the interior, having lingered to the point of becoming part of the house itself.

Ita swept a lock of unruly hair from her forehead, tsking as she subjected Cleona to an overall inspection that could have detected a missing eyelash. "I wouldn't have known you for the wee lass we met in Texas. Goodness, that was ages ago, wasn't it? You're looking a mite peaked, though, luv. We must work on that."

"I've been trying, Mum," Sinead said. "Believe it or not, she looks loads better than she did on Tuesday."

"It's the headaches," Cleona explained. "And my appetite isn't what it should be."

"Nor can pub food compare with good home cooking," Ita said, nodding. "I've a pot o' coddle in the oven and there's a fresh batch of soda bread. Nothing better to put a body to rights."

"I'm sure it'll work wonders." Cleona personally thought coddle was a bit heavy, as anything consisting of bacon, sausages, potatoes, and onions might be. However, as a comfort food, it was right up there with macaroni and cheese.

"Wonders, indeed, ' Ita said. "And to think, you surviving when so many others died. Why, it's nothing short of a miracle."

"That's what Susan—one of the other survivors—said, although I couldn't see the reason for such a miracle then. Still can't." A loud, inner chorus of protests made her wince but didn't set off on another headache.

Weird.

The things that *should* cause a headache didn't—yet another circumstance that defied logic.

"Well, whatever the reason, we're all so very glad we still have you," Ita said, crossing herself. "We can thank the good Lord for that."

Cleona nodded, but she suspected that a number of people saw the outcome in an entirely different light. So many lives lost. So many families destroyed...

She waited for the hum to resume, but it didn't. At least, not right away. Had they been observing a moment of silence to honor all who had died or only those who weren't haunting her? Did each one know what the others were thinking? Were they in communication with one another or only with her? They'd seemed to cooperate when Jacob Emhart had spoken. Perhaps his purpose outweighed the rest—unless that occasion was an isolated incident.

"Shall I show you to your room, then? You'll want to lie down for a bit before dinner. ' Sinead's anxious, cajoling tone suggested she was becoming accustomed to dealing with Cleona's momentary lapses. Either that or she was trying to keep her mother from noticing them, which was probably a wasted effort. Cleona had heard enough tales from Sinead to know that keeping Ita Mahoney in the dark would be about as easy as turning back time. Cleona could save everyone a lot of trouble by telling them the truth right then and there.

Nope. Not ready for that. Aside from the fact that she wasn't sure exactly what the *truth* was.

"A nap sounds pretty good, actually."

"Follow me, then," Sinead said. "We'll wake you in time for dinner."

* * * *

Shafts of sunlight filtered through curtains of Irish lace, bringing with them much sweeter dreams than the recurring nightmare that had plagued Cleona since the crash. Similar to her earlier daydream, they had a pleasant, gentle flavor—more romantic than passionate.

Time slid by as her fingertips threaded through the curls that blew past his scarred cheek. No man had ever affected her the way Kevan had done, causing daydreams and what now seemed to be a waking dream.

Experimentally, she brushed the flat of her hand over his lips. Bluish heat curled around her fingers like tufts of cotton candy. Looking toward the window, she raised the sash with the power of her mind alone. Curtains that had once hung limply now billowed upward on the breeze. Returning her gaze to his face, she reveled in a pair of deep brown eyes that promised greater delights and more love than—

A knock at the door awakened her with a jolt.

"Cleona," Sinead called as she knocked again. "Mum says supper's almost ready. About fifteen minutes or so."

Cleona was on the verge of asking if Kevan had arrived when her cousin pushed the door open a crack and peeked inside.

"Kevan just got here, and he doesn't smell a bit like his sheep." With a throaty laugh, she added, "But then, he always did clean up nice."

Cleona wouldn't have cared if he had dung on his boots. "Be down in a minute."

Snatching up her purse, she rose from the bed and approached the bureau, barely recognizing the pale face in the beveled mirror. Only when she raised a hand to smooth her disheveled hair did she acknowledge that the stranger's face was indeed her own.

For the first time since her arrival in Ireland she wished she'd heeded Sinead's urging to buy some makeup—at the very least something to add color to her cheeks. Unfortunately, it was a little late to make a good first impression.

Not too late for a second one, though.

She brushed out her hair, thankful that her shoulder-length blunt-cut didn't require much fuss and also had the virtue of being easy to put up, giving her less to worry about while keeping the university marketing director's office running smoothly.

Pausing in mid-stroke, she gaped at her reflection. This was the first time she'd given any thought to her job since leaving Dallas. The moment she wondered how her boss was coping without her, she realized she didn't care.

A revelation, indeed.

How would he react to her reluctance to board a plane back to the States?

She could hear him now.

"Get a grip, Mahoney. I need you back here in time to finalize the layout for the fall brochures. I still can't believe you'd up and leave at a time like this "

She had another week to sort out her fears and put them to rest or never go home again.

"You can't go home again."

Was that the name of a book or just the opening line? She didn't know and couldn't believe no one else was chiming in. Perhaps they were discussing the matter in committee before supplying the answer.

"Thomas Wolfe."

She couldn't help but laugh. The gaggle of voices in her head was like having her own private search engine. She didn't even need internet access.

"You all need a name."

Several moments passed. *"Just call us the Collective."*

"Seriously? Sounds a bit sinister. Like the Borg from *Star Trek*."

A chorus of disappointed sighs was still echoing through her mind when she was bombarded with additional suggestions.

"Assembly, congregation, enclave, gang, troupe, band, array—"

"Wait. I like that one."

"Array?"

"Yes."

"Then Array it is."

Fortunately, Sinead had closed the door before the seemingly one-sided conversation began; otherwise, she would've already been dialing up the nearest shrink.

With no rouge to be had, Cleona pinched her cheeks à la Scarlett O'Hara and headed downstairs.

Chapter 4

KEVAN HAD BEEN BAPTIZED AND CONFIRMED IN THE CATHOLIC FAITH, but the death of his parents and the scandals within the church hierarchy had reduced his attendance at Mass to nil, eliminating the need to ever wear his "Sunday best." Thus, the contents of his wardrobe only reflected his occupation, consisting mostly of pullovers, rugged trousers, and work boots. He didn't even own a suit or a tie and preferred to keep his visits to town at a minimum, only occasionally stopping in at a pub.

After a rigorous search of his closet, he managed to find a shirt and a pair of jeans that were both clean and relatively new. That he needed to shower before going to dinner with the Mahoney's was a given. He still couldn't figure out why he'd been invited—or why he'd accepted.

No. He knew exactly why he'd done it. He wanted to see Cleona again.

He showered quickly, leaving his hair damply curling while he shaved and dressed. A bottle of aftershave gave him pause. Not having used anything of the sort in so long, he wouldn't have thought he had any. And yet he did. As he picked up the bottle, he realized it wasn't his. It had belonged to his father.

A good many of his parents' belongings were still scattered about the house. The furnishings, of course, but also other personal items. The aftershave was one. He wore his father's heaviest jacket whenever the weather called for it.

Staring at his reflection, he questioned the need for any ablutions whatsoever. Cleona probably wouldn't even notice that he'd gone to so much trouble to look nice for her. The voice of negativity in the back of his mind told him he was wasting his time. No matter what he did, the disfiguring scars remained, some hidden by his clothing and some not, but his face was the worst.

Had he misread her interest? Was it only pity that prompted her to stroke his cheek?

No mere touch, that. More of a caress, actually.

And then there were the other things. Simply shaking her hand had brightened the world and lifted his spirits.

Had he imagined all of it?

That was another reason for going to dinner. To test the theory. To see if it was a fluke or a figment of his imagination.

Sinead had told him of Cleona's upcoming visit. She hadn't mentioned anything about dinner. Had that been a spur of the moment invitation? Or was it planned?

No. It was because of when they'd met.

Timing is everything.

But then, matchmakers didn't always keep their intended victims informed.

"Victims," he mused. "That sounds pretty harsh."

Perhaps that was all they were to one another. Both victims of terrorist attacks. Both survivors. The only difference was that his scars were visible. Hers probably went deeper.

But then, so did many of his.

Deciding there was nothing further to be done about his appearance, he left the house and climbed into his ancient Volvo, which, like everything else he owned, smelled of sheep. Funny how he'd never paid any attention to that before.

Once he arrived at the Mahoney's house, doubts assailed him once again. He was about to turn around and leave when Ita waved from the porch. He couldn't let her down. She was closer to being his favorite aunt than his nearest neighbor. To leave now would be rude in the extreme.

"There you are, Kevan," she shouted. "And about time too. Supper is almost ready.'

"A much better supper than I'd get at home, no doubt." He climbed out of the car and walked up the stone flags to the house.

Ita dragged him into a hug the moment he set foot on the stoop.

Those hugs had helped him adjust to quite a few changes over the years, and though several years had passed since the last one, he hadn't forgotten the effect. She had a way of hugging more than your body. Ita Mahoney could put her arms around your soul.

He nodded toward the open doorway. "Something smells delicious. But then, your coddle always was the best."

Ita replied with a soft slap on his arm. "Get on in with you, flatterer."

"I only speak the truth," Kevan insisted. "I'm sure anyone else would agree."

"I'll grant you that," she said with a grin. "Ah, Kevan. It's been too long since you came to dinner. I'd all but given up on you ever gracing my table again."

Kevan couldn't blame her for thinking that. Staying home was so much easier, even when sharing a meal with people who cared for him. "I'll try to stop making excuses, then."

"See that you do. Although if I'd only known it would take a visit from my pretty little niece to get you here, I'd have begged her to come sooner." Her expression clouded. "Of course, if she had come another time, she might have been spared."

"Don't be playin' that game, Ita," Kevan cautioned. "I've done enough o' that myself, and believe me, it's all for naught."

"Can't argue with that." With a brisk nod, she led the way to the kitchen where Sinead was setting plates on the table. "Fergus is washing up. Sinead, you can go wake Cleona now that Kevan's here." She gave the pot of coddle a stir, shaking her head. "Poor child had to lie down for a bit. She looked about done in."

"That's my fault," Sinead said. "I've run her ragged trying to keep her occupied." With a shrug, she added, "Seemed best to stick to the original plan."

"Keeping things normal," Ita said with a nod. "Aye. There's a great deal to be said for that."

Sinead started toward the steps, then turned back to give Kevan a hug that was nearly as comforting as one of her mother's. "I'm so glad you came," she whispered, then pulled away and darted up the stone steps to the upper floor.

Fergus came in from the sitting room, his face wreathed in smiles as he gave Kevan's hand a firm shake. Although Kevan hadn't seen him up close in months, he looked the same as he ever had—long, lean, and weathered with a thick thatch of wavy white hair. "Kevan, lad. So good to see you here again." With a wink, he added, "Haven't seen my niece yet. She was napping when I came in. I hear she's a pretty one."

Ita chuckled. "She is at that."

Fergus sat down at the head of the table, and Kevan had taken his usual place on Fergus's left when Sinead returned. "She'll be down in a minute."

Ita set the steaming pot of coddle on a trivet in the middle of the table. "Hope her nap has given her an appetite." She glanced at Sinead. "I got the impression she hasn't been very hungry lately."

"Who could blame her after that frightful business?" Fergus

asked.

"At least she isn't hurt." Ita shuddered. "To think we might be visiting her in hospital at Galway."

"Or going to her funeral," Sinead said. "I still can't believe she survived."

Ita sniffed. "Yes, and she should've been resting instead of gallivanting all over the county, poor thing. I hope you're planning to let her take it easy while she's here."

"We'll let her decide," Sinead said. "Although she did say she wanted to take a drive through the Black Valley."

Kevan was about to volunteer to take her there when Cleona came down the stairs.

Nothing had changed except her appeal, which had inexplicably tripled. Emotions flooded his entire being—desire, longing, and sexual excitement mixed with overwrought nerves and a healthy measure of fear—leaving him not only speechless, but breathless as well.

Fergus stood to greet her with an embrace that tugged at Kevan's heart. He'd done it so easily, so naturally. Then again, the man *was* her uncle.

Maybe I'm going about this the wrong way. Should I hug her or let it pass?

He'd risen from his chair just as Fergus had done, but swayed slightly, barely able to remain upright. Tingles of embarrassment crept up his neck to warm his cheeks as he gripped the table's edge. Cleona triggered something in him. Something latent and nearly forgotten that acted on him like wine and made him dizzy.

Was it love at first sight? Or simply lust?

Either way, he felt rather silly. *She* was the one who'd been in a plane crash. His own injuries had been inflicted long ago; he should have at least been able to stand.

"Better have a seat, pet. Supper's all ready for you to tuck in." Ita had been speaking to Cleona, although the brief glance she'd shot at Kevan made him wonder if she hadn't meant to include him as well.

Cleona smiled shyly "Thank you, Aunt Ita. Everything smells delicious."

Ita flapped a hand before scooting her chair up to the table directly across from Kevan. "Oh, pish. Drop the 'aunt' if you please. Makes me feel right ancient."

Sinead took the seat beside her mother, leaving the remaining empty chair for Cleona. With an inward groan, Kevan realized what he'd done. As was his habit, he'd positioned himself in such a way that no one had to look at his scars while they ate.

No one, that is, except Cleona, who would now be seated to his immediate left.

As she rounded the table, he took advantage of the fact that he was still standing and pulled out his own chair for her. "Better sit here, instead. You'll want to be closer to your aunt and uncle."

Despite seeming flustered by his suggestion, Cleona did as he asked, leaving him to push her chair up to the table.

Large enough to seat eight, the heavy wooden table was probably as old as the house, and given the chance, Kevan probably would've taken the seat at the opposite end instead of sitting beside the only guest. Unfortunately, like most seldom-used surfaces, the far end of the table had drawn clutter like a magnet, the accumulated stacks of magazines and letters giving him no choice but to sit next to Cleona.

Not that he minded. In fact, as a strategy, it was unsurpassed. Not only was she seated on his unaffected side, she would be in his line of sight anytime he spoke to Ita or Fergus.

Mentally patting himself on the back for being so inadvertently clever, Kevan waited while Fergus asked the blessing, even crossing himself at the appropriate times.

He'd all but forgotten what it was like to sit down to a family dinner. Memories of meals with his own family came surging back—laughter, easy conversation, fragrant flowers artlessly arranged in his mother's favorite vase, scones made just the way he liked them, rich mutton stew, steaming hot vegetables, and freshly baked bread.

His mother's garden no longer yielded vegetables or flowers. Only weeds grew there now. He'd told himself he didn't have time for gardening, but that wasn't the real reason. The garden reminded him too much of her, bringing back memories that should have comforted, but only triggered other memories, painful ones that were best forgotten. He dashed away the sting of tears like an annoying itch.

Kevan had never been able to separate the good recollections from the bad, so he rejected them all. Keeping the farm had been hard enough. His first instinct had been to sell out, but because raising sheep allowed him to earn a living while maintaining a relatively solitary existence, he'd chosen to stay on.

He questioned that solitude now. Cleona was so close, her scent reached out to him, awakening his senses as it bound him to her with invisible tethers. Where he had once been chilled, her radiant heat filled him with warmth. Her dark, shining hair begged him to learn its texture. He was at peace and yet he wasn't. Need and longing warred with the fear of rejection—a fear that seemed unreasonable since Cleona had abandoned a simple handshake to touch his scarred cheek.

Calm settled over him like a blanket of down. Whether or not she wanted more from him than that one tiny touch, she was good for his soul. Every sense he possessed swore it was true.

Sinead broke his reverie by offering him a plate of bread. After taking a slice, he passed it on to Cleona. If the plate had been made of copper, it couldn't have conducted the electric charge between them more efficiently. Had his hair had been shorter, it would have stood on end.

Her puzzled frown proved he hadn't imagined the connection. "Did you feel that?"

"A bit of a shock, you mean?"

She nodded. "I didn't think ceramics were good conductors."

"They aren't." Sinead handed him a bowl of coddle, then nudged the butter dish toward her cousin. "You'll love the butter, Cleona. Made with the best Irish cream you'll find anywhere."

Her attention successfully diverted, which had undoubtedly been Sinead's intention, Cleona gaped at Ita. "Don't tell me you make your own butter."

"I do indeed," said Ita. "Just enough for ourselves, mind you. The majority of our herd is beef cattle—Angus, mostly. I've no desire to run a big dairy, but I milk two Holsteins and make our own butter and cheese.

"It's a wonder you have the time," Cleona observed.

Ita shrugged. "I could buy it, of course—and would probably save money if I did. Milking is more of a hobby than a necessity."

Kevan's heart skipped a beat when Cleona turned toward him. "Like knitting sweaters from your sheep's wool?"

"Maybe," he said after assuring himself that his heart was beating once again. "That is, if I'd ever learned how to knit."

"You have to spin it into yarn first," Sinead pointed out. "I've tried spinning. It's harder than you'd think."

"I'm sure it is." Cleona sliced off a pat of butter and spread it on her bread. "I've never done anything like that. My job keeps me busy enough as it is."

"What sort of work do you do?" Kevan's question was more than polite conversation. He would have done anything to keep her talking. Her voice was like a soothing balm to his soul.

"I'm a university marketing director's assistant," she replied. "Which makes me a jack of all trades—or a traffic cop at the very least. I do everything from tracking social media to making sure the right forms get sent to the right people at the right time. Logo use and approvals—that sort of thing." A giggle escaped her. If her smile had made the world brighter, her laughter sent thrills zipping to the far corners of his body. "On a good day, I can anticipate what the boss wants even before he knows he wants it."

"I see," Ita said with a nod. "You're one of those people who work behind the scenes to keep everything running smoothly—like Radar O'Reilly."

Cleona's expression went blank. "Who?"

"Didn't you ever watch *M*A*S*H*? It's an American show. I'd have thought—"

Fergus cleared his throat. "A bit before her time, I believe."

"Mmm, yes." Ita conceded. "But what with the internet and all, you can watch anything nowadays. You just have to know where to look." Returning her attention to Cleona, she added, "I suppose much of your work is done online?"

"Most of it, actually. It's been kinda nice to get away from computers for a while." With a grimace, she bowed her head and muttered something Kevan couldn't hear. "Sorry," she said after a moment's pause. "I'm still not quite myself yet."

"Not to worry, pet," Ita said gently. "These things take time. Hopefully sooner rather than later."

Kevan didn't need the pointed look Ita aimed at him to know what she meant by that. Ten years had passed, and he still wasn't himself. She and Sinead had done their best to keep him from becoming overly isolated. Too bad those efforts had been for naught—until now.

Solitude had begun to grate on him almost from the moment he'd laid eyes on Cleona, a change that intrigued him as much as it would have delighted his neighbors had they known of it. Perhaps they did. The fact that he'd accepted this particular invitation after having refused so many others was an excellent clue.

Cleona's left hand lay in her lap. The impulse to reach over and give it a squeeze was so strong, action preceded awareness by a fraction of a second.

This time, their connection was less like an electric shock and more like flipping a switch or opening a floodgate. Ever so slowly, she turned to face him. The moment their eyes met, her pupils dilated, displaying a montage of flickering images.

"Welcome to the Array."

Chapter 5

KEVAN RELEASED HER HAND, BREAKING THE CONNECTION, BUT NOT before his stunned expression proved he'd heard the same voice.

Turning her thoughts inward, Cleona squeezed her eyes shut and prayed she wasn't speaking aloud. *You didn't say that. Please, please tell me you didn't.*

"He's a conduit, just like you."

That explained why the voices had been quiet when she'd touched him before. They were planning to use him the way they used her. Undaunted, she attempted to close her mind, which, unfortunately, wasn't quite as easy as closing her eyes.

"You can't shut us out," the Array protested. *"Even if you won't acknowledge us, we're still here."*

Haunting her was bad enough. Why did they have to haunt Kevan?

"He can help us," came the reply.

Yeah, right. Cleona was becoming more annoyed by the second. The poor guy had already been through enough to drive him insane. He didn't need the Array messing with his mind.

"We can help him."

Okay. Fine. Help us, then. Tell me where I can go to get rid of you.

A collective chuckle reverberated through her skull. *"A little while ago, you thought we were the next best thing to a search engine."*

She heaved a sigh. *You're right. I did say that. But we need to leave this conversation for another time. Preferably when I'm alone.*

"Gotcha."

Blessed silence followed. She opened her eyes an instant before Kevan averted his own. Clearly he was as weirded out as she was.

A quick glance around the table reassured her to some extent. No one else appeared to have taken any notice. Had they all chosen that particular moment to focus on their food? Or had they simply allowed a private moment between her and Kevan to pass without comment?

Whatever the reason, no one seemed to have the slightest inkling that they were harboring a madwoman. Granted, the conversation with the Array hadn't been lengthy, but Cleona couldn't help wondering if she might appear to be having seizures—the type that manifested as a momentary lapse as opposed to an all-out convulsion. She'd noticed several pangs near her right temple since she'd sat down to eat. What would a neurologist make of that? Probably nothing without a MRI or a CT, and she had no desire to be hauled back to the hospital for more tests. Too many CT scans and she could wind up with brain cancer.

Cheery thought.

Now that the Array had been given a collective voice, the babbling buzz had ceased, which was a miracle in itself. Putting her concerns on hold, she savored the silence, the food, and the sheer joy of sitting beside Kevan MacFinnin.

"This coddle is fabulous, Ita," she said. "The soda bread and butter are great too."

Kevan nodded. "Aye. Like the coddle of old."

She fixed her aunt with a speculative gaze. "Don't suppose you'd part with the recipe, would you?"

"I could," Ita replied. "Although I've heard it's tough to duplicate the ingredients in the States. Might taste different."

"Probably so," Cleona said. "The sausages and bacon back home aren't like these."

"Well, then, you'll just have to stay on, won't you?" Ita's lilting tone and twinkle-eyed smile suggested a tease, but Cleona had heard enough of the same from Sinead to know that mother and daughter shared similar hopes. Cleona still hadn't figured out why, unless it had something to do with the brooding chap to her immediate left.

"Might be worth it at that," she admitted.

Kevan shifted in his seat, drawing her eye.

"What do you think?" she asked him. "Is the coddle worth staying on in Ireland?"

"I believe it is."

When he actually smiled, Cleona nearly fell off her chair. As if it wasn't enough to be broodingly handsome, he was downright cute when he smiled. Charming, sexy, delightful to behold…and hold.

How could she possibly know all that? She'd only met him that afternoon and they hadn't exchanged more than a handful of sentences. Then again, when the chemistry was there…

No. Chemistry wasn't everything. Chemistry was just...chemistry.

"Nothing wrong with that. Chemistry is good. Go for it."

She counted to three and told the Array to mind its own business. This didn't concern them, whoever they were—unless they wanted to live vicariously through her, which was kinda creepy. She needed to have a good, long talk with them. Why were they stuck in her head? What was their purpose?

"We have tasks to accomplish and wishes to fulfill."

Didn't everyone? Cleona couldn't imagine that many lives ended without something left undone.

"It's important."

Some of it, perhaps. But all?

"It is to us. You lost five of our number with dinner."

Lost? So she *was* losing them. With fewer numbers, the clarity of communication had improved, which was a good thing, if a little disturbing. On the other hand, she couldn't help but see the humor. Had Ita's coddle truly been good enough to send five souls on to their reward?

The Array didn't bother to reply, possibly because Kevan spoke up first.

"Aye. A bowl of Ita's coddle can make you feel as though you've died and gone to heaven."

* * * *

Kevan regretted those words the moment they left his mouth. Given Cleona's recent brush with death, his use of that analogy was downright insensitive.

Unbelievably, she laughed. "That explains a lot."

He waited for her to elaborate, but she seemed content to leave it at that. Nor did she mention the peculiar internal voice that had welcomed him to the Array.

While he wanted to believe it was a dream fragment or the replay of some other deep-seated memory, he couldn't shake the notion that someone or some*thing* had actually spoken to him through Cleona.

The counselor who'd taken on his case after his parents' death would've had a field day with that one. The jumble of images he'd seen in her eyes could have simply been a trick of the light, but even chalking the voice up to his own imagination didn't help him make any sense of it.

Welcome to the Array? What the devil did that mean? Meeting

Cleona and shaking hands with her had improved his mood considerably. He could understand that. She was a lovely woman and his attraction to her was strong. But hearing voices when they touched?

That was weird.

Too bad it wasn't something they could discuss over dinner.

Ita barely missed a beat before snatching up the thread of conversation. "Does my cooking truly make you feel better, luv? If so, I need to go to work in a pub. Just imagine the good I could do."

"Aye, that you could," Fergus said with a smile. "But then I'd have to leave home *and* be fightin' a mob o' customers just to get a look at you—not to mention a decent stew. I'd much rather keep you to meself."

Ita sighed. "I suppose it would grow tiresome after a bit. Even something you love becomes work once you start doing it for a paycheck."

"And here I was plannin' on giving you a raise." Fergus took a bite of his bread, chewed it slowly, then swallowed. "Guess that's a no-go."

Cleona bowed her head and pressed her lips together, her shoulders shaking with barely suppressed laughter. Kevan was looking right at her when her sidelong glance caught him watching. He saw no strange, flickering images in her eyes, only mischief dancing beneath her lashes as she put a hand to her lips to hide her smile.

Entranced, Kevan returned her smile. Warmth stole through his body, and he was about to reach for her hand again when Sinead's peal of laughter broke the spell.

"As if Mum wasn't the one managing the money," Sinead said with a snort. Nodding toward her cousin, she added, "Don't let them fool you, Cleona. They really do love each other."

No longer hiding her amusement, Cleona giggled. "I can tell."

"There now, you've made her laugh," Ita said with a satisfied nod. "And would you look at that? If Kevan isn't grinnin' like the cat that got the cream."

His eyes met Ita's, catching the wash of tears pooling in her eyes. He'd been wrong to stay away. These people cared about him, almost as if he were their own son.

"Ah, now, Ita," he said. "You'll be makin' me blush."

"Better that than the sad face you've been showin' round the county." He could've sworn she winked. "More bread, luv?" She motioned for Sinead to pass the bread plate. "Perhaps Cleona might like another slice?"

Ita's tactics were as transparent as rainwater, but Kevan wasn't the least bit bothered by them. He was as curious as she to see if the same shock would result. After selecting a piece for himself, he offered the plate to Cleona, praying she wouldn't refuse.

Unfortunately, all she did was take a slice of bread without touching the plate, only a slight hesitation betraying her apprehension.

Ah, bugger it.

A glance at Ita caught her moue of disappointment. There were only so many ways to connect with the person seated next to you at the dinner table. Simply giving them a nudge was one, but following his inclination to drop an arm around Cleona's shoulders would've been as gauche as it was obvious. Several deep inhalations later, he buttered his bread while trying to ignore the need to wrap Cleona in his arms and hold onto her forever. He might have been back in school again, fighting for control of his raging teenage hormones.

Was there any excuse for a man to grab a woman? Probably not. Not unless she tripped and he somehow managed to catch her before she fell.

Perhaps she's a bit of a klutz.

No. She was graceful and beautiful and had descended those ancient stone steps like Cinderella.

Talk to her.

Small talk? How? What about? He'd already asked about her work.

"They certainly don't have anything like this back home," Cleona was saying. "Unless you go to an Irish restaurant, that is. Too bad my mother wasn't Irish. My father has never been very handy in the kitchen."

"Shame on him," said Ita. "Lettin' you grow up without havin' a taste o' the old country."

Cleona shrugged. "He can't help it if he's not the domestic type, which is probably just as well." She turned toward Kevan. "What about you? Can you cook?"

"If I couldn't, I'd starve," he replied. "I've had no one to cook for me since my mum died."

The loss was old, but it still hurt. Especially on holidays, when he had nothing to celebrate, save for being the one left alive. He suspected that holidays might be a whole lot more interesting with

Cleona around for the festivities.

"My coddle isn't as tasty as Ita's, but it's edible." He drew in a breath for courage. She'd given him an opening. *Don't make a shambles of it now, MacFinnin.* "So, Cleona, where's home?"

"Dallas, Texas." She grinned. "And no, I'm not a cowgirl. Never been on a horse or roped a steer or anything like that."

"Ah, a city lass, then." He smiled back at her. "No worries. We won't hold it against you." About the only thing he might have held against her was having a husband or a boyfriend, and he was fairly certain he wouldn't have been invited to dinner if she'd had either one. Nonetheless, he felt the need to ask. "Married?"

She shook her head. "Quite single."

Ita's sigh was like the cooing of a dove. Clearly this conversation was going in the direction she'd hoped it would.

The trouble was, when it came to chatting with eligible females, Kevan was beyond being out of practice. The best he could manage was, "Same here," even though it was completely redundant to say so.

"Tell me about your sheep," she said.

"I've about fifty ewes—though one less than I had yesterday. The meat is mostly exported and the wool goes to local cottage industries. There's a load o' work goes into raising them. I'm one of the younger sheep farmers around. Many have retired and their children would rather do something a bit less labor intensive."

"That's understandable, but it's good you decided to carry on. There's no job more worthwhile than raising food." Her expression grew thoughtful, her gaze aimed somewhere in the vicinity of the top button of his shirt. "People tend to forget that sometimes and take for granted that there will always be meat and vegetables on their tables." She cleared her throat in a self-conscious manner as a soft blush rose in her cheeks "Sorry. Didn't mean to get all preachy."

Preachy or no, she fascinated him. So much so that for a long moment, all he could do was stare.

"No need to apologize," Fergus put in. "I think everyone at this table would agree with you on that."

Cleona gave her uncle a shy smile before returning her attention to her dinner. She still seemed uncomfortable, though, bringing to mind the voice he'd heard when he'd held her hand. He had yet to make sense of it, if indeed there was any sense to be had. Merely another bizarre event in an otherwise normal life.

Normal, hell. There was nothing normal about either of their lives. Perhaps that was why they'd both reacted the same way. If they'd been alone, he would've asked her. As it was, that question left a gulf between them while at the same time creating a bridge. Perhaps she was unwilling to cross that bridge or to admit to the connection between them. No matter. He had a little time.

"How long are you staying in Ireland?" he asked.

"Until the end of May," Cleona replied. "And believe me, I'm not looking forward to the return flight. They had to sedate me to get me on the plane from Inisheer, and I couldn't face the flight from Connemara to Galway. Susan and Jillian weren't too excited about it either, so they took us there by car."

"Surely a disaster like that couldn't happen again," Ita said. "I mean, what're the odds?"

Slim to none, he'd have said, and if the subsequent exchange of opinions was anything to go by, everyone present agreed.

But there was something different about that crash. He couldn't say what it was or how he knew. The feeling was simply there, festering inside him like an abscess. Or simmering like the anger he still carried for the death of his parents and his own injuries. Now his sheep were being subjected to violence, the reasons for which weren't immediately apparent, but he couldn't shake the notion that there was something deeper, more sinister afoot. More so than mere butchery or criminal intent. A darker evil that touched everyone on the planet.

As though a cloud had passed overhead, his mind slipped back into the brooding depths where it had dwelt for so many years. Perhaps now was the time to seek the greater truths, the whys and wherefores, if indeed there were any. Somewhere in those depths, he saw Cleona as the key.

The key to what? To his redemption? His salvation? His return to sanity?

He studied her from the corner of his eye. What he felt for her was more than physical attraction. She was lovely, yes, but no more so than a thousand others. She possessed some other quality. Something eternal and serene. As he watched her, he couldn't help thinking she was the answer to everything. Every question, every problem, and more.

Perhaps even the meaning of life itself?

The cloud lifted and he realized the utter nonsense in which his thoughts had been engaged. No single person held the key to everything. Such a thing was impossible. Improbable. He was mad to even think it. And yet, there was something not quite of this earth that set her apart from the rest. No one else seemed aware of it. To them, she was simply a relative visiting from the States, one who could just as easily have grown up on a nearby farm.

Her father had been one of those to seek out a different life than the one his own father had lived. He'd not only left the farm, he'd left the country. Kevan could scarcely understand that. True, there were economic reasons for emigration. But to leave Ireland forever? He couldn't fathom such a sacrifice.

"So you'd like to stay on in Ireland?" The words were out of his mouth before he took the time to examine their deeper meaning.

"I would, actually," Cleona replied. "I just need to find a good enough reason to do it. Can't have everyone thinking I'm too chicken to fly home."

"You could take a boat," Fergus suggested.

"Not after what happened to the *Titanic*," Cleona replied. She stopped short and blinked. "Now, why on earth did I say that? Talk about an unreasonable fear..."

"Not really," Kevan said. "I'd say any fears you might have are reasonable at this point. Even modern cruise ships have been known to sink. I'm surprised you can stomach riding in a car."

"Casting aspersions on my driving?" Sinead had been uncharacteristically quiet throughout dinner. He wondered why, especially after she'd been so quick to change the subject when he'd remarked on the peculiar current that had passed between him and Cleona. Almost as if she knew something was amiss. Perhaps he was wrong to believe she hadn't noticed.

Kevan would have liked the opportunity to discuss his suspicions with Sinead, but for now, he deemed it best to give the conversation a nudge in a lighter direction.

Arching a brow at his lifelong friend, he said, "If the lead shoe fits..."

Chapter 6

CLEONA WAS MORE THAN HAPPY TO SIMPLY SIT BACK AND ENJOY THE banter being batted back and forth across the table. Too bad she couldn't say the same about the Array.

What was that bit about the Titanic anyway? If the Array was going to make her sound like an idiot, she wished they'd keep their pet phobias to themselves. *Only useful information from now on,* she scolded. *If you can't come up with a sensible addition to the conversation, for heaven's sake keep quiet.*

She'd been afraid to touch the plate again, not wishing to give the Array another chance to speak to Kevan. What she'd originally thought would save her from the buzz took on an entirely different perspective when they began to include him in their possession—or whatever this was—of her. She leaned forward, rubbing her temples to ease the discomfort.

"Still have the headache, dear?" Ita asked. "Perhaps a tisane would help."

Sinead nodded. "Mum makes a great headache remedy—a mix of peppermint, feverfew, ginger, and chamomile. Works wonders."

"It's certainly worth a try," Cleona said.

"I'm thinking the apple amber Ita made for dessert might help more," Fergus said. "Although I could be wrong."

"I'll take that as a hint." Ita rose from her chair and retrieved a pie from the baker's rack in the corner. "Made it this mornin'."

"*Very* traditional," Sinead added. "Sort of an apple mousse pie topped with meringue."

"Sounds great." With any luck, a single serving would enable a few more members of the Array to move on.

Perhaps I should have them make out a to-do list.

"I'll put the kettle on for the tisane," Ita added. "Might as well try everything."

Everything?

What if she were to kiss Kevan? Would she fulfill the final wish for enough of the Array to put an end to the internal dialogues?

"Sex would be better."

Thankfully, she had the presence of mind to close her eyes before rolling them heavenward. Then again, if Kevan was indeed a conduit, making love with him would cover the wishes of both genders. She could, in effect, kill two birds with—

Sorry. Bad analogy.

"No shit."

When Ita set a piece of pie in front of her, Cleona wasted no time picking up her fork and taking a bite. The delicious flavor had barely registered when a sharp pang knifed through both temples, causing her to suck in a lungful of air that nearly choked her. After a difficult swallow, she had just managed a breathy "Fabulous" when she finally figured it out.

The headaches… That's what happens when some of you leave, isn't it?

"Bingo."

Ita patted her on the shoulder. "Glad you like it, luv. And don't you worry. I'll have that tisane ready in two shakes."

The pain eased quickly and didn't recur with the next mouthful of pie. Apparently everyone on board who regretted dying without ever getting a taste of apple amber had already skedaddled.

That an important task undone or a purpose unfulfilled could have been something as simple as eating a home-cooked Irish meal seemed improbable. And yet, when viewed from the standpoint of having been denied such basic human pleasures, perhaps it made sense after all.

Well done, Ita.

Unfortunately, Cleona doubted the rest of the Array would be gotten rid of quite so easily. Case in point, Jacob Emhart. Among all the others, he alone had identified himself, and if she had to guess, he was still there.

Was he waiting until everyone else was gone? If so, why?

The one time Cleona would've welcomed a discussion, the Array didn't seem to be interested.

Unless they were trying to keep *him* quiet.

Great. I'm dealing with the spirit world version of a gag order.

Maybe not. Surely they hadn't all moved on—unless figuring out the headache aspect shut them up for good.

There was a lot to be said for that. Thus far, Jacob was the only one who had benefitted her, and he'd done it before he joined the Array.

Perhaps the reverse was true. The whole "it's important" thing seemed miles away when she recalled that their numbers had been significantly reduced at dinner.

I really need to get out of my head.

Ita had the tisane ready in considerably less than two shakes, and Cleona sipped it slowly. Her headache had already begun to ease, so she couldn't have said whether the concoction had any effect aside from being pleasantly soothing. Fortunately, no one in the Array appeared to be interested in trying out herbal remedies or drinking the tisane might have brought on a few more pangs. Once again, she let the conversation flow over and around her without contributing much. But Kevan's presence beside her was never far from her thoughts.

"It'll be gettin' dark soon," Ita said when Cleona finally set down her cup. "Sinead, why don't you and Kevan show Cleona around a bit? You two know this farm as well as me or Fergus."

Cleona had no problem agreeing to that suggestion. Strolling through the Irish twilight arm in arm with Kevan certainly had its appeal. And yet, he seemed as shy as an untamed colt. Not wanting to admit it had come from any mind other than her own, she left the origin of that particular comparison alone.

Kevan got up from the table and helped her scoot her chair back. The next best thing would've been his warm hand pressed against the small of her back. Her imagination took over and supplied the necessary sensations. To lean into his hand and then into his arms would be heavenly. The thing was easily done—a stumble would do it.

No. Too contrived. He would recognize the ploy for what it was. But would he mind what she'd done? Really? He might even welcome it. She'd gotten the distinct impression that he would enjoy a bit of feminine attention. Unfortunately, playing games wasn't in her nature, nor was being overly forward. The same could probably be said of Kevan.

As if on cue, Sinead hesitated. "Cleona's probably sick to death of hearing me talk. Think you could go it alone, Kevan? I'll give Mum a hand with the cleaning up." With a sly smile, she added, "Besides, Conall is picking me up in a bit. I do believe he's missed me."

The Array ganging up on her was nothing compared to a mother and daughter in cahoots with each other. If nothing else, she'd have expected Kevan to come up with something better to do.

He didn't object. "Sure. I'd love to." Holding out his hand, he said, "Shall we?"

* * * *

Kevan didn't know who to thank first, Ita or Sinead. Now, if Fergus didn't up and volunteer, he would have it made.

"You didn't have to do this," Cleona said as they headed toward the door. "I'm sure the tour could've waited for another day. You probably have loads to do at home."

"Nothing pressing." He wasn't sure what else to say. "I don't mind a bit."

"I'm surprised you aren't out watching over your sheep."

"To keep them from being killed, you mean? Funny thing, that. It's never happened again straightaway. Always a month or more in between."

"Still, it has to make you wonder, doesn't it? The who and the why of it, I mean."

"Aye, it does." He led the way down the cobbled walk from the house, then turned and walked beside her when the path widened out toward the barn, making a point of staying on her left side. No voices spoke to him, and the evening was quiet save for the chirp of birds, the far-off bleating of his sheep, and the occasional lowing of a cow. Nothing to cause alarm or distress. Only him with Sinead's lovely cousin.

"Must get lonely out here," she said.

"Sometimes." Should he say what was in his mind? Should he succumb to his need to hold her? "I've had my share of loneliness in recent years. I might go for days without seeing another soul."

"I've never been that alone," she said. "But then, I work in an office and live in a huge apartment building."

"Having someone around all the time is no guarantee against being lonely."

She exhaled a fervent sigh. "You got that right."

When was the last time he'd spoken to a woman like this? Regardless of how long it had been, it still seemed like an eternity. If he'd ever been any good at making small talk, he'd forgotten how. Most of his time had been spent avoiding the ladies. The best he could do for now was to be a decent tour guide.

"Ita's garden is over there," he said, pointing. "She's already got some radishes ready to harvest, along with spinach and kale."

Cleona gazed out over the stone-walled garden. "What's that tall, feathery stuff?"

"That'll be asparagus. The season is past now, though."

She walked purposefully toward the plants, then stopped to comb her fingers through the wispy leaves. A delightful tingle tightened his scalp as if she'd done the same thing to his hair.

"I've never seen it growing before," she said. "Only the spears in the grocery."

"It's quite pretty in the morning with the sun and the dew on it. Like a cloud come down to earth."

He pointed out a few other vegetables before they moved on.

"The broccoli and cabbages, I recognize," she said. "But the potatoes had me stumped. I've never seen them growing either."

"Not a farmer, then?"

"Not me or my parents. If it wasn't for his accent, you could almost forget my father was Irish."

"Does he miss Ireland?"

"I'm sure he does, but he's never found the time to visit. Perhaps it's for the best. He might remember more of what he loved about the country and less about why he left it. I think it would be very hard for him to come back now anyway. His life is with my mother in Texas."

Kevan could certainly relate to that. His life was there, in his childhood home, working in the pastures with the sheep, which was why he hadn't left the farm after his own parents were killed.

A tour of the barn followed. The smell of hay and grain, the cluck of chickens, the comforting sound of cows chewing their cuds. All those things he'd taken for granted, never noticing how wonderful it all was.

"Goats too?" Her question ended on a squeal as a nanny goat let out a loud *meh-eh-eh* directly behind her. Kevan caught her in his arms as she leaped sideways.

When she turned in his embrace and pressed her palms against his chest, his entire body reacted with the tight heat of arousal.

"Yikes, what a strange sound! I've never heard a goat before."

"You have now," he said. "Don't you like animals?"

"Oh, I like them well enough. I'm just lacking in experience."

Didn't that say it all? An experienced man would have lifted her face to his with a fingertip beneath her chin. Would have leaned closer while maintaining eye contact, willing her not to turn away. Not to pull back, but to flow into his kiss like a mountain stream into a loch.

A sigh escaped her as their lips met and fused. Moments later, he knew precisely how the asparagus leaves had felt and then some. Her gentle, caressing fingers threaded through his hair, sending wave after wave of sheer excitement rushing over his skin. The feeling was similar to when she'd stroked his cheek earlier that day, but with an entirely different response. The need to possess her threatened to overwhelm him. The need to make her his own…

Suddenly, he was engulfed, plunged into the sea amid a host of thrashing, desperate souls. The efforts of most were futile; only one was successful. All he could do was watch as one by one, the lives around him ended. The scene should have been terrifying and macabre, and yet somehow, it wasn't. It was silent, mystical, surreal.

"We are the Array. The voices of the lost have found refuge here."

There it was again. *The Array.* But what was it?

And then he knew. Beyond a shadow of a doubt, he knew. They were the dead. The doomed souls who had perished all around Cleona while she made her escape to life and freedom. But was this coming to him from her mind? Was he some sort of mind reader, or was she transmitting the knowledge to him? Or had the transference already occurred?

Whatever it was, he had absorbed it through her kiss mere moments before the soft swirling heat of his desire burst into flame. Resistance melted as she pulled him closer. Urgency and need boiled up inside him as he deepened the kiss to express his hunger, pain, yearning, and want.

Want? For sex?

No. For love.

She wasn't running scared; he hadn't frightened her. She was still there, clinging to him, arousing his passionate nature, a dormant aspect of his persona that needed only her and the soft texture of her skin to be awakened. He'd so carefully avoided touching her before. But why? He paused for an instant to pose that question to himself. Unable to think rationally, he ran his hand over her back in long, sweeping strokes. A purr resonated through his head, although he couldn't have said whether it came from her or from him. Time flowed through him like sand escaping a smashed hourglass as invisible fingers both hot and cold played over his skin. Bizarre, spinning sensations whirled him around before hurling him back down to earth with a resounding thud as he was shoved from behind.

Stumbling against Cleona, he somehow managed to regain his balance without dropping her. A glance behind him revealed the culprit. Not the nanny but the billy goat.

"Come to fight over who gets dibs on the females in the flock?"

Cleona giggled. "I think you'd win this female. No contest."

Kevan wasn't sure if that was a commentary on his own appeal or the dearth of desirability in the goat. For the moment, he thought it best not to ask.

So he asked the other question, one that was first and foremost in his mind, even though he was reasonably sure he knew the answer.

"So, tell me, Cleona. What the devil is the 'Array' and what does it have to do with you?"

She took so long to reply, he was beginning to believe she suspected him of being completely mental, an opinion he was leaning toward himself. "You heard them, then."

"Aye, that I did. Mind explaining?"

"I would if I had any idea..." She ran a hand through her hair, gripping her forehead. "No. That isn't true. I know exactly what they are. I even helped choose the name." Raising her head, she fixed him with a slow, assessing stare. "Unfortunately, I only know what, not who, the Array is—except for the one, of course."

"Family?" he suggested before recalling that she'd had no loved ones aboard the flight.

She trembled in his arms as she drew in an unsteady breath. "Not family. A scientist named Jacob Emhart. He...he saved my life. And now he's in the Array." Her voice diminished in volume as she spoke, ending on a whisper.

Kevan considered himself a practical, down-to-earth sort of man, but he couldn't deny that the supernatural was all around him every day. He felt it in the breeze, the scattered raindrops, and smelled it in the scent of gorse. He'd yet to see a leprechaun and didn't particularly care to. But he was in tune with the rhythm of life around him, which might explain why the murder of his sheep had struck such a discordant note. Farmers lost livestock all the time. Not every calf or lamb survived. But this was different, disturbingly so.

"He saved your life? How?"

"At the time, it was as simple as handing me a life jacket," she replied. "But I think there was more to it than that. I don't know how or why, but his purpose must have been more significant than that of the others. Granted, they all had tasks to fulfill and dreams to realize—a number of them moved on after Ita's excellent dinner— but his is the only name I know, and I only know it because I bought his book in Kenmare." She sucked in another uneven breath before continuing. "He told me to pick it up and look at it. I recognized him from the picture on the back flap."

Just when a man should be patting himself on the back for having had the gumption to kiss a pretty woman, the hair on his nape rose instead. "He spoke to you directly?"

She nodded. "I know it sounds crazy but—well, you must know something—*believe* something—for them to speak to you."

"Aye. 'Welcome to the Array,' they said. Had me a bit…" He was hesitant to describe his reaction for fear that she might lose the will to confide in him and end the discussion just when he was getting somewhere.

To his surprise, she filled in the blank without missing a beat. "Weirded out? Yeah. It's like being possessed or haunted, but without the spooky stuff. It's more…" She chewed at her lip while appearing to search for the right word. "…*organic* than that. I can't explain it any other way." Reaching up, she pressed a fingertip to his temple, ramping up the heat between them once more. "When they leave, I feel it there." With a wry grin, she added, "I lost several with that kiss. Apparently a good many of the ladies in the Array came to this country hoping to kiss a handsome Irishman."

She thought him handsome? Despite the disfiguring scars? His throat tightened. When he spoke again, need roughened his voice. "And you? Is that why you came?"

She shook her head. "I came because Sinead has been bugging me to visit for years. But now that I'm finally here, I'd be out of my mind to turn down a kiss."

"Only one kiss?"

Her smile came dangerously close to being coy. "You mean there are more where that came from?"

"Oh, aye. Hundreds…thousands, even." He bent his head closer to hers and pulled her tight against his chest. "But who's counting?"

"Certainly not me." She closed the gap between them until her lips brushed lightly against his. "I'd like to lose count completely."

Joy washed through him, lifting his spirits higher than they'd ever been before. "Well then, Cleona. We'd best be gettin' started."

Chapter 7

GREAT. THE ARRAY MIGHT SHUT UP WHEN SHE WAS IN CLOSE contact with Kevan, but they obviously weren't being quiet on his end.

Still, if kissing Kevan MacFinnin hadn't been on her bucket list, it should have been because the second kiss was even better than the first. More hands, more tongue, more passion, and it was a given no man had ever made her knees weak before—especially not good ol' Billy Everest. Every erogenous zone she possessed awakened with Kevan's first kiss and became downright demanding with the second.

She was beginning to consider the possibility of a roll in the hay when Billy the Goat butted Kevan again, which was probably a good thing since she doubted Kevan had come to dinner with a condom in his pocket. The Array didn't say anything, although she did give some thought to whether they might have jumped over to possess the goat.

"We have no need to do that when we have the two of you."

No worries. I was only kidding. Although she might have guessed the goat remark would get their attention, if indeed *remark* was the right word.

Aloud, she said, "We should head back to the house. These goats are freakin' dangerous."

Kevan nodded. "That they are. And cows are even worse. They can be very aggressive."

"Yeah, well, if I knew someone was planning to turn me into hamburger, I might be a little aggressive myself."

"You have a point—although I doubt they know what's in store for them."

"I dunno… Stranger things have happened. I mean, we have dead people talking to us. Cows could be next."

Kevan burst out laughing, something Cleona suspected he didn't do very often. Whether it was a common occurrence or not didn't matter. Laughter took years off him, not to mention the weight she suspected he'd been carrying on his shoulders for every bit as long. She could have sworn she even heard a chuckle from the Array.

Kevan dropped a casual arm around her shoulders and steered her toward the barn door. "Guess we'd best be getting on before that happens."

The nerves and hesitation were gone. Amazing what a few kisses could do to bring two strangers closer together. She put her arm around his waist and gave him a quick hug, all the while wondering what Sineac and her parents would think if they were to walk into the house that way.

Probably be tickled pink. She was rather pleased by it herself.

"Any plans for tomorrow?" he asked.

"None that I know of, although Sinead may have something in mind. She mentioned a drive through the Black Valley. I don't know how soon, and to be honest, I'd like to chill for a bit myself."

"Been runnin' you ragged, has she?"

She shrugged. "There was a lot to see. Wish I had another month left of my vacation instead of a week."

"So do I."

She waited for him to elaborate, but he didn't. Upon further reflection, she decided he probably didn't need to.

Was it really going to be this easy? After all this time alone? Well, no, she decided. An Irish sheep farmer and an American woman on holiday… Not easy at all.

"Mere technicalities."

Oh, hush up.

"Does the Array talk to you?" she asked Kevan. "They keep popping in with comments here and there. It's kinda weird."

"I suppose it would be," he said. "But to answer your question, in the beginning, I only heard them when I was touching you. Something happened when I kissed you, though. I think some of them may have transferred to me."

Astonishing, yes, but that certainly jibed with the "we have the two of you" rejoinder. "How so?"

"I can't be sure, of course, but I seemed to have experienced the plane crash through them."

"How awful! I wouldn't wish that on anyone." The shudder that swept through her suggested it might be best to lighten the mood, for her sake as well as his. Grumbling, she added, "And here I thought you were overcome with passion."

"That too." He pulled her closer and dropped a kiss on the top of her head. "And let me tell you, it's been a very long time since I felt anything of the kind."

"Same here." She was about to say something along the lines of the two of them having been meant for each other, although even in her own mind the words sounded trite. Then again, perhaps the Array had something to do with the attraction. When all of the Array's goals or tasks were completed, would she and Kevan still share the same bond?

She waited for the Array to chime in, but either they didn't know the answer or they didn't want to be the bearer of bad tidings. Her money was on the latter.

When they reached the house, rather than releasing her as Cleona expected, Kevan held on until the last second before opening the door. "Let me know what you'll be up to tomorrow," he said. "I'd really like to—"

Cleona was waiting for him to finish when Sinead popped in from the kitchen. "Coming over again tomorrow, Kevan? I'll wager your sheep can spare you for a bit."

Kevan gave Cleona's hand a quick squeeze. "With fewer and fewer of them, I'm thinking they could dispense with me altogether."

"Surely not," Cleona protested. "Don't you have to feed and vaccinate them or deliver lambs or something?"

"Not at this time of year. The lambing is over and they're mostly out grazing."

He left the part about the possibility of their being butchered on the hillside unsaid. He probably couldn't do anything to prevent it anyway. Cleona was mulling over the possibility of surveillance cameras when Ita peeped around the corner.

"Irish stew for tomorrow's dinner," she announced. "And sticky toffee pudding for dessert."

Kevan used the hand Cleona had so recently been holding to smite his chest. "Yer killin' me, Ita. Truly, you are."

"Well now, we can't have that, can we? Guess you'd best be stayin' home."

Obviously accustomed to Ita's teasing, he shook his head. "Not to worry. I'll be here." As Ita disappeared back into the kitchen, Kevan turned to Cleona and took her hand in his warm grasp once more. "Lovely meeting you, Cleona." Raising her hand to his lips, he pressed a kiss on her fingers. Without another word, he was out the door.

Sinead exhaled a breath she might have been holding for days.

"Ha! I knew it!"

Not wanting to jump to the wrong conclusion, Cleona asked, "Knew what?"

"That you and Kevan were a perfect match," she replied, her eyes dancing with glee. "I couldn't be more thrilled if I'd won the lottery."

"I dunno," Cleona said. "According to the sign in the store yesterday, the lottery's got a humongous jackpot this week. Not sure Kevan and I are a perfect match either." She was being less than truthful, of course, but saw no point in getting her cousin's hopes up only to have them dashed when the month was out.

"Don't be downplaying it," Sinead said. "I saw the look he gave you—*and* the kiss."

If she thought that was a kiss..."He was only being polite," Cleona insisted.

"That may be, but I believe there's more to it." She grinned. "Humor me, will you? As happy as I've been with Conall, I can't help wishing the same happiness for you."

"Okay, then," Cleona said with a conciliatory nod. "We're madly in love and plan to marry on Saturday."

Sinead rolled her eyes and sniffed. "Even *I* don't believe that. I mean, you do like him, don't you?"

"What's not to like? He's..." She paused long enough to blow out a breath even bigger than Sinead's had been. "Gorgeous, sexy, and very sweet."

"No problem with the scars?"

Cleona shrugged, shaking her head. "Adds to the mystique." As if anything between them needed to be any more mystifying. She was still a bit freaked out that in addition to hearing the Array, he may have acquired several of their number. Not that she minded having them jump ship to be with him, but kisses and such could really be weird in the wake of such a singular event. At least none of them were related to either of them in any way.

That would really *be weird.*

"I'll be sure to tell him you said that. He's practically been a recluse since he left the hospital." All mirth left her, leaving her tone wistful. "I can't tell you how wonderful this is. I haven't seen him smile like that in so long. Sure hope it works out."

"We'll see," Cleona said cautiously. "After all, I only met him today. A lot could change."

"Aye, that's true. But at least there's hope now." At the sound of a car pulling into the drive, she glanced toward the door. "That'll be Conall," she said. "Care to meet him?"

Her casual tone didn't fool Cleona for a second. "Are you kidding me? After all I've heard about him in the past week? Of course I do."

Sinead grinned and took her cousin's hand, practically dragging her out the door. "I'm glad you and Kevan are hitting it off. Otherwise, I'd be afraid you might try to steal Conall from me."

"No chance of that," Cleona said. "I wouldn't spoil your happiness for the world."

* * * *

Kevan drove home, stopping briefly along the road to search the hillside for any sign of trouble among the sheep. Seeing nothing beyond Mac watching over the placid flock, he continued on to the house and parked the car.

Poor Mac. Kevan suspected the dog felt responsible for the deaths, and, not for the first time, he wished his collie could talk. A short whistle brought him running.

"Did ya see anythin', Mac?"

The dog's quiet pant and a wide-legged stance suggested that there was nothing untoward going on, but then, he hadn't alerted Kevan to the previous incidents either.

"Tis a fine shepherd dog *you* are," he chided, lapsing into the broad brogue he tended to use when speaking to animals. "Lettin' some scurvy bastard butcher me sheep."

Mac replied with a yawn and a wag of his tail, clearly denying culpability.

Kevan heaved a resigned sigh and reached down to rub the collie's ears. No. None of this was Mac's fault. He was only a dog, and while he could go in and out of the house as he pleased, apparently on the nights in question, it had "pleased" him to stay inside. Kevan could hardly blame him for that, although Mac usually stayed out at night during the summer months. Perhaps he knew enough to steer clear of madmen with sharp knives.

The best Kevan could hope for was that the killings would end as suddenly and mysteriously as they had begun. He'd done his best to salvage what he could from the loss of fine, healthy ewes, although fearing that the meat might be tainted in some way, he'd saved only the fleece and burned the carcasses.

Such a waste...

He'd even taken to locking his doors, something he'd never

bothered with before. Anyone willing to murder sheep might take a notion to go after other prey. The keys jangled in his pocket as he retrieved them and unlocked the deadbolt. Save for the squeaky slam of the screen door, the kitchen was quiet as he entered. The spicy scent of the soap he'd showered with still lingered, overriding the more homey aromas of bread and bacon. He left the main door open, letting the night breeze blow the sweet scents from the hillside in through the screen.

He swept the kitchen with his gaze. Nothing much had changed since his grandparents' day; the rough wooden table and six sturdy chairs stood in the center of the room as they had always done. Back then, the kitchen had been filled with voices and laughter. Then his grandparents had died one by one, followed by his parents, leaving only himself. He closed his eyes, imagining what it would be like to come home and find someone waiting for him with supper on the table and the kettle on the boil. Finding *Cleona* waiting for him with a warm smile and a fond embrace, and—dare he even think it?— their children clamoring for his attention.

Mac's toenails clicked on the stone flags as he went over to his water bowl, slurping noisily as he lapped up a drink. Had he always been that loud? Or was it simply the stark contrast to the silence?

No. His house was always that quiet. The increase in volume was simply a matter of perspective.

The whole Array thing leaned heavily on perspective as well. If he hadn't heard the voices himself, he'd have thought Cleona was completely daft. She wasn't, of course, unless they'd been drinking the same hallucinogen. Aside from that, there was no other explanation. He couldn't say why he believed some of them had popped over to him—at the moment, they weren't chiming in with much of anything—but he suspected they would when the time was right.

Tasks undone and dreams unfulfilled… Was it truly possible? Just when he should have been waxing poetic about having kissed a woman for the first time in years and possibly making plans for some sort of rendezvous, he was mulling over the possibilities of why she, and subsequently he, had acquired several…

What were they? Passengers? Or had he been possessed? Certainly a benign possession anyway. Might even prove helpful.

If they could only help me figure out what's happening to my sheep.

"All in good time."

"Ah, so you *are* there," he said aloud. "I thought as much. All in good time, you say? I'd rather know the answer now so I can put a stop to it before I lose any more ewes. Or are you more interested in me getting together with Cleona?"

A ripple of decidedly masculine laughter was the only reply.

"I'll take that as a yes." He glanced at Mac, who was eyeing him with interest from his position on the hearthrug. "And, no, I haven't gone *completely* mental. Just a wee bit."

Mac yawned and stretched out with his head between his paws.

"Now, when *you* start talking to me, I'll know I need professional help." To be honest, he wasn't sure he didn't need help already. About the best he could say was that the Array was more concise than wordy. He was fine with that. He would much rather they remained in the background, especially when he was kissing Cleona.

Crossing to the fridge, he took out a Guinness and popped off the cap. One long pull on the bottle had him right back where he should have been.

Fantasizing about Cleona Mahoney.

Caressing her alabaster skin. Gazing into her fathomless brown eyes. Holding her close. Making love to her until he had no strength left in his body. She was beautiful, inside and out. He didn't have to know her well to know that; he could feel it in the depths of his soul. Something about her made him whole again, made him believe in destiny and fate. Her lack had made his life mundane and predictable. Her presence gave him hope and joy.

Now all he had to do was figure out how to keep her in Ireland long enough for her to fall in love with him.

He had until the end of the month to convince her to stay. Given the circumstances of her arrival, boarding another plane was probably the very last thing she wanted to do. However, he saw no need to take advantage of her fears. He would simply do whatever was necessary to keep her from having to take that step.

"Any suggestions?" Although he'd aimed his request at Mac, he was fairly certain the Array was listening. "Surely one of you has been in a similar situation."

"You're on the right track. Go for it."

Then it occurred to him that the Array was made up of passengers aboard a plane. They had no specific qualifications he could research, no history of success he could verify.

"What the devil do you people know?"

Again, the collective, masculine chuckle.

"Yeah," Kevan said. "We're just a bunch of ordinary blokes who don't have the first clue about the workings of the female mind."

He couldn't help laughing himself. Granted, he wasn't alone, but he doubted the help was any better than what he could've gotten by buying his mates a round at McCarthy's pub. Contrary to popular belief, he did go into town for a pint now and then. He just didn't try to chat up any of the ladies present. He had an idea his appearance frightened them—although he suspected Sinead was right about his perpetual scowl keeping them away.

"Yes, but women adore a brooding, wounded hero."

Sure, they might adore a man like that, but would they truly love him or only admire him from afar?

Cleona hadn't been content to stand back and observe. She'd touched his face mere moments after they met. She was different, special.

She was The One.

Chapter 8

CLEONA CLIMBED INTO BED AT THE END OF A VERY UNUSUAL, eventful day. Sinead's boyfriend, Conall O'Mara, had proven to be a pleasant, attractive fellow who appeared to be every bit as taken with Sinead as she was with him. Cleona was very happy for them and more than a little pleased at the improvement in her own love life. On that agreeable note, she fell into a deep, slumberous repose that opened her mind to dreams, allowing her to drift among them like seaweed amid ocean waves.

Kevan became part of her recurring dream, telling her that the dog's name was McKnight. No longer the slim greyhound of her previous dreams, the dog resembled the Mac she knew, the border collie that was Kevan's virtual shadow.

But what did the dog have to do with anything? What did any of it mean? As she asked herself those questions, she became aware that this was yet another waking dream. One she could control to some extent.

She stroked the dog's head. "What are you trying to tell me?"

The collie remained mute, meeting her gaze with steady, solemn eyes.

She glanced at Kevan and saw him whole, unblemished by scars. No more or less handsome, he was the same, and yet somehow different. Unscathed, perhaps? Or was he simply undisturbed by the memories of his tragic past?

He placed a gentle hand on his dog's back. Mac merely thumped his tail in reply, that action drawing her attention to her surroundings for the first time. She knew where she was, even though she'd never been there. She was in the kitchen of Kevan's house—similar to Ita and Fergus's cottage, but with the evidence of a bachelor existence all around her. Surprisingly neat and tidy, the pans he always used were on the stove. One plate and cup in the drying rack along with only one set of flatware and a spatula. One mat lay on the table, the rest of the surface was bare. Oddly, it was a place at the side, not the head of the table. Had he kept on at his same place after his parents died, not moving over to take his father's seat? Was it habit or deference to his parent's memory?

Returning her attention to the injured dog, she touched a sore on his back, which healed instantly. An amazing event, to be sure, but one that was quickly overshadowed by a rising wind that tore through the kitchen. Eevan's dusky curls blew across his face, covering his cheek the way it had done at their first meeting. His eyes smoldered with anger—or was it passion?

Again, Kevan reached out to stroke the collie's fur. At his nod, she did the same.

The air around them stilled as lightning struck nearby, illuminating the room with intolerable brightness. In its wake came a roaring thunder like the sound of mountains colliding.

Now fully awake, she blinked, although the afterimage remained. The man, the dog, and the symbol she'd seen in a dozen other dreams, that of an oddly-shaped castle.

Except that the mention of Baja, California was gone now, replaced by that of Ballycarbery Castle.

She remembered it now.

She'd been there. Even took pictures of it. One up close, and another taken from a distance while standing atop the outer wall of the Cahergall stone fort. The castle was a crumbling ruin with irregular, step-like crenelations above ivy-covered walls. Viewed on a cloudy day against a dark, foreboding sky, she recalled thinking that if ever a castle should have been haunted, that was the one.

No spooky vibe had attached to the other castles she'd toured. She'd kissed the Blarney Stone and felt no peculiar aftereffects, not even the gift of gab, which kissing the stone was purported to bestow. Bunratty Castle and the surrounding Folk Park had been full of tourists. No ghostly images had shown themselves there, even though she'd climbed alone to the very top. Ballycarbery Castle was fenced off, entrance forbidden, undoubtedly due to the treacherous nature of the ancient building.

But was there more than that? Was it truly haunted? Had people run screaming from the castle gates or plunged to their death from the battlements?

Oddly enough, she wasn't the least bit frightened by those possibilities. They were the stuff that fascinated people from all over the globe, drawing the type of tourists who were only looking for a thrill. Having experienced what was possibly the ultimate adrenaline rush and lived to tell about it, she didn't understand the attraction.

Perhaps it was the lack of a safety net that made such things attractive. Although roller coasters sometimes failed, the safety features were built in and no doubt scrupulously maintained. She'd seen people climbing the fence around Ballycarbery Castle and picking their way through the ruins without a second thought.

She hadn't been one of them. Again, any need she might have had for excitement had already been fulfilled in the worst possible way. She wanted to forget about it and enjoy the beauty of Ireland rather than its terrors.

The room was still now. The howling wind had gone, leaving a tiny breath of a breeze in its wake, just enough to stir the lace curtains.

Had the wind been real or was it part of the dream?

Glancing around, she could see nothing amiss, although she might have missed something in a room lit only by the night sky. Funny how clouds could brighten the night even more than the stars. She rose from her bed and checked the casement, then the dresser top where various ornaments sat. Nothing appeared to be overturned or damaged in any way.

Only a dream.

A dream that could easily have been tweaked by more recent events.

Maybe.

Then again, the castle symbol hadn't changed, only her recognition of exactly which castle it was. Too bad it was located on the other side of the county—of the Iveragh Peninsula anyway—and a good hour and a half drive away. Not that she really needed to go there again. At least, she didn't think she did. After all, she'd had no earth-shattering revelation on her previous visit.

But she hadn't met Kevan then, and the fact that his dog's name was McKnight might make a difference. Perhaps the castle held some special meaning for Kevan. Maybe he was the one who needed to go there.

And maybe I'm seeing significance where there is none.

She checked the clock, a little surprised that it read three forty. Her dreams usually occurred later, often right before her alarm went off. Something else was different this time.

A soft bark sounded from beneath her window.

Pushing the window open, she leaned out. Kevan stood in the yard below with Mac sitting beside him. Both were gazing up at her window.

Okay. Now this *is* weird.

"Could you come out, Cleona?" He hadn't raised his voice, and yet she heard him perfectly. She was considering, not the impropriety of the situation, but how the acoustics might have affected the way his voice carried, when he held out his arms. "Please."

The thought of refusing him never entered her mind. "Just a minute."

Snatching up her sweater, she pulled it on over her nightgown and then stepped into her slippers. Her feet made no sound on the stone steps as she crept downstairs. The kitchen was dark, but the aroma of Ita's coddle still lingered as she passed through to the outer door. She pushed it open and went out, pausing only a moment to get her bearings before running lightly down the broad flagstones to where Kevan was waiting.

"I was dreaming about you," she said as she approached him. "And here you are."

The clouds parted briefly, allowing a shaft of moonlight to shine down on him as he smiled. Damn the man, he was even more handsome in the dark.

"I couldn't sleep," he said. "Couldn't wait until daylight to see you again."

If it was a line, it was a good one, and she fell for it. "I must have had the same problem. You were in my dream. Mac was hurt, but he was healed when we touched him. Then there was lightning and thunder and I woke up."

He nodded. "I had the same dream. I'm thinkin' we may need to pay a visit to Ballycarbery Castle."

* * * *

That particular dream wasn't the only reason Kevan was standing beneath Cleona's window like some lovesick Romeo. He'd been feeling that way even before he somehow managed to fall asleep, so her appearance in his dreams wasn't the least bit surprising, nor was the fact that she'd had the same dream. What had him up and dressed before he realized where he was headed was the *nature* of the dream. Although he told himself he was only there to discuss any possible meanings, even he didn't believe the lie.

He was there because he didn't want to spend another night apart from her.

No evidence of shock or disbelief showed in her face or in her stance. "I might have guessed you'd know all about it. As crazy as it sounds, the Array seems to have opened a channel between us."

"You can't read my mind, can you?" Despite the note of levity in his question, he hoped the answer would be no. That would be carrying intimacy uncomfortably far.

Her wry smile proved she understood the humor. "I could make a reasonable guess, of course. But no, I can't tell what you're thinking. We only share the dreams."

Perhaps it was the darkness or the vision of her in a nightgown that made him bold and deepened the timbre of his voice. "I'd like to share more than dreams with you, Cleona."

"Oh? And what would that be?" Once again, he was sure she understood him perfectly.

"Everything," he replied. "Starting with this."

He pulled her into his arms and kissed her ruthlessly, like some swashbuckling hero of days gone by who had finally caught his heroine alone and unprotected. She clung to him as any fair maiden would have done, encircling his neck with her arms and kissing him with a fervor that spoke of years yearning for this one fleeting moment alone with her true love.

His body was already primed for a clandestine meeting. Nevertheless, even more heat surged to his groin, demanding release. He couldn't do that, of course. Making love with Cleona, right here, right now? The idea was absurd. And yet that was exactly what he longed to do. Lie her down on a bed of flowers and taste and feel all she had to offer.

This time, there were no goats or other livestock to intervene. Only the night and hot, frenzied hunger. He'd never kissed anyone like this. Never even imagined a kiss could be so emotionally charged as to make him forget everything except the woman in his arms. Her scent filled his head, deluging him with the need to taste, to feel, to *know*…

He knew the moment she surrendered. Softening in his embrace, she melted against him, rippling tremors betraying the unsteadiness of her legs. He could have done anything with her then, even something as outrageous as making love to her in Ita's garden in the middle of the night. Letting her slip to the ground, pulling him down with her…

He was a heartbeat away from doing just that when reason prevailed—her reason, not his. Breaking the kiss, she eased back to rest her forehead against his chest, her deep, rapid breaths proving she was as overcome as he. With a tiny gulp, she slid her hands from his neck to curl them around his waist and glide up his back.

"You feel so good," she whispered. "Like you— Like we—" She paused, shaking her head. "I don't know...*belong* together or something. The first time I touched you, the Array finally shut up. I wasn't sure why then. Now I wonder if it was because they recognized the uniqueness of our connection." She hugged him hard, as though demonstrating just how real that connection was.

All Kevan knew was how perfect she felt with her arms around him and his arms around her. Joined. United in a way that defied description. Was this how everyone felt when they found the love of their life? How would he know? How could he possibly know?

And yet, he did. He knew it for a fact. Even if every voice in the Array hadn't assured him that it was true, he would have known. He didn't need them to explain his reaction to Cleona. She was an explanation in herself. The missing piece of his heart that he'd lost so long ago.

"I'm sure you're right," he said. "I only hope they stay quiet. Imagine how embarrassing that would be."

"Earlier, I thought that if touching you had that effect, I never wanted to let go."

"As good a reason as any. You certainly won't hear any complaints from me."

She took a deep breath as if to steady her nerves, although as shaky as that breath was, he doubted it did her any good.

"Not now, though," she said, her voice warring between firm and wistful. "Maybe later."

He pressed a lingering kiss to the crown of her head. "Later today?" Surely, it was after midnight.

"That depends."

"On what?" he asked.

"On how big a risk-taker you are. Do you want to delay this until we have protection? Or are you willing to accept the consequences of your actions right here and now?"

"My, how...legal that sounds."

She shrugged. "I suppose it does. Nonetheless, it's a question that needed to be asked—one we both need to answer."

Kevan took a moment to gather his rampant wits before replying, then decided he wasn't in the right frame of mind for making rational decisions. "You first."

"Chicken," she chided. "Making me be the sensible one."

"That's usually the case, isn't it? The woman is always more sensible than the man."

"I doubt that, but for now, I'll concede." A different kind of tremor shook her body. The heat had cooled somewhat, leaving her vulnerable to the chilly night air.

"Guess I need to be the sensible one now." he said. "You'd best be getting back inside. Wouldn't want you to catch cold."

To his surprise, she laughed. "If a plunge into the Atlantic didn't give me the sniffles, I can't imagine the night air in County Kerry would cause me any problems. You're right, though. I should be getting back to bed." She reached up and ruffled his hair. "And so should you. We'll talk more tomorrow."

"Aye, that we will." Kevan hoped they would do more than talk. However, for the moment, he tried to be satisfied with hugs and kisses. He knew it would take more than that to truly satisfy him. A lot more. Only a lifetime of making love with her would suffice.

He would settle for nothing less.

"Goodnight, then." She lifted her face to his, clearly expecting another kiss.

Kevan did his best not to disappoint her, and although the kiss wasn't quite as passionate as those that had gone before, it held promise and further strengthened the bond between them.

"Sweet dreams."

"Yeah. Hopefully they'll be about something other than dogs with saddle sores and pictures of castles on their collars." Lowering her arms, she released him and took a step backward, shaking her head. "What a weird freakin' dream."

"I'll not argue with that," he said. "When Mac asks me to saddle him up, we'll know we've all gone completely mad, but I do think we should take a drive over to the castle in the morning. There's something significant about it. Some connection I'm missing. It's right there on the edge of my brain. Just can't seem to put my finger on it."

With a tiny giggle that held more sarcasm than mirth, she said, "I'm sure the Array could tell you."

"What? You mean consult the resident brain trust?" he scoffed. "That would be too easy."

"It's worked for me before, although there were more of them then. The brain trust has shrunk a bit, so they probably aren't quite as good as a search engine now."

Kevan wondered who was left. The scientist, perhaps? Either way, none of them were talking. He could think of no reason for their dormancy other than to offer some privacy during a midnight rendezvous. He certainly didn't believe they had all been waiting for him to kiss Cleona before moving on to a higher plane.

"Tell me again…how do you know when they've gone?"

She tapped her temple. "I get a pain here when they leave."

"Hmm, well, I haven't felt that, so I guess they're still with me. Then again, with something as strange as this, there probably aren't any hard-and-fast rules."

"I think they're making up the rules as they go along."

Kevan was reminded of the *"All in good time"* admonition he'd received. "You're right, I'm sure. It isn't as though they'd had time to read the instruction manual." He barked out a laugh. "Would you listen to us? Out here in the middle of the night talking about being possessed by spirits when we could be doing far more interesting things."

Her teasing grin and subsequent wink made his heart flip over. "Yeah. Like crawling into bed for a little more shuteye."

"I had other things in mind." Taking her hand, he pulled her close.

"So do I, but we've already decided that isn't a good idea right now."

"Okay. One more kiss and I'm gone."

"Make it a good one. It has to last us until morning, you know."

Kevan did his best, throwing every emotion he possessed into one long, slow, deep, wet kiss that lasted far longer than he'd intended and left them both breathless.

After which, the Array cheered.

Chapter 9

THE MORNING BREEZE STIRRED THE CURTAINS IN CLEONA'S bedroom, carrying with it the heavenly aroma of bacon and eggs. And, if her nose didn't deceive her, scones, rich with butter and slathered with clotted cream and topped with strawberry jam. She would probably lose a few more of the Array after eating that, although she suspected a few of them were holding out for Ita's version of Irish stew. Either that or they were waiting for some serious nookie with Kevan.

She was a bit anxious for that herself. God only knew when or if she would ever find another like him, and despite the logistics of the match, she had every intention of hanging on tooth and nail.

Donning a pair of jeans and a sweater, she trotted downstairs to catch Ita in the act of taking a tray of scones from the oven.

"Good morning, Cleona," Ita said. "Sinead and Fergus are out with the cows, but they'll be in shortly. I think they have a sixth sense for when the scones are done."

"I must have the same sense," Cleona said. "Woke me right up."

"We thought it best to let you sleep as long as possible." She grinned. "Didn't imagine you'd want to help feed the cows."

She said no more, and though her manner didn't betray her, Cleona couldn't help wondering if Ita hadn't been privy to some of the goings on in her garden during the wee hours of the morning. Not that it mattered. As fond of Kevan as the family was, they probably wouldn't have batted an eyelash if he'd come down to breakfast with her.

A sudden wave of longing washed over her. What would it be like to have breakfast with a man after so many years spent alone? Married couples often complained that marriage wasn't what they'd hoped it would be, but not having to meet somewhere or go out on a date to see one another had to be an advantage. She'd heard more than one male celebrity who'd dated dozens of women before finally settling down remark on how wonderful it was to be married. To know the person you loved was no more than an arm's length away from you all night and would still be there when you woke up.

She remembered something like that. Or at least seemed to, similar to the porch swing memory that wasn't her own. Granted, it may have only been a fantasy, but it didn't feel like that. More like a cherished memory.

She hadn't had any memorable dreams after finally tearing herself away from Kevan and going back to bed. Apparently one weird dream a night was enough. Either that or time spent with Kevan kept them at bay.

"Did Kevan say when he'd be back?"

Briefly startled by Ita's question, Cleona opted for a cautious reply since the discussion about going to Ballycarbery Castle had taken place while everyone else was asleep. "I don't think he said for certain."

"I bet he'll be here soon, though." She bustled about the kitchen, setting out plates and pots of jam. "Didn't want to leave last night, did he? I think he's right smitten with you."

Not half as much as I'm smitten with him. "You think so?"

"I do indeed." She nodded toward the table. "Have a seat, luv. Might as well get started." At the sound of footsteps and running water, she clucked her tongue. "That'll be them washing up now," she said with a nod toward the scullery. "Definitely a sixth sense."

Moments later, Sinead and Fergus entered the kitchen, bringing with them the sweet aromas of hay and molasses-laced cattle feed. Both father and daughter were chuckling, proving they'd heard at least the last of Ita's comments.

Sinead gave her mother a quick peck on the cheek. "A scone sense, maybe?"

"More like you know how long we'll be out." Fergus gave Ita a firm hug, winking at Cleona over his wife's shoulder. "But then, she's always telling me I can smell her scones from the next county."

Ita gave him a playful slap. "As if you ever *go* to the next county. Now, sit yourselves down and eat it while it's hot."

Cleona took a seat next to the empty chair that Kevan had been sitting in the night before. His presence seemed to have lingered to the point that she could almost feel his heat, see his smile, and watch as the muscles flexed beneath his clothing. The last time she'd been with him, she'd had her hands all over that man.

Well…perhaps not *all* over him. There were a few places her fingers and lips hadn't explored, and she looked forward to finding them all. The intensity of their attraction still astonished her. She'd never felt such magnetism before, not with anyone. She suspected the Array might have something to do with that, but was she utilizing the strength of their emotions? Or was she tapping into a heretofore unused portion of her own persona?

After one bite of a fresh scone topped with clotted cream and jam, her taste buds might have reached a state of nirvana, but her mind had already begun to drift elsewhere. Across rolling hills carpeted with green grass and studded with stones...

The images were so real, so detailed, her mind's eye might have been a movie camera. As she watched, a man got out of an expensive-looking vehicle, walked across the pavement, and passed easily through the gate in the wire fence. His dress was an unremarkable shirt and jeans, his complexion swarthy, his hair cropped short—nothing about him to raise any concerns other than his surreptitious glance toward the road. Cleona waited long enough for the man to circle the ruined structure and vanish from sight before following him.

Awake or asleep, her imagination had never been so vivid. She truly felt as though her feet were moving over the grass—dodging a stone here and avoiding a shallow depression there—but always a dozen or so steps behind her quarry. What was he doing there? Trespassing was forbidden. Hadn't he read the sign? For that matter, why hadn't she obeyed its strictures?

The clatter of a spoon on a china plate whisked her back to the present.

She'd been to that same castle and hadn't noticed anyone like that. Or had she? Was this her memory? Thankfully, a swift perusal of the table proved everyone was paying more attention to what was on their plates than they were to her momentary lapse.

A moment was all that could have passed or the cream surely would have dripped from the scone she still held in her hand. Was she seeing her own memories more clearly? Or were these images from a different source? A search of her own experience there showed her three people standing inside the fence close to the castle. Did they have permission or were they in blatant violation of the law? She remembered discussing the possibilities with Sinead, but that was all. She certainly hadn't climbed the fence to follow any of them, nor had she waited to speak with them when they returned.

Someone in the Array must have done what she had only been imagining. That person was trying to tell her something. Why didn't he or she just come out and say it? Was the danger such that risking their "host" was too great? Perhaps the Array needed to convey a message of some sort, but the tale couldn't be told in words, they could only show it...

The realization that the voices in her head had stopped struck her with an impact both swift and sure. She'd told them to hush up, and they had done just that. She never imagined her admonition would work or that she would regret having said it, especially now when she had so many more questions. Had the voices all transferred to Kevan, leaving only dreams behind?

The vision she'd just experienced—she was at a loss to put any other label on it—proved that someone had concerns about the goings on at Ballycarbery Castle, whatever they were. She reminded herself that anyone in the Array would have died in the crash, never having made it to Ireland. Therefore the event she'd just witnessed must have taken place in the past. But when? Years ago? Months ago? There could have been any number of Irish tourists or businesspeople aboard that plane. Any one of them could have witnessed something that hadn't seemed significant at the time, but had grown in importance when viewed in retrospect.

A man going into the castle...for what?

She caught herself pushing a tiny bit of bacon around her otherwise empty plate with a fork, barely remembering having eaten anything after that first bite of the scone.

"More bacon, Cleona?"

Something in her aunt's tone made Cleona look up from her plate. No doubt about it, Ita had noticed.

"No, thank you. I'm stuffed. That was absolutely delicious." At least she thought it might have been. The scone was the only thing she could truly vouch for.

"Glad you enjoyed it." Ita's voice held no trace of sarcasm, making Cleona wonder if she'd imagined the odd inflection in her aunt's question.

Only then did she notice that Fergus and Sinead had already risen from the table and were putting their dirty dishes in the sink.

I must've missed that.

At that point, it hardly mattered whether she was caught daydreaming. She certainly had plenty of things to think about, and her budding romance with Kevan gave her an even better excuse. Telling the truth about the Array was out of the question. She never would have mentioned anything to Kevan if she hadn't known the

Array had already spoken to him.

"What are your plans for the day?" Fergus asked.

"I'm not sure we have any." Cleona aimed a questioning glance at Sinead. "Do we?"

How was she to explain that she wanted to visit a castle she'd already seen? She hoped Kevan would have some ideas. Of course, she wouldn't have to explain anything if she went out for a drive with him. Alone.

"Not unless there's somewhere you want to go," Sinead replied. "Dad's been missing my help while I've been in Sneem. He might even beg for your help if we don't come up with something quick."

"I'll not be made the culprit here," Fergus declared. "For all we know, Cleona may have a deep abiding desire to learn about the cattle business."

"Can't say that I do," Cleona said with a wag of her head.

"Is it sheep you'd be more interested in?" Ita never looked up from her task as she rinsed another plate.

Cleona cast a sidelong glance at her aunt, who, despite appearing to be preoccupied, was too perceptive by half. "What makes you think that?"

Ita put the plate in the drying rack and nodded toward the window above the sink. "It's just that Kevan is makin' his way up to the door. He doesn't have any sheep with him, but you never know..."

At that point, Cleona would've bet any amount of money that Ita had witnessed her late-night tryst with Kevan, and she thanked her lucky stars they'd had sense enough to stop before removing any clothing. Even so, her cheeks prickled with embarrassment as she recalled just how heated those kisses had been—the kind of kisses that normally only happened behind closed doors.

Behind closed doors...

The mere thought of what else might happen in private unleashed a deluge of rampaging hormones into her system, compounding the yearning to discover what she'd been missing all her life.

"If he's free for the day, I wouldn't object to giving you up," Sinead said. "It's true I have a fair amount of catching up to do here at home. You know how it is when you've been away for a bit."

Considering that Cleona lived in an apartment without so much as a plant to water, the only thing that might be piling up in her absence was junk mail. She wouldn't be faced with the real pile-up until she went back to work. Her job and all it entailed seemed a lifetime ago now. The crash of Oceana Airways Flight 2324 had been a life-changing experience. She truly was a different person with different needs and wants.

Better make that several different persons.

At least, there *had* been several. So many they had to form a collective entity. Now they were silent, and the only possible catalysts for that change were either when she'd told them to hush up or when she'd kissed Kevan MacFinnin. Her money was on the latter.

A tap at the door had her surging to her feet. "I'll get it," she said, praying she didn't sound quite as breathless as she felt. Her heart pounding, she ignored any puzzled frowns or knowing grins on the faces of her relatives and forced herself to walk purposefully to the door instead of hitting the ground at a dead run.

Would he have changed his mind? Was he coming to tell her that last night's rendezvous had been a mistake?

She yanked open the door and the moment her eyes met his, she knew her fears were groundless. Brooding passion smoldered behind his smile, luring her into the deep, treacherous waters of his embrace.

"Careful now," he said before she could launch herself into his arms. "We wouldn't want to astonish the family so early in the morning."

His deep brogue was like a balm that both soothed and stimulated. The man was dangerously attractive; so much so that she could easily forget every dictate of polite society in order to kiss him one more time.

After a difficult swallow, she opened the door wider. "Won't you come in?"

He arched a wicked brow. "As if anyone could keep me out."

No, he hadn't had a change of heart, and the intensity with which he growled out those words as he crossed the threshold proved he was every bit as anxious as she to pick up where they'd left off the night before. Her knees threatened to abandon her; only her white-knuckled grip on the old-fashioned door handle kept her from falling.

"You're too much for me, you know. Too much to resist." She paused, gulping in an unsteady breath. "Not for long anyway."

"With any luck, you won't have to." His light touch on her shoulder sapped her strength even further. The fear that she might collapse at his feet almost became a reality when he traced the length of her arm with his fingertips. Taking her hand, he raised it to his lips. Such a chaste kiss had never seemed like an intimate gesture before. Now, as his smoldering gaze remained riveted to hers, promising myriad delights even beyond the seductive press of his lips, she understood.

* * * *

Kevan knew the layout of the Mahoney's cottage as well as his own, although he'd never appreciated the fact that the front doorway wasn't visible from the kitchen. A glance in that direction proved it.

"Do we dare take this any further?" he whispered.

A rosy blush blossomed in her cheeks. "We won't have to. Ita is about to make a suggestion that will give us all the privacy we could possibly want."

"This should be interesting," he said. "Lead on."

Cleona led the way to the kitchen, the slight sway of her hips speaking to him in a language he'd all but forgotten.

"Good morning, Kevan," Ita said. "Seems like old times having you here twice in as many days."

Better make that three. "Feels like old times too." Except that he'd never been in love with Sinead. They'd always been the best of friends, but his heart had never leaped at the sight of her. Not the way it did whenever he looked at Cleona.

"I hope it stays that way." With a sigh, she added, "What a shame we've too much work to do to keep Cleona entertained today. She's sure to be bored out of her mind."

"Oh, I doubt that," Cleona protested. "I have books to read and—"

Cleona might never have spoken as Ita continued, "Don't reckon you'd have the day free, would you, Kevan?"

"Happens I do," Kevan replied. "That is, if she doesn't mind mucking about with a sheep farmer."

"She seems to have taken an interest in sheep," Ita said as though the thought had only just occurred to her. "But then, fuzzy little lambs appeal to most people."

"I have several of those." Although he doubted that any time spent with Cleona would involve sheep. "What about it, Cleona?"

To her credit, Cleona didn't take the bait at once. "I suppose I could. That is, if it wouldn't be too much trouble…"

"None whatsoever," he assured her. "I'd be more than happy to be your guide for the day." And the next day, and the day after that…

"Well… If you're sure, I guess it would be okay." Her show of reluctance was so convincing, he might have believed her if he hadn't known better. By the same token, he doubted that Ita had fallen for the ruse anymore than he bought her "we're too busy" line of gobshite.

Ita wiped her hands on a towel, smiling. "That's all settled then. Anythin' you'd like to see today, Cleona?"

Cleona chewed thoughtfully on her thumbnail before making her reply. *Damn, she's good.* "I suppose we could take a drive through the Black Valley. I've heard so much about it, seems a shame to miss it when I'm this close."

"We could do that," Kevan said. "Haven't been over that way in a while now. Plenty of places we could go for lunch afterward, especially if we drive on to Killarney."

"Just as long as you have her back in time for supper," Ita cautioned. "You'll stay to eat with us again, Kevan?" Her inflection may have made it a question, but he wasn't fooled into thinking she intended it to be anything other than a direct order.

"Wouldn't miss it," he replied.

Ita beamed. "There now. You be sure to show her your sheep as well."

"I'll do that." He glanced at Cleona. "When would you like to leave?"

"I'm ready whenever you are." Once again, her shrug was a study in nonchalance that any aspiring actress would envy.

"Might want to take a jacket with you, luv," Ita suggested. "It can be chilly in the mountains."

"It's not like we'd be climbin' them, Ita," Kevan said.

"You never know what you might take a notion to do."

A loaded statement if he'd ever heard one, especially given the nature of his "notions." "Now, Ita. You know I'll take good care of her."

Ita actually reached up and pinched his cheek—something she hadn't done since he was ten years old. "See that you do, laddie. That's my favorite niece you're talkin' about."

Sinead laughed right on cue. "Your *only* niece."

"Ah, go on with you then," Ita said with an admonitory wave.

Cleona took the hint and ran upstairs, returning promptly with a small leather handbag and a light jacket. "All set."

When she grasped the hand he held out to her, he fought the

impulse to kiss her hand once more. Knowing that he would soon be alone with Cleona tempered his desire.

After all, better kisses awaited him, and God knew he was a patient man.

Chapter 10

"THAT WENT WELL," CLEONA SAID AS THEY STARTED DOWN THE stone steps to the driveway. She nodded toward Kevan's battered Volvo. "I see you intended to take me for a drive whether Ita insisted or not."

"Pays to be prepared." Kevan opened the car door and gestured her inside. Truth be told, he was prepared for a lot more than a drive through the Irish countryside. "So...the Black Valley or Ballycarbery Castle?"

She grimaced, looking simultaneously chagrined and adorable. "I'd say both if I hadn't checked the map again. Those two places are only close in the sense that they're both in County Kerry. Not sure we could make that big a loop before dinnertime."

"You could always say you'd changed your mind."

"And come across as a flighty woman? Never."

In Kevan's eyes, *flighty* was the very last description he would've chosen for her. "Been called that a time or two, have you?"

"Oh, God, no," she replied. "But I don't care to risk it. I've been the rock that keeps the boss from going off the deep end for years, and I"—she came to a sudden halt, both in her gait and her speech—"I'm not going back, am I?"

"What d'you mean?"

"I mean, I don't think I *can* go back. There's something here..." Pausing again, she turned a full circle, gazing off toward the horizon at every point of the compass. "The Black Valley," she whispered. "Ballycarbery can wait until tomorrow—or another day, perhaps. We have to go to the valley today."

He arched a brow, but only out of habit. Nothing was ordinary anymore. "If the lass says she needs to go to the valley, then the valley it shall be."

Nodding slowly, she headed toward the car like a woman possessed, which, of course, she was. Sort of.

Kevan slid behind the wheel thinking how strange Cleona would have seemed if he hadn't understood her predicament—the Array anyway. This seemed different, although he couldn't have said how.

Her concussion, perhaps? For all he knew, her injuries might have worsened. "Any headaches today?"

She gaped at him for a long moment. "No. Not yet." Again, she hesitated. "The Array isn't speaking to me anymore. The dreams are all that's left—at least, I think that's what's happened." Fixing him with a penetrating gaze, she asked, "Are they talking to you?"

"Some," he replied. "But not as often as before." He still had yet to decide whether that was for the best. The Array was significant—its very existence proved that much—and for them to be silent was…baffling.

"And neither of us has a clue as to what that might mean." Her rueful smile twisted his heart, making him wish he had the power to keep her from ever smiling that way again. "Never thought I'd ever be worried because I *wasn't* hearing voices."

"D'you miss them?"

"Maybe. I feel like their mission got aborted for some reason." She blinked and swept a lock of hair behind her ear, increasing his longing to touch her again—to hold her until every bad memory left her. "Like it's over and done with before it even began."

"Or maybe it changed." Once again, he marveled at the peculiar nature of their conversation. Given the sexual tension between them, the Array and its purpose should have been the very last thing on their minds. When he gave into the need to take her hand again, he had no qualms about kissing it. "Give it time. This may only be an adjustment period."

"Possibly." She gave his hand a squeeze before releasing it and turning toward the window.

So much for better kisses.

Kevan started the engine, backed the car into the turnabout, then pulled out onto the main highway. He hadn't driven the Black Valley road for a while now, but he hadn't forgotten the way. Those mountains had called to him more than once since a terrorist bomb changed his life forever. Endowed with a stark beauty all their own, the black, rocky crags stood as a reminder that long after the valley road crumbled to dust, the mountains would still be there, and the lochs would still fill with rain that flowed down the rugged slopes. Time might weather the peaks, but the mountains wouldn't fall unless an earthquake toppled them.

He found that comforting. Hopefully, Cleona would feel the same way.

She was quiet during the drive—a reaction he understood completely—taking a few pictures now and then, until suddenly calling out for him to stop.

He should have guessed she would have wanted a closer look at this particular place, as it was one where he had often come seeking solace. Up ahead in one of the more crooked stretches of road, a low stone bridge arched over the stream that wound its way through the grassy, boulder-studded bottom before flowing into the loch beyond. Forbidding black mountains loomed high on either side, acting as guardians of the loch. He parked the Volvo in a pull-off just past the bridge.

She got out of the car without a word, walking back toward the bridge, barely taking note when he caught up to her and grasped her hand as she stood by the parapet. If anything, he seemed superfluous, unnecessary, merely the impersonal driver who was only there to show her the sights.

Wind lifted her hair and blew it across her face. She brushed it away absently, her distant gaze seeming to encompass the entire valley.

"What *is* this place?" Her tone was hushed, reverent.

He doubted she was asking for a lesson in geography, but he gave her one anyway. "It's called the Gap of Dunloe. From here, the road goes north to Dunloe, and then the Gap Road intersects the Ring of Kerry, which goes around Lough Leane to Killarney. Interestingly enough, there's a place along the way called Mahony's Point that juts out into the water. Same name as yours, but spelled without the 'e.'"

Kevan knew he was babbling, but her peculiar demeanor was unsettling to say the least. Especially when her eyes met his almost as though seeing him for the first time.

"You've been here before, haven't you?"

He nodded. "Spent many an hour right here on this bridge. Seemed the best place to contemplate things that made no sense at all."

"Weird, isn't it?" She paused as a frown furrowed her brow. "No. Not weird at all. We're connected to this place somehow."

The skin on the back of his head and neck tightened, creating a prickling rush of tingles. "Aye, that we are. Dunno how exactly, but, yes." Kevan didn't fully understand what he was saying or even what he was agreeing to. The words seemed to come from somewhere else—some*one* else.

He drew her off the road and onto the verge. "Stand over here and feel the earth beneath your feet."

She did as he instructed, going one step further by removing her shoes and curling her toes in the grass. When she looked up at him, her dilated pupils were no longer black, but a rich, mossy green—the same green as the grass beyond the bridge—encircled by the deep brown of the iris. The color could have merely been a reflection of her surroundings, but it seemed to be so much more than that.

The water beyond the bridge shimmered, rippling with darkness and light. In a flash of insight, he saw it, the same shape he'd seen painted on the fleece of four butchered ewes. Only this time, he knew it for what it was.

Ballycarbery Castle.

Why he hadn't realized it before, he couldn't have said, but he knew it now. He started to blurt out this revelation when a movement caught his eye as Cleona stretched her arms toward the sky.

"I'm here," she whispered. "I'm all around you. My bones are there beneath your feet. Send your roots deep and feel the strength emanating from the core."

Her voice had an odd ring to it, not like her normal voice at all. Was she talking to him or to herself? "Cleona—"

The word had scarcely left his mouth when she turned slowly, just as she'd done earlier, facing first north, then east, south, and west, like the needle on a compass. He didn't need to consult an actual compass to verify her accuracy.

With uncanny certainty, he *knew.*

* * * *

Cleona's soul stretched deep into the ground. Past rocks and minerals, soil and turf. Closing her eyes, she inhaled the essence of the planet in deep, swirling breaths. Rooted to the spot and yet arching upward to the sky, her arms lengthened and stiffened into branches. Bark thickened and split as she grew. Leaves budded, swelled, and unfurled, only to fall in a shower when she shook her head. Fingerling roots emerged from her toes to push through the rocky ground, splitting the grains to dust, sucking moisture and heat from so far inside, the depths could never be measured.

I'm a tree?

"You are the tree of life."

Oh, surely not... There were no trees around anywhere, only scrubby tufts of grass and gorse.

The voice continued—not like the Array, but as a hollow, resonant gong that reverberated through every cell in her body. *"It is true. Believe what you imagine. Feel what you touch. Know that you belong here in the light, the abundant and eternal light. Only in the light can you understand both the question and the answer."*

"What are they?"

"You will know when the time comes. You will know..."

At the moment, Cleona only knew that her mind had turned to mush—or was it stone? No. It was wood. She had a wooden head. Thick as a post instead of dumb as a box of rocks. She almost laughed at the absurdity. Those things weren't dumb at all. They held the secrets. Secrets they wouldn't impart to just anyone, especially since so few could actually hear them speak.

As she stood there a gentle rain began to fall, feeding both the stream and the grassy bed through which the water meandered. She registered each drop as it fell on her hair, her face, her hands. Nourishment flowed over her before being absorbed by her skin.

"I feel so...alive."

"You are the Carrier of Life's Preservation. Use it well. Heal what is sick, mend what is broken."

"It isn't too late?" Cleona didn't understand the question, let alone her reasons for asking it. Nevertheless, she grasped its importance.

"It is never too late," the voice replied. *"Not while a spark of life remains."*

Whose life? No, wait. Somewhere inside, she knew it didn't matter. Life was life. Precious and unique. And so easily snuffed out.

Her roots began to retract, her arms returning to their original length. Extending first one foot and then the other, she discovered that she was as mobile as she'd ever been. Sounds that had been muffled before sharpened to become the murmur of water rushing over a rocky creek bed, accompanied by the high, thin call of birds circling above. The rain slowly ceased, and a shaft of pale sunlight shone down on the bridge. Crickets chirped their usual chorus, but were their songs louder and more joyous than before? For that matter, what could possibly make a cricket feel joy? Did they even experience that emotion?

She glanced at Kevan. "Are crickets happy?"

His eyes widened briefly.

"Sorry," she said before he could draw breath to speak.

"Not at all." With a smile that was genuine rather than

condescending, he added, "I've often wondered that myself. But anything that sings as much as they do must be pleased about something."

"Did I—" How should she ask if he'd heard any of the bizarre conversation in which she'd been engaged? Then she remembered who she was with. "Did you hear anything else?"

"Aye, but the dialog was a bit one-sided."

"I'm not sure I can fill you in completely. It was a little…strange."

"Try me." He led her back onto the bridge and leaned against the parapet with his arms folded across his chest. The mere sight of him standing there as the breeze tossed his unruly curls threatened to steal her breath, her sanity.

A brittle laugh escaped her. "What would you say if I told you I was the 'Carrier of Life's Preservation?'" she asked, punctuating her new "title" with air quotes.

"Figured it was something big," he said as though he was often privy to such claims. "What I mean is, no one surviving a disaster of that magnitude picks up souls just so they can enjoy Ita's cooking before moving on to a higher plane."

"You'd think that, wouldn't you? Seems like only a greater purpose could have that effect." She chewed her lower lip, still trying to puzzle out exactly what that greater purpose might be. Too bad the voice in her head hadn't given her a job description or a list of pertinent duties along with the title. "I'm supposed to use that designation well, healing what is sick and mending what is broken. Unfortunately, I haven't a clue as to how to go about actually *doing* any of that."

He shrugged as though he gave advice to crazy people on a daily basis. "You'll muddle through somehow. Just be ready for the instructions whenever they come."

"Sounds simple enough, but I'd like to be a bit more proactive than that. I hate having stuff creeping up on me. I prefer to be prepared." Her job required her to be one step—preferably two or three—ahead of whatever came across her desk. No matter what her new purpose was, it was bound to be more important than anything she'd done in the past.

"Could be this is one of those things you can't prepare for," Kevan said. "The kind of thing that strikes like a bolt from the blue when you least expect it or only occurs when your mind is open." He paused, clearing his throat before he spoke again. "Speaking of bolts from the blue, I had one just now. The symbol on the sheep…it's the outline of Ballycarbery Castle."

She turned to lean against the parapet beside him, needing more support than her hands had to offer. "I'm not surprised, what with all the visions we've been having of that place." Her head began to pound as she gazed southward over the valley. "Must've lost another one," she said, massaging her temples.

Kevan smiled. "And sometimes a headache is just a headache."

"True. Wish I could tell the difference." She looked up at him, once again struck by the sheer male beauty of him. "Are you having headaches too?"

"Some. Had a few twinges last night."

The arm he slid around her shoulders was comforting in its warmth and thrilling in its intimacy. Somehow or another, she'd managed to forget the tryst in the garden the night before—blocked out by other earth-shattering events.

She remembered it now.

"Aren't we a pair? Standing here contemplating the fate of life on earth—at least, that's what I think we were doing—when we should be doing what other"—she hesitated, casting about for a word to replace the one that was first and foremost in her mind—"*people* would be doing in our situation."

"Other lovers, you mean?"

Obviously he wasn't afraid to say the word aloud. "Is that what we are? So soon?"

"Maybe. Could be that's another of those things we should take on faith."

Her sigh expressed a lifetime of being disappointed by love. Was this—she was reluctant to call it an affair—different from the others? "I'd sure like to. You know…dive in headfirst and damn the consequences."

"And what consequences would that be?"

She shot him a scowl. "Playing devil's advocate now?"

"Could be," he replied. "But if we're going to consign those consequences to hell, we should at least know what they are."

"Okay, then. To start with, disappointment, broken hearts, depression—"

He pressed a finger to her lips. "I was thinking more along the lines of a future together with love, family, and children."

Tears stung her eyes as she gazed up at him and whispered her reply. "Oh, God, if only. .."

"We'll never know if we don't give it a try."

His vision of the future was so enticing that she ached for it to become a reality. She had nothing to lose but her heart—and possibly her sanity, which was already compromised—and, of course, her job. But did keeping a job mean anything when what he offered was worth so much more? "What should I do? Go for broke and move in with you?" She left out the "until I head for home" part of the question.

"You'd get no arguments from me," he said—a response she could have predicted.

She rested her head against his shoulder. How marvelous it would be to stay with this man forever. How absolutely *marvelous*... "Just wish we had more time."

Linking his hands behind the small of her back, he pulled her close until nearly the full length of their bodies pressed together. "Didn't you know? Time has no meaning here." The deep rumble of his voice breached her defenses, beating any protest she might have made to the punch.

Desire stole through her, curling her toes and melting her fears. "Seems that way, doesn't it? Like anything is possible, or nothing else really matters. I'm not sure which." At the moment, she wasn't sure of anything except the need to discover whether making love with Kevan would be as earthshaking as she thought—no, *hoped*—it would be. And not in the back seat of a car—or even a secluded spot nearby. "But I do know one thing."

"Oh, and what would that be?" His brogue was more pronounced than usual, and a funny little half smile quirked the corner of his mouth—both of which she found equally endearing.

"I think you know," she replied.

"Want to go check out where you'll be livin', then? Evaluate the closet space and such?" His lilting tone teased as well as enthralled. "I'll warn you, it's your typical sheep farmer's house, complete with antibiotics in the fridge and skeins of wool hanging from the rafters."

"Sounds perfect."

Another car approached the bridge and passed by them, one of the few they'd encountered on that lonely road. In its wake, the murmur of the stream rose in volume, drowning out every other sound. Not a soul intruded to interrupt a kiss that began as a light brush of the lips before deepening to become something far more intimate. Swirling, tempestuous desire engulfed her, making her forget why they had come there and all the other places compelling them to visit.

So much remained for them to do. So many mysteries were still unsolved—mysteries that hammered at her, a reminder of her duty, her destiny.

Not now. I'm busy.

Threading her fingers through his hair, she used those dusky curls to pull him even closer—to taste, to enjoy, to *devour…*

Cleona was about to melt into a puddle at his feet when Kevan framed her face with his palms and broke the kiss. "Do you want to take the scenic route through Killarney or go back the way we came?"

"That depends," she replied, amazed her mouth could form words after being so thoroughly kissed.

"On?"

"Which way is quicker."

Chapter 11

IN THE END, THEY TOOK THE ROUTE HE'D DESCRIBED, PASSING through Killarney before making a loop to the east and heading back to Kenmare. Time-wise, that route was about the same as retracing their original path, but it had the virtue of being a straighter road with a higher speed limit. Plus, there were restaurants along the way, and even though stopping for lunch prolonged their trip by another hour or so, Cleona didn't mind. Any time in Kevan's company was time well spent, and she looked forward to enjoying the rest of the afternoon in his arms.

Nevertheless, she grew more and more anxious as they neared Kevan's farm—anxious to pick up where they'd left off and take their relationship one giant step forward.

By the time he'd parked the car, Cleona's hands and feet had transformed into trembling blocks of ice and her heart threatened to beat its way out of her chest. Fortunately, her knees didn't fail her and she was able to walk to the door, but the moment she crossed the threshold, she let out a cry as her hand flew to her temple. Staggering, she would have fallen if it weren't for Kevan's grip on her arm.

"Whoa, that was a bad one," she gasped. "Apparently several of the Array gang just wanted to see inside your house." Regaining her balance, she added, "Seems like they would have waited for the chance to see a lot more than that." Kevan without his jeans was surely a sight worth seeing.

Ranks pretty high on my bucket list anyway.

Chuckling, Kevan relaxed his hold on her arm and pushed the door closed. "Should I lock it to keep any more of them from leaving prematurely?"

"Not sure that would help. They don't seem to respect any earthly boundaries." Despite the pain in her head, she managed a grin. Surprisingly, her hands and feet had returned from the polar regions and were warm again. "Might keep Ita out, though."

"I doubt she'd come looking for you unless we're late for

dinner."

"Better set an alarm then. I don't want to miss that either." Although truth be told she'd have willingly missed any number of meals if it meant being with Kevan. How had it happened so quickly? She didn't believe in love at first sight—or insta-love, which seemed to be the current slang equivalent. Love needed time and nurturing to develop, didn't it?

Possibly.

On the other hand, there was a great deal to be said for chemistry and living in the moment.

As though guided by a magnetic pull, her gaze was immediately drawn to the far wall of the living room where an upright piano stood, silent and waiting for... What? Someone to play it? Crossing the room, she skimmed her fingertips along the fallboard. "Do you play?"

"Not anymore," Kevan replied. "I was never any good, so I gave it up when I was about twelve. Mum was the one with the talent."

"I never even took lessons. I wanted to, but we didn't have room in our house for a piano. Wish we had." Cleona's sigh was as wistful as the sudden urge to sit on the bench was overwhelming. "Do you mind? I never miss the chance to 'tinkle the ivories' as the saying goes—or is it 'tickle the ivories?' I've never been sure."

"Probably both, dependin' on where you heard it first." He nodded toward the instrument. "That one is old enough that the keys are real ivory instead of the plastic they use these days." If he was anxious for her to do something other than play the piano, it didn't show in his face. "Tickle away—although it's sure to be sadly out of tune."

Cleona smiled to herself as she seated herself on the bench. Raising the fallboard, she imagined a very young Kevan doing the same thing before putting sheet music on the rack and playing scales or whatever it was people did when they first learned to play.

"Ohh-h..."

She sat up straighter, scouring her mind for the source. The Array was speaking again? Although technically, what she'd heard was more of a sigh than a word.

Closing her eyes, she placed her hands on the keys and pressed down. Her eyes flew open as a harmonic chord sounded—a bit out of tune, as Kevan had said, but a chord, nonetheless. Although stiff on the keys at first, her fingers stretched and flexed as she played a scale.

"You're better than I ever was," Kevan said. "Never could get the fingering down."

"Me either." Cleona hesitated, almost afraid to say what she was beginning to suspect. "I've never done that before," she said flatly.

"Coulda fooled me. Keep going."

He knew. Somehow, he knew.

Taking a deep breath, she closed her eyes again and let her hands take over. They played—not just a simple song, but the resounding opening bars of Grieg's *Piano Concerto in A Minor*.

Her memories of any piece of music had never been so detailed, so precise—even with regard to the title. The tune she played wasn't merely recognizable, it was performance quality.

Goose bumps tightened her scalp and flooded down her back. She snatched her hands from the keyboard. Astonished, overwhelmed, and more than a little freaked out.

"I don't know this song. I mean, I know what it is when I hear it, but I never—"

Kevan's low whistle echoed her own amazement. "So…someone in the Array was a concert pianist?"

"Ho-ly *cow*…" Tenting her fingers, she pressed them to her lips as her heart thumped wildly in her chest.

"Any headache?"

A quick survey of her feelings revealed nothing. "Nope. Maybe I have to play the whole song."

"Or not," he said. "Maybe this 'talent' is permanent." He reached into a basket beside the piano and pulled out a piece of sheet music, dog-eared and yellowed with age. "Here. Try this one," he said as he placed it on the stand. "Mum's favorite."

Bless him for his patience. Any other man would have been chomping at the bit to do something else—*anything* else. But he wasn't any other man. He was Kevan MacFinnin, and he already knew how she felt about him. Romance could wait for a bit, and it would be just as good, perhaps even better, than it would have been in the heat of the moment. What was happening now was…incredible.

"I can't read music," she protested. "I wouldn't know a bass clef from a hole in the ground." But she did. She stared at the page before her and heard the notes clearly—as if they were being played on a piano in her mind.

The song was one she'd never heard before, and yet the symbols on the page were being interpreted for her, telling her exactly how it should be played. She'd gotten past the introduction when Kevan began singing the words in a rich, flawless baritone. She didn't have to ask why he wasn't singing for a living—the reason was obvious—but *still*...

She kept on playing, enthralled by his singing and her uncanny ability to play. When the final chord died away, she looked up at him. Tears streaked his cheeks with shining rivulets, but he was smiling.

"That was so…perfect," he whispered. "I can scarcely believe it." He leaned down and placed a kiss on her lips—a kiss that conveyed both gratitude and awe. "I haven't sung that song since she died. Thank you for playing it."

"You're welcome," she said, grateful for an automatic response when her feelings were anything but commonplace. "Just hope it lasts."

Even if it didn't, she'd had this one magnificent moment when she could play like she'd always dreamed of playing—a virtuoso performance that came from someone else's knowledge, someone else's skill, and someone else's heart, but it touched her soul nonetheless.

His kiss moved from her lips to her hand before he helped her to rise. "I have a feeling it will." He smiled. "Guess I'd better call a piano tuner."

His smile was contagious, passed easily on to her. "Not yet. Better wait a few days to see if it sticks."

"Even if it doesn't, you could still learn. After all, I do have a piano."

His meaning was clear. If she stayed with him, she would have music and much, much more. "I'll keep that in mind."

She slid from behind the keyboard and into his arms. Such a simple, delightful move and, oh, so easy. Their lips met in a kiss as thrilling as it was natural, like she'd been kissing him for years. Making love with him would probably feel the same way—not stale or redundant, but filled with emotion and comfort.

She was about to find out.

Kevan swept her off her feet and carried her across a wooden floor worn as smooth and solid as the one in the Mahoney's cottage and up a similar flight of stone steps. His bedroom was decorated in a more masculine style than the lace-curtained room she'd slept in the night before, but the bed was soft, and she sank into the down coverlet with a sigh. Kevan stretched out beside her, toeing off his boots even as he scattered kisses over her face. Emotions welled up within her, some she was sure she'd never known before. Not with a man. Not like this. Need and longing mixed with passionate fire. That alone told her how right this was, that he was surely the one she'd waited for all her life.

Was he an experienced lover or a virgin? The question passed through her thoughts only briefly. What he'd done before had no meaning now, just as her past hadn't prepared her for the onslaught of molten fire coursing through every vessel in her body. Kisses weren't enough. Hands weren't enough—not on clothing anyway. She craved the contact that only skin on skin could provide.

Unlike the sureness of her fingers on the ivory keys, she fumbled with buttons determined to thwart her and drive her mad with their reluctance to part. Finally, they relented, allowing her to push back the fabric to reveal his lean, muscular chest, liberally dusted with crisp, dark curls. Her own shirt and bra seemed to have vanished—the how and when of their disappearance a mystery she saw no need to solve. What a blessing to have survived to be in this man's bed. A renewed joy of simply being alive gathered her up and thrust her skyward as between them, they dispensed with the remainder of their clothing.

Kevan's warm, wet kisses trailed from her neck to her breasts, escalating her desire and opening her soul to him. Time itself ground to a halt, anticipating the moment toward which her entire life had been focused, the silence broken only by his breathing as he donned protection. She accepted the need for it but despised its presence. She wanted nothing to come between them. Nothing but their own skin.

A nudge of his knee opened her to his blissful penetration. *No.* Penetration was too coarse a term for something so hot and smooth, as though it had been designed specifically for her. Warmth flooded her core, followed closely by greater need and pleasure so exquisite that her eyes stung with tears. A moan escaped her lips.

"Okay?" he asked, his voice a deep, bone-melting rumble.

Her sigh left her with barely enough breath to speak. "So much more than okay. Absolutely *perfect*."

His satisfied groan set off a tingling wave that began at her nape and only stopped where their thighs met. Nothing urgent as yet. Just a steady glide that ramped up the tension, then released it before coiling tight once again. Never-ending, breathtaking pressure, growing and expanding in joyous fulfillment. She might as well have been a virgin, so different was this from any previous encounter.

Opening her eyes, she gazed up at his face and traced the scarring on his cheek with a fingertip. His scars represented tragedy, disaster, and devastating loss, yet those same scars had saved him for her and no one else.

"So beautiful," she whispered. "And you're really mine?" The words had hardly left her lips when she wished she could call them back, longing to give them the conviction they deserved rather than using them to pose a question.

Black, tousled curls grazed her hand as he turned to kiss her palm. "Body and soul."

Would he have said the same thing even if she hadn't asked? Somehow, she thought he would have.

Spearing her fingers through his hair, she pulled him down and kissed him, teasing his lips with her own until he returned the kiss with a fervor that was echoed with each stroke as he thrust into her. His pace increased, and she marveled at the knot of heat forming at the center of her being. Her breath caught in her throat as her mind expanded, just as it had during those last frantic moments after the plane went down. This time, no souls flew in with a cacophony of voices, flowing outward instead, reaching for stars and planets as yet unnamed. No pain accompanied their departure, only peaceful sighs of pure contentment that merged with Kevan's climactic cry.

Another vision drifted in on the wake of the exodus. One she'd seen before, yet not in its entirety. She saw it all now, although she still didn't know what it was. Numbers, symbols…she'd never been good with such things, but now they flipped past her mind's eye like pages in a book.

They *were* pages in a book, each number and symbol located on the opening page of numbered chapters that corresponded to letters spelling out Jacob Emhart's name.

A code, but for what? Some sort of formula? That it related to solar energy was a giver, but why hide it in code? Why make it such a secret?

She waited for Jacob to respond, but heard nothing. He hadn't spoken to her directly since she'd picked up his book at the store in Kenmare. She'd assumed he'd been usurped into the Array before possibly being transferred to Kevan.

Now would be a good time to speak up, Jacob.

Still nothing. Could he only communicate in symbols and numbers now? Actually speaking to her had been so much more helpful. Perhaps his persona had transferred to Kevan, leaving only the code behind. He might even have been among the mass exodus that had just occurred.

Interesting timing.

Had the entire Array been waiting for her to make love with Kevan before moving on? If so, they must have all been a bunch of hopeless romantics. She really hoped the pianist wasn't among them, although in all likelihood, a pianist would be more of a romantic than most. Was Jacob a romantic?

She blinked against the light from the window at the foot of the bed. What a time to be thinking about the romantic nature of a man she barely knew. She should be thinking about the man lying beside her, not the man who'd sat beside her on a plane and had died along with so many others.

The voice that had spoken to her in the Black Valley had told her to keep an open mind. At the moment, her mind was more open than it had ever been, and the connection to Jacob was still there. She was certain of that. Perhaps he was only waiting for the proper time to speak up.

And this wasn't it.

* * * *

Kevan had no problem giving his body and soul to Cleona. He wasn't so sure she would want his mind.

A mind that chose the post-orgasmic period—when his thoughts should have either been satisfyingly blank or engaged in warm, fuzzy feelings for the woman with whom he'd just made love—to replay of the most tragic event of his life.

Except this time, he saw something he hadn't seen before; a man standing in the shadows just beyond the blast zone. He was holding what Kevan could only assume was a detonator, and he appeared to be pleased with himself to the point of high-fiving the man standing next to him.

Was this "vision" simply a figment of his imagination? Or had he actually seen the man at the time? If so, he'd blocked the memory—although just why he would have done that was anyone's guess. Perhaps he feared reprisals if he were to claim that he could identify the perpetrator. The Garda had obviously believed he knew more than he was telling. They'd questioned him at length about any suspicious characters in the vicinity. He hadn't been able to help them then, and he wasn't completely sure he could do it now. After all, ten years had passed since the bombing. People could change quite a bit in that length of time, although the possibility that he could pick the guy out of a lineup did exist. The trick would be convincing the Garda to take new evidence in a ten-year-old crime seriously, especially when that evidence came from his own, somewhat faulty, memory.

And then there were the odds of finding the suspect—let alone bringing him in for questioning—which were essentially nil.

Unless the man was suspected of a different crime with similar details and credible witnesses.

The amount of research he could have done—*ought* to have done—was nothing short of astounding. Surely a few terrorist cells had been discovered and their members arrested since then. His parents' killer might have been among them. He should have studied every photograph that appeared in the news with the hope of jogging his memory.

Actually, that might not be a bad idea now…

Well, not *right* now, but soon. Right now, he'd better be paying more attention to Cleona or she was liable to get up and leave.

He rolled over to find her staring at the ceiling, biting at her lip as though also deep in thought.

Clearing his throat, he said, "I'm almost afraid to ask."

She blinked and turned toward him. "I'd say you don't want to know, but you probably do."

"About…?"

"What's been running through my head for the past few minutes. It's a little…strange."

"Same here."

"Is that good or bad?"

"No clue." He stretched out his arm and she scooted closer to lay her head on his chest. The arm she draped over his stomach proved she wasn't upset with him, nor was she disappointed. At least, he thought that's what it meant. He gave her a quick squeeze. "You go first."

She shook her head. "Might be best if you did." With a bark of mirthless laughter, she added, "I'm still not sure I can explain my—whatever it was."

"Okay then, I was remembering the day my parents died."

"That doesn't sound good."

"Wait, it gets better. For the first time, I remember seeing a man nearby holding what I'm guessing was a detonator. I must've been blocking the memory for years."

"Any idea why?"

"I've been asking myself the same question. There are plenty of reasons why I would want to forget everything that happened that day, but only one reason why I would remember it now."

She raised her head, and for a moment he was too lost in the depths of her eyes to continue.

"Go on," she prodded.

Placing a finger beneath her pert little cleft chin, he tipped her head back and kissed her slow and deep, savoring her scent and the intoxicating flavor of her lips. Whatever god or spirit or fate was responsible for bringing them together didn't matter. She was his as much as he was hers.

"The reason is you."

Chapter 12

FIGURING OUT CLEONA'S CONNECTION TO HIS OWN "VISION" DIDN'T take a rocket scientist, and God knew Kevan could have been more than a sheep farmer. Case in point, he and his parents had been visiting the university because he'd set his sights on a degree in geology. Those plans were temporarily put on hold while he recovered from his injuries, and then put on an indefinite hold when he finally left the hospital. Life at a major university would have been tough enough as it was. He had opted not to find out what it would be like for a recently orphaned teen with disfiguring scars.

Since then, his life had settled into a predictable rhythm that ebbed and flowed with the seasons. As he grew older, he realized that only his choice had kept him from obtaining that degree. He could have put the family farm up for sale and moved to the city at any time, but the love of the land prevented him from abandoning the farm and going off to university, even to learn more about the rugged landscapes that surrounded him.

And now, he had found Cleona. Had his life taken a different path, they might never have met.

Scary thought.

"You're probably the reason for my…vision too," she said. "I was told to keep an open mind, and you really did it to me." Chuckling, she gave him a poke in the ribs that proved making love hadn't diminished their camaraderie. Rather, the intimacy they'd shared intensified the bond between them, which was as it should be.

"Glad I could help. So, are you going to keep me in suspense forever, or are you gonna tell me about your 'vision?'"

"I could explain it better if I had Jacob Emhart's book handy," she replied. "We should head back over to my aunt and uncle's house so I can test my theory."

The involvement of Emhart's book was certainly interesting, but the episode at the bridge in the Gap of Dunloe intrigued him even more. "Does this have anything to do with being the 'Carrier of Life's Preservation'?"

"Maybe. I didn't tell you the whole story of that either. I felt like I was a tree growing roots and branches, becoming one with the planet. I know it sounds crazy, but I think Earth was speaking to me."

In Kevan's opinion, no entity short of God, Earth, or Mother Nature could have spoken to her in such a manner. The crazy part was that anyone had spoken to her at all. Ordinarily, he'd have thought her completely mental. But his own experiences told him otherwise.

"That is a mite strange, I'll grant you, but given everything else you've been through, not entirely unbelievable."

She gazed up at him with awe. "You simply take it on faith that I'm not stark raving mad, don't you?"

"What choice do I have when I'm right there with you?"

"None, I suppose." She pressed a hand to her forehead. "This is all so weird. I was just getting used to the Array commenting on practically everything, then they got quiet, and now, if I'm not mistaken, they've all abandoned me."

"All? Are you sure?"

"I think so. I felt them flying away. Their loss was like waking up from a dream and remembering less and less with each passing moment. Then I saw numbers and symbols. I think it's a formula of some kind. Seems mathematical anyway. Like I said, I need to check that book to be sure. There's a code in it—or something of that nature—which makes me suspect there's a whole lot going on that we don't know about."

"Okay. You've lost me now, lass."

"Remember what I said about being crazy? I have a feeling I'm not the only one. After all, three of us survived that crash. What if Susan and Jillian are having weird dreams or have an Array of their own? Maybe they think they've gone completely bonkers. If it weren't for you, I'd be thinking the same thing. But you heard the Array and you even picked up some of them. That's proof, isn't it? I mean, insanity isn't a contagious disease, so we couldn't be insane."

At the moment, Kevan wasn't entirely sure that was true. After all, catching the Array from her had been as easy as catching a cold. A bit of affirmation wouldn't go amiss. "Maybe you should call them."

"I will. In fact, I should call them right now." With a groan, she slumped against him. "My, isn't this romantic? The freakin' earth moves and we're sitting here trying to figure out which of us can tell the craziest story."

Chuckling, he pulled her closer and kissed the top of her head. "I'll admit, it's one of the more bizarre forms of pillow talk, but it seems to work for us."

"I can't argue with that. We seem to have more expected of us than to simply fall in love. We have mysteries to solve, and, if I'm not mistaken, a planet to save—the life on it anyway."

In Kevan's mind, love was neither simple nor expected. Love was a gift that took some doing to maintain. Still, it paled in comparison with the saving of life on Earth.

"Guess we should head back then," he said, all the while wishing they could spend several days right where they were. "How much of this are you planning to tell your family?"

"Nothing for now. They'd probably have me committed, and I wouldn't blame them." She rose up on her elbow and gave him a quick kiss. "You're my partner in this. For now, you're the only one who needs to know. Except for Susan and Jillian." She paused, her brows knitted together in concentration. "I think I should call Jillian first. Susan insisted the crash was deliberate, but she was speaking from her knowledge as a flight attendant. Jillian had a connection with another passenger's dog—someone she'd been sitting beside on the plane. I questioned her about it at the time because it seemed so peculiar. Looking back, her rapport with the dog could be explained by that woman being part of *her* Array—like she incorporated that ability the way I acquired the knack for playing the piano."

Her silky hair, smooth, unblemished skin, and delicate curves as she sat up were even more breathtaking than before, despite her resigned sigh. "Guess that's another theory I need to test." With a rueful grimace, she added, "I'm almost afraid to."

"I don't blame you for that." He motioned toward the door. "Loo's across the hall."

"Thanks." Not seeming the least bit shy, she made no attempt to cover herself as she gathered up her clothing.

Kevan gazed at her until he realized that he too, was completely exposed—condom, scars, hairy chest, and all. Heat flooded his face as he snatched up his shirt to cover himself.

"No need for that," she said. "You look positively delicious."

As if to prove her assertion, she pushed his shirt aside, peeled off the condom, tossed it in the bin by the nightstand, and bent down to suck him into her mouth. After a few ecstatic swipes of her tongue that left him gasping for air, she released him and smacked her lips.

"Been wanting to do that for a while now." With a wink, she swung her jeans over her shoulder and sauntered from the room.

As a result, several minutes passed before Kevan could collect his wits enough to move, let alone stand, which wasn't surprising given that an event for which he'd been waiting throughout his entire adult life had finally taken place.

And if the pain in his right temple was any indication, several members of the Array had been waiting for it too.

* * * *

Cleona finished in the bathroom in record time, mainly because she was afraid that, like a normal dream, her grasp of the code contained in Emhart's book would fade before she held the book in her hands. Otherwise, she would have happily spent the remainder of the afternoon snuggling with Kevan.

The other reason for her haste was to see if she could still play the piano now that the Array had left her.

Abandoned might've been a better word to describe their defection. Granted, every soul wanted to go on to their ultimate reward—was their presence in her mind proof of heaven's existence or was it proof of reincarnation? She hadn't been privy to that kind of information, although it was possible the Array didn't know what was in store for them after they had fulfilled their purpose and completed their tasks. Nothing made sense anymore. Nothing cut and dried and easily proven by using her own senses to evaluate their worth.

Heedless of the danger, she ran down the steps to the living room, but stopped short at the sight of the piano. She'd told herself whether she could still play or not didn't matter. She'd done it once and had enjoyed every thrilling moment. Perhaps that ability was a temporary gift, a reward for doing some talented pianist the favor of playing their favorite composition one last time.

Did Jillian still have the same rapport with the schnauzer she'd rescued from its cage before it sank? That question served as a reminder to give Jillian a call, but how did one begin such a conversation?

Hey, Jillian… A funny thing happened on the way to Sneem…

She reminded herself that all she had to do was ask after Jillian's health. The rest would come naturally.

Yeah, right. The accompanying eye roll might not have been visible to anyone, but she felt the need for it all the same.

"Must prioritize," she muttered. "Piano first, code second,

Jillian third." She put Jillian last so she would have something concrete to tell her aside from hearing voices and growing roots like a tree while Earth spoke to her.

And meeting Kevan MacFinnin.

Jillian was supposed to meet with the son of another woman she'd met on the plane—one who, like Jacob Emhart, hadn't survived. How did that go?

The more she thought about Jillian, the more convinced she became that she should have called her a long time ago. She should do it now—

No. Piano first.

Fear washed through her. What if she couldn't play? Would the world still turn? Would she even care?

With a purposeful stride, she crossed the room and sat down on the piano bench. She hadn't closed the instrument earlier. Her fingers were already on the keys. What should she play? Some other piece of music, perhaps? Another concerto? Or should she stick with something simple like "Chopsticks" or "Old MacDonald?"

Without warning, the introduction to "Auld Lang Syne" rolled off her fingertips without a hitch, then came the melody, complete with harmony. She was even singing. Why, among all the songs ever been written, was that particular song the one she'd chosen to play? Did it hold a greater meaning for someone in the Array? The pianist or someone else?

Or was this simply the pianist's way of saying goodbye?

Crap. She was going to forget every note, every chord.

Figuring she might as well enjoy it while she could, she played the rest of the song, then launched into another. She had just finished the third song when Kevan came up behind her and placed his hands on her shoulders.

"Your technique is marvelous," he said, nuzzling her neck. "But that thing is in dire need of tuning."

"Tuning it would probably jinx me into forgetting how to play," she said. "And I *really* don't want to forget."

"I dunno… Could be your 'teacher' would rather you played on a well-tuned instrument.'

"I suppose so. I just feel like I have to keep on before I lose it. Sort of like bingeing on cupcakes when you start thinking about going on a diet."

He chuckled in her ear, sending a rush of tingles flowing down her back. "Thought you wanted to take a look at that book before dinner."

"I do. I just…" Was she truly torn between the desire to play the piano and her duty to save the planet? That decision should have been easy. But it wasn't that simple. Music was real. Kevan was real. The way he made her feel was real. The voice in her head had laid a heavy burden on her. What the hell was the Carrier of Life's Preservation anyway? She wasn't some kind of superwoman. She wasn't extraordinary in any way.

Why me?

"Want to enjoy life?" he suggested, bringing her back to her original thought.

"*Yes*," she said on a breathy exhale. "I'm alive when I shouldn't be. Seems like I should do something to celebrate."

His quiet chuckle became an all-out laugh. "I thought we just did that."

Once again, his laughter was contagious. "You'll get no arguments from me, but you see what I mean, don't you? I should be cherishing and enjoying every moment that I can draw breath."

"I do know what you mean. I didn't do that after my brush with death—too much grief and loss. Seems like I'm doing it now, though."

"I'm glad you finally got around to it." Cleona closed the piano with a great deal of reluctance. "Too bad we have to soldier on for the greater good and all that jazz. Just wish I knew exactly what I was soldiering on for."

"That's what we need to find out." He held out a hand. "Ready?"

"Ready as I'll ever be." As she grasped his hand, his touch reminded her that, come what may, she would no longer be facing the future alone, a revelation that gave her strength as well as comfort. "Lead on."

* * * *

Ita looked up from the bread she was kneading as Kevan and Cleona entered the kitchen. "Did you enjoy your day out?"

Her smile and tone seemed innocent enough, but Kevan was quite sure she knew exactly what they'd been up to. First off, they'd been gone far too long for a simple drive through the mountains. And second, Cleona was positively glowing.

"Very much," Cleona replied. "The Black Valley is spooky, but amazing, and we had lunch at this terrific little pub in Killarney."

"Nice to see that Kevan still knows how to show a girl a good time." She glanced toward the clock on the wall, proving she knew precisely how long they'd been away. "And did you take the long way back?"

If he was suspicious before, he was convinced now. She *knew*. "We came through Glenflesk and Kilarvan."

"Ah, yes. Pretty country through there, isn't it?"

If Ita was fishing for discrepancies, she was doomed to disappointment. Cleona had been as taken with the countryside as she had been with his piano.

And other things...

"I haven't seen any part of Ireland yet that wasn't pretty," Cleona remarked. "The people are wonderful too."

Her saintly expression would have convinced anyone but Ita Mahoney—although perhaps Kevan's guilt made him see suspicion that didn't exist. He figured he was safe as long as no one mentioned music.

"We went to Kevan's house after that," Cleona went on. "He has this fabulous old piano. A bit out of tune, but—"

"I didn't know you played piano," Ita interjected. "How lovely. You must play for us sometime."

Kevan waited a beat to see how Cleona would talk her way out of that. Being able to play a recognizable tune was one thing. Cleona's talent was something else altogether.

To his surprise, she laughed, not even bothering to deny Ita's assumption. "We'd need to get a piano tuner to work on it first, although it does have a nice tone." She hesitated as though startled by her own observation, which was the sort of casual comment a seasoned pianist would have made. "I—I'm a bit rusty."

Rusty, hell. She was an artist.

The problem wasn't whether she could play, but what would happen if she were to suddenly lose her newfound ability. Short of claiming to have suffered nerve damage to her fingers, she would have a tough time explaining that, although a concussion could manifest itself in any number of ways. That explanation would be so much easier to swallow than telling her family she'd been possessed by the Array.

He left the thought dangling, curious to see whether the Array would take the bait.

They didn't.

He was beginning to suspect they had all departed that afternoon, which, oddly enough, didn't please him. Like Cleona, he'd grown accustomed to their comments, to the point of expecting them—even missing them.

Perhaps it was due to the loneliness of his existence prior to Cleona's arrival. He hadn't realized how much he missed the ordinary, bantering conversation among friends and family, which may have been what the Array was attempting to convey with their silence.

If so, point made.

"That bread dough smells wonderful," Cleona said.

"It's the yeast that does it." Ita continued working the dough, clearly intending to let Cleona's blatant change of topic pass without comment. "I usually make soda bread, but I thought I'd do something a bit different this time."

"I've never made bread of any kind before, unless you count banana bread. I used to let bananas get spotty on purpose just so I could have an excuse to make it."

Ita grinned. "Fergus does the same thing, although I'm always the one to make the bread."

"I kinda figured that." Cleona hesitated, then glanced at Kevan. "I'll go get that book and be right down."

"Reading romance novels to him now, are you?" Ita suggested, her lilting tone signifying her approval of their burgeoning romance.

Cleona shook her head. "Nope. It's a book on solar energy."

That tidbit actually disrupted Ita's rhythm for a moment. "Planning to go solar, Kevan?"

"I might," he said. "Be nice to produce my own power instead of paying through the nose for it."

"I suppose it would," Ita agreed. "But are there enough sunny days here to make it worthwhile?"

Kevan shrugged, figuring he might as well go along with the ruse. "That's what I want to find out."

Ita continued her kneading for a few moments before directing yet another question at Cleona. "How came you to have a book on solar energy, pet? I wouldn't have thought you'd be interested in such things."

This much, he knew Cleona could tell the truth about, although she might need to gloss over some of the finer points.

"The man I sat beside on the plane was a solar scientist, and he'd written a book on the subject. Since he saved my life by giving me his life jacket, I figured the least I could do for him and his family was to buy his book."

Kevan had to stop himself before responding to her edited version of the story with an appreciative whistle. The one detail she'd omitted was that most of the communication between them occurred *after* Jacob's death.

"My, that was very heroic of him, wasn't it?" Ita commented. "But why didn't he use the jacket himself?"

"Some luggage fell on him when he leaned forward to reach under his seat. I couldn't tell how badly he was hurt, but I think he must have known he was dying."

Again, just enough information to satisfy Ita's curiosity.

"Such a dreadfully sad business," Ita said with a wag of her head. "Go on up and get that book, pet. Hopefully something good can actually come out of such a terrible tragedy."

In Kevan's opinion, something good already had—at least, on a personal level.

However, if his suspicions were correct, the ultimate impact of that disaster would have global effects.

Now all he and Cleona had to do was figure out what they were.

Chapter 13

CLEONA STARTED TOWARD THE STAIRS, WONDERING IF SHE SHOULD ask Kevan to accompany her rather than waiting in the kitchen. Somehow she doubted they could speak freely with Ita in the room. Even the main sitting room was too close. What they really needed to do was take the book back to Kevan's house. Granted, she could tell him how to break the code himself, but working on it together held a much greater appeal.

In the end, all she said was, "Be right back."

She trotted up the stairs only to discover that, despite the changes her entire world had undergone that day, her room hadn't altered a bit. No leprechauns had invaded her space to work their mischief on her belongings. The book was right where she'd left it on the padded window seat.

She opened it to the back flap and addressed the author's photo. "Well, Jacob…You sure picked a great time to communicate with me. Couldn't you have waited until tonight and told me all that stuff in a dream?"

Disappointment met her head on when her question received no reply. Did his silence mean she was back to normal? Just when she'd begun to enjoy being a bit loony? A glance at her reflection in the mirror proved there had been at least one change for the better. The roses were back in her cheeks.

Amazing what a day with Kevan MacFinnin can do.

A quick recap made her smile. In one day, she'd become a tree, communed with planet Earth, made love with Kevan, played the piano like Rachmaninov, and now she was about to decode a secret formula.

Somehow, in the wake of tragedy, she'd managed to have the best and certainly most interesting day of her life. No wonder her senses were singing.

She gave her hair a quick brush and ran back downstairs to find Ita plying Kevan with tea and biscuits in an apparent attempt to make up for all the years she hadn't been able to feed him. He seemed to have taken care of himself well enough without her help. Not too thin, not too fat. Just right—a fact she knew from hands-on experience.

Close observation had revealed other things as well. The scars on his cheek weren't the only ones on his body. Almost his entire left side had been burned, and her heart ached for the pain he must have endured. His ordeal surpassed hers by a mile, and she vowed to spare him further pain, mental or physical, in any way she could.

"*The Green Solar Earth*," Ita quoted from the book cover as Cleona laid it on the table. "Sounds lovely, doesn't it?" By this time, Ita had finished her kneading and was shaping the dough into two loaves with well-greased hands.

"Aye, that it does," Kevan replied. "We take our world too much for granted. It's time we showed it more respect."

Was he saying that because of her bizarre "tree" episode, or had he always believed it? Both, possibly, although she suspected the latter carried more weight. He lived off the land, in tune with his flock, a simple man with simple needs. Would that there were more like him in the world.

Already, she could see her life melding with his—planting seeds in his neglected garden growing food for his table, filling his heart with her love, and giving birth to his children. If she'd been asked a week ago, Cleona never would have said her goals and aspirations were that simple. But they were now. Perhaps they always had been.

The life she would have with Kevan wasn't anything like the life she'd left behind in Dallas. The fast pace, the stress—all for what? Marketing a university? Did it really need marketing? Probably not, although marketing brought in revenue, hopefully to keep the buildings maintained and tuitions low—that was the theory anyway. But did it really? Or did someone other than students profit?

Cleona was rapidly approaching the point where she didn't care—at least, not like she used to. She might not know a thing about sheep or gardening, but she could learn. Ita would make an excellent mentor, and so would the rest of the family, Kevan included.

He picked up the book and nodded toward the living room. "Mind if I look at this in there?"

"Go right ahead," Ita replied. She gave one of the loaves a final pat before placing it in a baking pan. "Take the tea and biscuits with you, if you like." She smiled at Cleona. "Shall I pour a cup for you, pet?"

Cleona glanced at Ita's buttery fingers. "No need. I can get it."

"Might be best." Grinning her approval, Ita went to work on the second loaf.

After pouring herself a cup of tea, Cleona followed Kevan into the front room.

He held up a pad of paper and a pencil. "Figured we might need these."

"Good idea." She settled herself on the sofa beside him. "As I recall, the symbols were at the beginning of each chapter. How many chapters are there?"

Kevan flipped to the table of contents. "Twenty-six."

"My, how convenient," Cleona drawled. "First, we need to give each numbered chapter a corresponding letter of the alphabet—'A' would be Chapter One, and so forth."

"Unless he decided to be tricky and start from the last chapter."

Despite the scowl she shot at him, she couldn't deny the possibility. "We'll do it both ways. This way first."

"Do you know what this is supposed to look like when we're done?"

"Sort of. I saw it written out, so I have a general idea, but that's about it."

"Better that than nothing," he said. "So if his name is Jacob, we should start with Chapter Ten."

"Ooh, you're good. I'd have to count on my fingers to do that."

He laughed. "How do you know I didn't?"

"I don't. Although the Array could have been doing the math for you."

"Yeah. Where the devil is Jacob when we need him?"

"Strangely silent," she replied. "I haven't heard from him directly since I bought the book."

Kevan appeared to consider this. "Maybe that's all he needed you to do."

"Maybe. The dream or vision or whatever post-orgasmic, stuporous imagining that was filled in the rest."

"You were in a stupor?" If his smile was any indication, he seemed inordinately pleased by that possibility.

"I guess so. Not sure what else you could call it."

With a self-congratulatory grunt, he muttered, "I must be better than I thought."

She made a face at him. "Let's not get cocky now. You had some sort of stupendous, stuporous event too, which must mean I'm pretty good myself."

"We'll call it a draw, then." He peered at the page. "So what is it we're looking for?"

She pointed to the chapter heading. "See those little squiggles before and after the chapter description? That's what we want."

"Could've used a larger font," he complained. "I may need a magnifying glass to see them."

"No one said this would be easy. I mean, it *is* supposed to be secret."

"I still don't get why all the secrecy was necessary. If this is such an important formula, it should be backed up somewhere or even published." His expression grew thoughtful as his voice trailed off. "Where do you suppose Jacob was headed when he boarded that plane?"

Cleona shrugged. "No idea. He wasn't what you'd call chatty during the flight, and he hasn't been very talkative as a member of the Array. For a while there, I thought he was gone, until that…" Her voice sank to a whisper as the sound of water running in the kitchen served as a reminder that they weren't alone. "…vision thing."

Kevan followed her gaze toward the kitchen and nodded his understanding. "What if he was keeping the formula secret until he could sell it to the highest bidder? Any of his work has to be something significant to the solar energy field. A new technique for producing solar cells or some sort of major improvement to current technology."

"Sounds reasonable," Cleona said. "Maybe he was afraid someone was trying to steal it from him."

"Or maybe it was what got him killed."

Kevan's words echoed through an eerie, ominous silence.

Cleona shook her head in disbelief. "An entire 747 filled with innocent people crashed into the sea just to kill one man? That's, that's—" She hesitated, searching through her working vocabulary for a word bad enough to describe such a thing. "Overkill" was the first that came to mind. "—horrific" was the second.

"It is indeed," Kevan said. "But to people for whom money and power are more important than human life…" He paused, clearing his throat.

Cleona knew he was thinking about another horrific event. One that had changed his life forever. Despite the impulse to hug him, she settled for squeezing his hand.

"Let's figure this out first," he finally said. "No one knows we're trying to decipher the code, so we're probably safe for now."

"But what do we do with the damn thing when we finally figure it out? Post it on the internet?"

"That's actually not a bad idea. If the formula is made public, we can't be targeted for knowing it exists."

She stared at the book lying open on his knee. "Sure would be nice to know what it is before we do all that. I can't imagine it would be something bad, like the formula for some sort of doomsday bomb. I mean, if I'm the Carrier of Life's Preservation, I can only assume that Jacob is one of the good guys. If he worked for an oil company, I'd believe otherwise. The Array survived the crash for a reason. At least, that's what they told me. If I'm—" She gasped as realization struck. "Holy cow... What if this formula *is* 'life's preservation?'"

Kevan's eyes widened for an instant, then he nodded. "Makes sense. After all, you *were* the carrier."

"And you were the catalyst that made me remember it."

He nodded. "Like you made me remember more about the university bombing." With a sideways glance, he added, "Seems we're quite a pair, you and I."

"Aren't we, though?"

Kevan leaned closer as though intending to give her a kiss when approaching footsteps warned him off.

Seconds later, Ita passed through the front hall, having traded her apron for a barn coat and a pair of stout leather gloves. "I'll be out in the garden for a bit while the bread is rising. Don't study too hard, now."

With that cheery admonition, she left through the front door, closing it behind her.

* * * *

When his heart and lungs finally resumed their normal functions, Kevan grimaced. "That was close."

Cleona giggled. "Makes me wonder if we should just 'fess up and be done with it."

"That would certainly simplify things." Hoping to recall himself to the task at hand rather than succumbing to the desire to cover her with kisses, he tapped the pencil on the notepad. "Although we do need to finish this so you can call Jillian."

"You're right." She sighed. "Not looking forward to that either. I'm still not sure what to tell her or even how to begin."

"Can't say I envy you that." He copied down the symbols from Chapter Ten, then moved on to Chapter One.

Cleona nodded her approval. "You're getting good at this."

"Too bad I have no idea what any of this means. Should've paid more attention in math class." To be honest, he wasn't sure whether the formula related to math or chemistry.

"We'll figure that out later," she said. "Keep going."

Kevan flipped back and forth through the book, doing his best to avoid making any mistakes. The numbers were easy enough, but the symbols meant nothing to him, which probably meant that Jacob hadn't hopped over to him during the transfer.

When he'd finished, he handed her the notepad. "What d'you think?"

She stared at what he'd written. "Something's missing. It should be longer than that."

Not, I *think* it should be longer, but it *should* be longer. He didn't bother to ask how she knew that.

"That's all the letters in his name," Kevan said. "I even included his middle initial. What d'you suppose the 'D' stands for…"

He turned to the biography on the back flap. After giving the bio a quick read, he shook his head. "Nothing here, although there is a website listed."

"We could look there or Google him," Cleona suggested. She fished her phone from her handbag and swiped the screen. "Not much of a signal here," she said after a moment's scrutiny. "I could probably make a call, but I can't get online. I'm getting a WiFi signal, though. Don't suppose you know the Mahoney's password, do you?"

"Sure don't." Kevan grinned. "I'm sure Ita would tell you what it is, but it might be best to go back to my place and use my computer." He had an ulterior motive, of course, although no one could blame a bloke for trying.

She hesitated, biting her lip in the most endearing fashion, seemingly oblivious to the innuendo. "Maybe I should just call Jillian. If she's in on this Array thing, she may know something we don't."

Considering Cleona had been the carrier of Jacob Emhart's spirit, he doubted Jillian would know anything about the man. However, with no other suggestions to make, he could only nod his agreement. "If nothing else, it should be an interesting conversation."

"No kidding." She tapped the screen before holding the phone to her ear. "Hello, Jillian?" she began. "This is Cleona Mahoney."

Putting the call on speaker probably wasn't a good idea, but the moment Cleona paused to listen to Jillian's reply, Kevan wished he'd suggested it.

"Physically, yes," Cleona said. "Otherwise, I'm not really sure *what* to think. Some really strange things have been happening."

After another pause, she went on, "I'm still in Ireland, at my aunt and uncle's farm near Kenmare." Cleona's deep breath didn't stop the quaver in her voice, proving she'd been more nervous about making the call than he'd suspected. "I've been seeing things, hearing things, and having the strangest dreams. I know things I couldn't possibly know. I'm either losing my mind or, well...it sounds crazy, but—"

During the next pause, Cleona glanced at Kevan. "Would you mind if I put this on speaker? There's someone else here with me. He's also...involved."

And then some.

Cleona nodded, then laid the phone on her knee and tapped the speaker. "Can you hear me?"

"Yes," Jillian replied. "Listen, if you don't mind, I'm going to put my phone on speaker too. Ranjiv Tenali is with me. He's...well"—she paused, chuckling—"he's also *involved*."

"More than that, I'd say," a male voice with a decidedly British accent chimed in a moment later. "She just asked me to marry her." After a beat, he added, "I said yes."

Stifling a giggle, Cleona aimed a speaking glance at Kevan. "Congratulations. Kevan and I haven't gotten that far. But then, we only met each other yesterday."

Kevan blinked, mentally computing the time he and Cleona had spent together. Astonishingly enough, they truly had only met on the previous afternoon.

"Kevan MacFinnin is my cousin Sinead's nearest neighbor," Cleona said. "They were childhood pals, and I think Sinead—"

"Was playing matchmaker," Kevan interjected. "Seems to have been a good plan too."

Jillian laughed. "Glad to hear it. Ranjiv's mother did the same thing." She cleared her throat. "So, Cleona...you've been hearing voices?"

Chapter 14

CLEONA WAS RELIEVED TO DISCOVER THAT JILLIAN NOT ONLY DIDN'T think she was crazy, she'd had similar experiences, including a spiritual event that was a lot like Cleona's "tree" episode, except hers had happened at Stonehenge.

"I was getting a 'save the planet' vibe," Jillian said. "And our other adventures seem to be related to it in some way. Viewed in that light, your connection with Jacob Emhart makes a lot of sense. I don't know how closely you've been following the news—"

"Hardly at all," Cleona admitted. "I probably should have, but—"

"Oh, I know what you mean," Jillian said quickly. "Seeing my picture on the front page of *The London Times* was unnerving to say the least. But I'm not afraid anymore." The squaring of her shoulders was almost audible. "Anyway, what you might not know is that Emhart was on his way to Paris for an energy summit after a stopover in London. There were other participants aboard, and although the summit has been postponed—"

"Oh, let me guess," Cleona drawled. "The oil company representatives were all on a different flight, right?"

"Several different flights, actually," Jillian replied, her ironic tone mirroring Cleona's own. "But none were aboard the plane that went down. Ordinarily, I'd have assumed it was just a bizarre coincidence, but after everything else that's happened, I have my doubts."

Cleona's belief in coincidence was losing strength with each passing hour, particularly given her suspicion that Earth itself had dubbed her as the Carrier of Life's Preservation—not something to be taken lightly, whatever the source.

"Same here," Cleona said. "Kevan and I have been working on deciphering a code in Jacob's book that appears to be a formula of some kind. Not sure what it means exactly, although it's obviously important enough to keep secret. Something's missing, though. The code corresponds to the letters in his name. We have that much, but it's too short." Cleona gave a brief thought to why Jillian wasn't questioning how she knew as much as she did, but dismissed the notion as quickly as it surfaced. Having dealt with voices in her own head, Jillian obviously knew the drill. "We're still working on it, and we think what's missing is his middle name. The book only lists his name as Jacob D. Emhart."

"We could check on that from here," Jillian suggested. "I also have some thoughts as to what we should do with the formula when you finish with it. Might even help us learn what it's for."

"Kevan and I have been talking about that too," Cleona said. "We thought about going public with it. You know...run it up the flagpole and see who salutes? After all, it can't be something bad for the planet or Earth wouldn't want us to figure it out."

Jillian chuckled. "Makes sense in a bizarre, mystical sort of way, doesn't it?"

"No kidding. Everything that's happened since we boarded that plane has been bizarre and mystical." A glance at Kevan triggered a warm flush that flowed through Cleona's entire body. Her immediate bond with him was perhaps the most amazing thing of all. "We seem to have each been rewarded with our lives and a partner in crime, so to speak."

"The perks of being Earth's chosen ones, you mean? If so, I'm good with that." Jillian was openly laughing now, making Cleona wonder whether Ranjiv was as gorgeous as Kevan.

Probably so. Different, perhaps, although no doubt every bit as perfect.

"Me too," Cleona said. "Think Susan is part of this?"

Jillian didn't hesitate. "I don't see why she wouldn't be. She seemed so sure that the crash wasn't an accident. Given the nature of the major terrorist attacks in the past twenty years, anyone could've made that assumption, but she was pretty definite about it."

"Yeah. Like it wasn't a guess—not even a reasonable one. She *knew*."

Kevan leaned closer to the phone. "Don't suppose you've talked to her, have you?"

"Not since we landed in London," Jillian replied. "I've thought about it several times. I've just been so wrapped up in everything that's been happening here. Things didn't really settle down until today."

"And then I called you." The irony of the situation twisted Cleona's smile. "Timing is everything, huh?"

"I suppose so, although I had an idea this was one of those tip of the iceberg things. There had to be more to saving the planet than solving an eleven-year-old murder."

Cleona nodded. "Like there has to be more to it than—" She stopped mid-sentence as the connections seemed to meld in her mind. "—terrorist bombings and murdered sheep."

"Excuse me?" Jillian squeaked. "Murdered sheep? Seriously?"

"Aye, four of them in as many months," Kevan replied. "All killed in the same manner, and all with the same symbol painted on the fleece."

"Symbol?" Jillian echoed.

"A rendering of Ballycarbery Castle. We're headed there tomorrow." This time, Kevan was the one to clear his throat in a rather ominous manner. "We both had a dream about it—or a vision if you prefer."

"Actually, I had two," Cleona said. "One dream, one vision."

Kevan frowned. "You didn't tell me about the vision."

Her eyes widened, then narrowed, furrowing her brow. "You're right. I didn't. Guess I got distracted by…other things." If Kevan had any sense at all, he would know precisely what those other things were, himself being the primary culprit. "At breakfast this morning, I had this…I guess we're calling it a vision. It was like watching a movie, only I was the one behind the camera. I saw a man pass through the gate and go into the castle, and I followed him. I never did see why he was there, although I do remember his face—dark, swarthy, and exotic. Not bad-looking, but hardened and grim."

"Middle Eastern, perhaps?" Jillian prompted.

"Maybe," Cleona said. "I'm not sure."

"Could have been Indian or Arabic as well," Ranjiv added. "Even those of us who are from that part of the world can't always tell the difference by appearance alone. Language sets us apart as much as anything—that and style of dress."

Cleona shook her head. "No clues there; he was wearing an ordinary shirt and jeans." She closed her eyes, and the image was right there behind her eyelids. "Blue shirt. Long sleeves rolled up to just below the elbow. Average height. Lean build. Black hair, dark complexion." She opened her eyes and shrugged. "Nothing remarkable. No tattoos or other identifying marks, and he didn't appear to be armed. He was wearing some sort of bracelet, although it struck me as unremarkable as the rest of him. Except for his eyes; they were shuttered and secretive."

"Which would be appropriate if he was going into the castle," Kevan remarked. "Trespassing being illegal and all."

"So you didn't see this one, Kevan?" Jillian asked.

"No, I didn't," Kevan replied. "Although I did have what you might call an enhanced memory of the bombing that killed my parents. While Cleona was seeing the code for Emhart's formula, I was seeing a man holding a detonator." With a glance at Cleona, he added, "Interestingly enough, your description would also fit him. D'you suppose they're the same person?"

Cleona shook her head slowly, frowning. "I dunno... Seems like too much of a coincidence, doesn't it?"

Jillian's snort signaled her disagreement. "Listen, if there's one thing I've learned in the past week, it's that there's no such thing as coincidence. Everything has meaning. Every weird feeling, assumption, craving—you name it—is there for a reason, and everything is connected. Trust your instincts, Cleona. They won't steer you wrong."

Cleona couldn't help admiring Jillian's conviction. Too bad she wasn't quite ready to share it. Still, the suggestion that the man at the castle and the one present at the university bombing were one and the same seemed reasonable, albeit in a bizarre, surreal, save-the-world-while-communing-with-the-planet sort of way. What she had yet to figure out was the source of her "vision" and its connection to the crash.

Did that memory belong to a random witness who just happened to be in the Array? Or was it someone who was actually involved?

She waited a few seconds for the Array to chime in with that information.

Which, of course, they didn't.

Guess we're on our own now.

"Okay then, if that's true and there *is* a connection, does that mean this guy is our target? Or would he be our contact? Forgive me, I'm new to this sort of thing." Cleona would have liked to have given it a name like, "our mission" or "our destiny" or something of that nature. However, at the moment it was just too freakin' weird to hang a label on.

"No worries," Jillian said. "But yeah. I think you need to find him. Somehow."

Kevan gave Cleona a nudge. "Are we still on for the castle in the morning, then?"

"I suppose so," Cleona replied. With a wry grin, she added,

"Although that may change depending on what kind of dreams I have tonight." Or visions she might have while awake.

Obviously, falling asleep wasn't a prerequisite.

* * * *

The connection between his enhanced memory and Cleona's vision made so much sense, Kevan wished she'd told him about it sooner. No doubt she would have mentioned it eventually—probably during the drive to Ballycarbery Castle. "I think we should pay a visit to the castle no matter what you dream about."

"I agree," Jillian said. "We'll see what we can find out online. And Kevan, if you'll give me the date and location of the bombing, we'll do some research on that too."

Kevan didn't have to dig very deep for that information, relaying it promptly and with surprisingly little emotion. Perhaps the more recent tragedy had given him a different perspective, allowing him to see the bigger picture.

That there *was* a bigger picture was becoming more obvious by the minute. Everything Jillian had told them pointed to it, and in that light, any connections on their end made perfect sense. The strange thing was, while the IRA had been among those blamed for that bombing, they'd never claimed responsibility. Add that to the fact that the man he'd seen holding the detonator didn't look the slightest bit Irish, and the links to the current disaster were even stronger.

"I can run some searches when I get home later tonight," Kevan said. Would Cleona come with him when he left? He hoped so, mainly because he had an idea that she wouldn't be spending the night in the Mahoney's spare bedroom if she did.

"Sounds good," Jillian said. "Guess we'd better get started. Keep in touch."

"Will do." Cleona ended the call, then leaned forward with her knuckles pressed against her mouth as if trying to keep her words from tumbling out. After several moments of silence, she heaved a ragged breath and grasped his hand. "The plot thickens."

"That's putting it mildly." Her fingers were cold as he raised them to his lips, and when he wrapped an arm around her shoulders, she snuggled into his embrace, even drawing her feet up beneath her. "You're trembling."

"I know." Her teeth chattered as she spoke. "This is getting scarier all the time—terrorist bombings, plane crashes, murdered sheep. I'm not sure which is more terrifying, nearly dying in the crash or living in the aftermath."

"I doubt you have anything to fear now, and perhaps I don't either. We're both survivors, and we survived for a reason. That much is becoming increasingly clear."

Raising her head, she gazed up at him, her dark brown eyes threatening to capture his soul. "You think we have some sort of protection?"

"I can't be sure, of course, but it would make sense if we did."

She nestled against him again, seeming to belong there. "Not sure I'd want to put that theory to the test—especially against a bunch of terrorists."

"Something tells me we already have—and we survived. I'm not saying we should do anything foolish, but do you see what I mean? If we have some sort of purpose, we need to live long enough to accomplish it."

"Or die trying?"

Her trembling had subsided and her tiny chuckle proved she'd relaxed enough to find a bit of humor in their situation. Gallows humor, perhaps, but humor nonetheless.

"Oh, I hope not." He kissed the top of her head only to note that he seemed to be doing that quite a lot—a circumstance that pleased as well as excited him. Having her close enough to kiss was delightful, giving way to all manner of carnal imaginings that had nothing whatsoever to do with, as she had put it, terrorist bombings, plane crashes, and murdered sheep.

When their mission was accomplished, would they still be together like this? Or would they part ways, her returning home to Texas and him resuming a solitary existence tending his flock? Either way, their time was limited—somewhere between a lifetime and a week. They shouldn't waste it.

He closed his eyes, willing himself to focus on the present rather than the unknown and possibly dangerous future. He'd meant what he said about being protected. But by whom? Planet Earth? Mother Nature? God? Those entities hadn't saved anyone else—at least not that he'd ever heard. People lived and died by chance, and sometimes even chance was overcome by strong purpose—not to mention emotions ranging from love to hate.

Then there was the Array. Cleona hadn't heard from them for a while and neither had he. They'd each been given a taste of what it was like to have an internal coaching staff helping them find their way—only to realize that the ultimate solutions to the difficulties they faced wouldn't be handed to them on a platter. Whoever was pulling the strings obviously enjoyed the sweat of human endeavor, as well as testing the problem-solving capabilities of the human mind.

Thus far, they'd solved a puzzle, made connections where there had previously been none, and managed to find each other in the process. Their mutual attraction had been immediate and intense. Was that planned? Was it necessary or merely incidental?

He had no answers to those questions, but for now, he would cherish this moment, this respite, this calm before the storm. The house was so quiet; the creaking timbers as the building settled were like crashing cymbals. On the wall above them, a clock ticked off the seconds, proving that time continued to slip past them, its progress unimpeded by anything anyone could do or say.

Constant and eternal...

Like a camera coming into focus, his mind's eye revealed the castle walls looming on the hill above. The tide was out, stranding clumps of seaweed amid the rocks of the shallow inlet to west. He passed though the rusted wire of the surrounding fence and floated like a ghost on the wind, hovering above, then swooping down to find *him* there, just as Cleona had described.

He was undoubtedly the same man from Kevan's own memory, although older now; the smooth curves of his face had become a collection of sharp, chiseled planes. A hand with a puckered scar removed a stone from the wall, behind which was a recess large enough to conceal... What? A plastic bag? At least there appeared to be a sheet of folded paper inside it rather than a stash of pot or cocaine. The man turned, glaring up at him as he hovered. Kevan doubted he could be seen, not when he only existed as a wisp of thought. Perhaps the man only glared at the sky, which was threatening rain. The brick was quickly replaced and the bag stuffed into a pocket without a glance at its contents.

Whoever he was—*what*ever he was—he was obviously very well-paid. The smarmy bastard drove off in a shiny new BMW X6— black, of course, as befit any successful underworld operative.

What he didn't fit was the stereotypical terrorist mold. Terrorists always seemed to have plenty of money for bombs and other weaponry, but fancy cars?

Hmm...

Too bad he couldn't follow the bloke. Whatever consciousness had witnessed this event seemed to be tied to the castle, like a phantom doomed to haunt the crumbling ruin for all eternity. Kevan was no expert on the supernatural, although given that everyone in the Array had drowned in the North Atlantic, a local spirit seemed an unlikely candidate.

But not impossible, especially if Earth's own spirit was the one in charge.

"Bloody hell," he said aloud. "The ghost of Ballycarbery Castle has joined the Array."

Chapter 15

FOR ONCE, CLEONA'S MIND HAD BEEN BLISSFULLY SILENT. No voices. No visions. Nothing apart from the comfort to be had from being curled up beside Kevan MacFinnin—until he started talking about ghosts.

She waited the space of perhaps five heartbeats before asking the obvious question. "Oh, and what makes you think that?"

"No one else could have put such a dream in my head."

"And that dream would be...?"

"One very much like the one you had this morning, only I was able to see what our terrorist friend was up to at the castle."

Another finger-drumming wait. "Are you planning to tell me, or are you gonna let the ghost do it?"

"There was some paper in a plastic bag behind a loose stone in the castle wall. He took it and then drove off."

"A *ghost* told you this?"

"Aye." At her arched brow, he added, "And what would the rest of the Array be besides ghosts?"

He had a point. "True. But why a ghost from the castle and not the plane crash?"

"Seems obvious enough to me. If the entire planet is running the show, it could call on any ghost it chooses."

"Hmm... Sort of like the Stonehenge spirits that spoke to Jillian?"

"Something like that. Or your own experience in the Black Valley."

She snuggled closer and hugged him as best she could, considering she could only use the arm that was draped across his chest. "You truly are one in a million, my friend. Best cohort a girl could ever have. You even believe in spooks."

The Cowardly Lion from *The Wizard of Oz* had nothing on Kevan when it came to believing in spooks.

I do believe in spooks. I do, I do, I do...

For a moment, she was sure the Array had spoken, although her own recollection was undoubtedly responsible for that quote. She'd seen that movie as many times as anyone.

"I'm glad you think so, but what choice do I have when there's so much that can't be explained any other way? In the vision I just had, I saw our man as though I were hovering above him. Only a ghost could have seen anything from that viewpoint—or someone in a helicopter. And since none of the original Array died in that castle, none of them would be tied to it. The only explanation is that a ghost from the castle supplied the visual."

"Works for me," she said. "All wrapped up neat and tidy. Did the castle ghost have any ideas as to what was in that plastic bag?"

"None whatsoever," he replied. "Although I suppose that could change."

"Could've been payment or a map. Instructions, maybe."

"Or government secrets?"

"Real James Bond stuff?" She nodded. "That or a contract of some kind."

Contract. She froze as the implication sank in like an icicle through her chest. "Holy cow... What if it's the *other* kind of contract?"

Kevan responded with a low whistle. "Like hiring a hit man, you mean?" With her nod, he added, "Or a terrorist for hire?"

She nodded. "Scary thought, isn't it?" Quite terrifying in fact, which was probably the desired effect. "Think about it. Several terrorist groups have already claimed responsibility for the plane crash. What if some of them are bogus?"

"A ring of assassins posing as terrorists," he mused. "They might even be keeping quiet while the other groups take the credit. We really need to do some research and find out who else died in the bombing aside from my parents. I can't remember any names, but I know there were others." Seconds later, Cleona felt a tremor rip through his body. "D'you suppose the 'new' version of what I remember from the bombing came from someone else? Someone who either survived only to die when your plane went down, or—"

"—someone who died in the bombing and latched onto you?"

Groaning, he pressed the heel of his hand to his forehead. "They're only communicating with me now? Surely if it was Mum or Dad..."

"I'm guessing it wasn't," Cleona said gently. "They would have made themselves known before this if it had been one or both of them."

His nod was slow, almost reluctant, as though he wasn't ready to abandon the possibility just yet. "Perhaps the one I picked up was the intended target."

"Makes sense." She sat there, fretting her lower lip with her teeth. As much tissue as she was nibbling away, she was surprised she didn't draw blood, until a metallic flavor touched her tongue, stopping her. "And you're right. We really do need to do some research. You were at a university, therefore I'm gonna take a wild guess and say the intended target was a professor. I'll even take it a step further and say he or she was researching alternative forms of energy."

"Jillian did say everything would be connected. Just never thought it would go that far back."

"Yes, but the murder case she and Ranjiv solved happened eleven years ago," Cleona reminded him. "The bombing occurred *after* that. This strikes me as a long-standing battle between—"

"Good and evil?"

"Maybe. Although I was thinking more along the lines of a war between greed and the greater good."

Kevan drew a breath to speak, but was cut off by the sound of the front door being unlatched. Ita came bustling in and began toeing off her boots on the mat by the door.

"There now," Ita said. "The bread should be nicely risen by now. Did you find what you were looking for in that book?"

"Most of it," Kevan replied. "I'll need to know more before I commit to anything. Seems promising, though."

Cleona marveled at how smooth a liar he was until she realized he was telling the absolute truth. He was simply answering a different question.

"Solar power would certainly be lovely," Ita said with a pensive smile. "It's the start-up cost that stops most folks from converting."

"You're right there, Ita," Kevan agreed. "That and the space needed for the collectors."

Cleona blinked. Was that it? Would Emhart's formula make solar power more affordable? Decreasing the size of solar collectors while at the same time making them more efficient? She tried to imagine powering a car with a cell the size of a headlight, or using a collector no bigger than a satellite dish—perhaps even smaller than that—to power the average house.

"Smaller and more efficient equals feasible and affordable."

Widespread conversion to solar power would greatly reduce the dependence on fossil fuels. That was a given. But would the oil producers retaliate? And if so, how?

Terrorism already had everyone in the western world on edge. Why not capitalize on the existing fear?

It made sense, all right. Too much sense. No doubt terrorist organizations were delighted to have someone pay them for their efforts. They could eliminate anyone the oil companies considered a threat, and then use those acts of terror to support any ideology they chose.

Meanwhile, the environment would continue to be destroyed.

And now Earth is fighting back.

Although Cleona hadn't had any say when it came to choosing sides, she doubted she was on the losing team. She was, after all, the Carrier of Life's Preservation.

No hotshot oil tycoon could claim *that* title.

Ita shook her head, her lips pressed into a grim line. "It's a crime the way what's good for people costs more than the things that cause them harm. It ought to be the other way 'round, don't you think?"

"Absolutely," Kevan replied. "But then, we aren't the ones in charge, are we?"

"No, we're just the poor sods who have to work for a living and have very little to show for it when we're done." Ita snorted with disgust. "What little we have could all be gone in the blink of an eye."

"But if solar power *was* affordable..." Cleona completely lost her train of thought as she recalled the last mention of "affordable" in her thoughts.

Only it hadn't come from her own imaginings. It had come from the mind of Jacob Emhart.

No one in the Array had spoken to her for some time. Was that really him or merely her own recollection of something she'd read in his book?

Oh, come on, Jacob! Say something! We could use your help here.

After waiting several moments without receiving a reply, she concluded that her entreaty either didn't warrant a response or the Array was only allowed one comment per day.

Mighty specific rules.

But who was making those rules? Mother Earth?

Without missing a beat, Kevan picked up where she'd left off.

"Oh, aye. If everyone had the money to install collectors, the world would be a far better place."

"I certainly can't argue with that," Ita said. "Wish there was more we could do about it than wish and hope."

Her aunt's wistful sigh was echoed within Cleona's own mind, proving that the Array hadn't been completely silenced.

"There may well be." Kevan tapped the book with a fingertip. "I believe the answers are right here."

Was he saying that for Cleona's benefit or Ita's?

Ita's probably. He knew Cleona believed it. She had to.

Why else would she still be alive? For that matter, why else would *he* still be alive?

Definitely food for thought.

* * * *

"I hope you're right about that," Ita said, then aimed a concerned look toward Cleona. "Not feeling well, luv?"

That Cleona was having one of her mental lapses was perfectly clear to Kevan. Obviously, Ita noticed it too.

"I–I'm tired, I guess."

"Hungry too, I'll wager. Here I am talking your ears off when I should be gettin' that bread in the oven." As Ita smiled at her niece, Kevan chastised himself for having been such a hermit. He had almost forgotten how sweet Ita's smiles could be. "Dinner'll be ready as soon as the bread's done. You might want to rest up until then."

"I'll do that," Cleona said before covering a yawn. As far as Kevan was concerned, she could rest up right where she was if she was truly tired, which he doubted. He was betting on the Array being responsible for her bout of woolgathering.

He waited until Ita was out of earshot. "So…been hearing voices?"

"Maybe. Although even if none of them are talking, I'm pretty sure I've figured out what Emhart's formula is for. 'Smaller and more efficient equals feasible and affordable.' I may have read it in the book, or he may have whispered it to me just now, but that's what his formula does. It reduces solar collectors to a fraction of their current size and makes them exponentially more efficient."

"Makes sense. We'd need to prove that, though—or at least get the formula to someone who would know what to do with it." With a short laugh, he added, "Last time I checked, I was naught but a sheep farmer."

"Not exactly my area of expertise either," Cleona said. "Too bad I don't know many professors where I work, although I'm sure I could ferret out a few if I put my mind to it. The trick would be explaining how I came to have the formula. Wish we could just post it online as a meme of some sort."

"That's a thought." He sat back, preparing to assume the role of devil's advocate. "Let's say we could do that without becoming targets ourselves. How can we guarantee the right people will see it?"

"Hmm... good question," she replied. "I suppose we could set up a blog and post it there, but without a decent following, no one would ever see it." Her eyes lit up. "Maybe Ranjiv could help. After all, he *is* a reporter, and if he doesn't know how to spread the word, well...we're screwed."

She had a point, although one tiny little problem remained. "Are you forgetting that we don't have all of the formula? You said it was too short."

"We only need to find out what Jacob's middle name is. How hard could that be? In fact, I'm surprised Jillian hasn't called me back already." She grimaced. "Wish we'd taken the book back to your place to begin with. We could have done the search ourselves."

"We still can. Bread takes at least forty-five minutes to bake. We can head over to my place and still be back in time for supper."

"You're sure?"

"Absolutely."

"Then what are we waiting for? Let's do it!"

Chapter 16

"BINGO," CLEONA ANNOUNCED AS SHE PEERED OVER KEVAN'S shoulder. "Jacob David Emhart. We probably could've guessed that, but we really need to be correct. This formula has to work, and someone in the know has to see it."

A search of Emhart's name had yielded an astonishing number of results. Even so, having learned the man's middle name, the next step was something of a puzzle. Kevan scrolled down the page, looking for a promising link while doing his best to tamp down his body's reaction to Cleona's close proximity. The last time they'd been alone in his house, he'd carried her to his bed. Immediately. Now, her intoxicating scent filled his head and her warmth reminded him that there were far more pleasant activities to share with her than surfing the Web.

Clearing his throat with an effort, he forced himself to focus on the task at hand, marveling at the level of self-restraint it took to keep his hands off her. "Let's see if he has a website… There." As the page loaded, he couldn't believe their luck. "Look, there's even a blog on it. Too bad we can't post anything other than a comment." He glanced up at her. "Unless he's shared his password with you."

The gritting of her teeth conveyed her frustration. "No, he hasn't. Yet another time when a more talkative Array would be terribly useful. It's as though having set us on the quest, he and the rest of the Array have deserted us."

"Maybe, although anyone trying to save the world has to put in a bit of sweat and toil, wouldn't you say?"

She squeezed his shoulder and gave him a tiny shake, apparently oblivious to the bolt of electricity she'd sent spiraling downward to ignite in his groin. "There you go being all reasonable. I'm ready to do this *now*. I mean, the polar ice caps are melting as we speak."

Polar ice isn't the only thing heating up.

"I'll not argue with that," he said after regaining some semblance of control. "But we aren't going to change anything overnight, Cleona. I wish we could." Chuckling, he added, "Are you always this anxious to finish what you start?"

"Hey, my college buddies didn't call me 'Miss Proactive' for nothing. I like being a step ahead. Always have. Sitting around waiting for stuff to happen goes against the grain, big time."

"There are those who say it's already too late."

"According to Mother Earth, it's never too late, not while there's a spark of life left in the world. That's what being the Carrier of Life's Preservation is all about: bringing us back from the brink of extinction." She drummed her fingers on his shoulder, once again seemingly unaware of her effect on him. "Maybe there's something else we know that we don't *know* we know."

"Like what?"

"Oh, I don't know... Some sort of carbon dioxide scrubber for the atmosphere or something that could be introduced into the atmosphere to filter out or reflect some of the sun's radiant energy. Anything to stop the polar ice from melting."

"I doubt that's feasible, and it might even cause more harm than good." He shook his head. "Any beneficial effects would probably take too long, if they worked at all. No, the problem is that once the melting starts, it initiates a continuous feedback loop that can't be stopped. The polar ice normally reflects the sun's rays to keep the planet cool. A smaller ice pack means more dark sea water to absorb the heat and accelerate the melting process." He paused as an image flitted through his mind, one that had nothing to do with his previous train of thought, even to the point of driving it from his head completely.

Mirrors.

"What if something man-made could do the same thing?" he mused. "If everyone on the planet pitched in to build it..."

"Ooh, I like it," Cleona exclaimed. "Solar panels in space?"

"Possibly. Although I was thinking more along the lines of mirrors."

Kevan could scarcely believe the words that were issuing from his lips. The scope of these ideas went far beyond anything he'd ever contemplated before, leading him to suspect—

Okay. Whose idea was that? Come on now, don't be shy.

He waited for the Array to speak. However, as before, they remained silent.

I'm no scientist. I'm only a sheep farmer who once wanted to study geology. It had to be one of you.

Cleona gasped. "That came from the Array, didn't it?"

Kevan wasn't the s ightest bit surprised that she would reach the same conclusion. She of all people should know the signs.

"I believe so," he replied. "They aren't saying, but I saw it—" Did one image qualify as a vision? Or was it a dream fragment? "—in my mind's eye. A vast array of mirrors."

"Wouldn't even need to be mirrors," she said after a moment's hesitation. "Any shiny white surface would do it. Sort of like reverse solar panels."

He nodded. "Reflect rather than absorb. Aye, it could work... A huge undertaking, of course, although desperate times call for desperate measures."

"Yes, but there are still people who insist global warming is a myth. Is the situation desperate enough to get the necessary backing?"

"Probably. People who live on islands would consider it to be a more pressing problem than those who live on the larger continents. They can move inland. We don't have that much land to spare here in Ireland. If the ice caps melted entirely, I'm guessing Kenmare would be under water."

She nodded. "Think of all the coastal cities that would vanish: New York, Miami, San Francisco. Venice wouldn't stand a chance, and the Florida Keys would be gone."

"River levels would rise too. Cities like London, New Orleans, and all the cities along the Danube...all gone." A glance at the lower corner the computer screen reminded him that their time was limited. "It's getting late. We'd better head back or Ita will send out a search party."

He was already closing the laptop when Cleona clutched his shoulder. "Wait a minute...there on the side bar. He has a Twitter account. What if we posted the formula on Twitter using his handle? He's bound to have plenty of followers."

Kevan shook his head. "That's considered a 'mention,' which his followers wouldn't see, although a 'solar energy' hash tag might reach the right people. Looks like he also has a Facebook page. We could probably post it there. The meme is a good idea. Too bad most of those symbols aren't on the standard keyboard."

"In special characters, maybe?" Cleona suggested.

Kevan opened the word processor and clicked on the pi symbol. "Aye, there's all sorts of stuff here. We should be able to duplicate the formula well enough to copy and paste it anywhere we like."

"The trick will be doing it anonymously."

"Not sure we can avoid being involved," he said. "Then again, if we emailed the meme to several friends and asked them to post it, no one would know where it originated."

"And then the terrorists would target all of us," she said with a grim laugh. "We may have to set up an account under a false name to post without repercussions."

"False name? Sounds a bit underhanded."

"I dunno… Authors set up accounts with their pen names. Why can't we set up a Save the Planet account or even a page?"

"Might already be stuff like that. Posts we could comment on and such." He typed a few keywords in the search box and came up with several related pages. "Lots of them here. We still may need to set up an account under a pseudonym for our own safety, but this is doable."

With a nod, she let out a long, slow exhale as though attempting to calm herself. "At least we have a plan now. Having this information and not knowing what to do with it was about to drive me nuts—as if I wasn't crazy enough already."

"You aren't crazy," he said firmly. "You're Earth's last best hope. Nothing crazy about that at all."

The fact that she was making *him* crazy was irrelevant.

* * * *

Cleona bent down to kiss his cheek. "Bless you for that."

Kevan was such a dear, sweet man, and his unquestioning belief in her made him even more precious. Although their attraction to one another had been immediate, she was beginning to understand why people brought together by adversity tended to become romantically involved. The meeting of the minds required to make it through difficult times created a closeness and camaraderie far beyond that of the casual dating scene. Despite knowing that any disagreements could destroy that bond as quickly as it formed, for the time being, the possibility seemed remote. She needed him and his support. Doing any of this alone—or even with Jillian's help—would have been impossible.

Recalling the Array's comment that, like her, Kevan was a conduit for them made her wonder…

"About that mirror thing," she began. "Are you sure you've never thought about it before?"

"Not that I can recall."

"You didn't remember the man with the detonator either. What if the mirror idea is related to that memory?"

Varying emotions flitted across his features, beginning with stunned disbelief and ending with grim acceptance. "As in from the same source? Aye, that would make sense. Would help to know who it was, though. D'you suppose Jillian has found a list of the people killed in the bombing yet?"

"I wouldn't be surprised. She's a woman on a mission, for sure."

Kevan chuckled. "And you aren't?"

"I suppose I am. Her situation is different, though. She's staying in London with Ranjiv. They're working on this together, and me, well, I want to spend every moment with you, but I feel like I'm neglecting my family. I've come so far to see them, and I—" With a half-hearted snort of a laugh, she added, "Like that's the most important thing going on here. The trouble is they don't know anything about what we're trying to do. All they know is that I seem to prefer your company to theirs." She smiled as she feathered his hair with her fingers. "Not that they blame me, I'm sure."

"Let's head back for dinner, then." Kevan closed the computer and rose from his chair. "On the way, you can figure out how much, if anything, you want to tell them. Although no matter what you decide, I'm going to Ballycarbery Castle tomorrow, and I'd much rather you were with me."

"Oh, I'll be there. I'm just wondering if we shouldn't come up with an alternate destination. Maybe even a reason of your own— apart from my sightseeing expedition. After all, I've seen the castle."

"I could say I needed to make a run to Cahersiveen. The castle isn't far from there."

She nodded. "Sinead and I didn't spend much time in that area. Just passed on through. I could say I wanted to see more of the town."

"Sounds good. As long as we keep our stories straight, we shouldn't arouse any suspicions."

Cleona burst out laughing. "Ya think? They probably have all sorts of suspicions about what we might be up to—and I'm guessing that saving the world is at the bottom of the list."

"Imagine their surprise when they learn the truth," he murmured.

"Yeah, well, we have to actually save the world first. Not sure they'd believe a word of it otherwise."

"I wasn't talking about saving the world." A wicked twitch of his brow was Cleona's only warning as Kevan tugged her into his arms, bringing his mouth close enough to lightly brush against hers. "I was talking about *this*."

She caught one glimpse of his smoldering gaze before her eyelids fluttered shut. If a kiss could save the world, Kevan's could have done it. Deep, succulent, and demanding, his kiss left her no choice but to fall under his spell once more. Having already experienced the full force of his passion, she would have expected mere kisses to lose some of their potency.

Not so. If anything, they had gained in power and strength. Was it confidence brought on by greater intimacy, or had something else changed?

Either way, her brain was turning to pudding along with the rest of her. Much more of this and she'd be a helpless puddle at his feet.

A puddle of pudding.

The thought brought a smile to her lips—or would have done if they hadn't already been engaged in a far more exciting pastime.

"Do you have any idea what you do to me?" His deep, rumbling question reverberated though her body, causing her to feel his words as well as hear them.

Did he really expect an answer when his effect on her was so clearly evident? Did she even need to reply? She sucked in a breath. "Oh, yeah," she whispered. "You do the same thing to me."

Anything else she might have said was obliterated by the overwhelming passion and complete loss of control that came from being kissed by Kevan MacFinnin. Wave upon of wave of desire flowed through her, rising to one peak and then another, each of them higher than the last. Breathless with need, she coiled her arms around his neck in a desperate attempt to remain standing while her blood sizzled in her veins.

"We'll be late for dinner."

Why he cared about food when he was devouring her was an enigma she chose not to explore, especially when he held her so tightly against his chest that her feet barely touched the floor. In that moment, she gave up any pretense of trying to stand and wrapped her legs around him.

"Not if we're quick about it."

* * * *

"We did tell Ita where we were going," Kevan added.

Granted, they'd only told her they wanted to discover more about the author of the book, but if Ita couldn't guess why they might be delayed, she wasn't as savvy as Kevan thought she was.

Seeing no need to climb the stairs to the bedroom, he opted for the sofa.

Nor did they take the time for foreplay. The entire day had been one long lesson in delaying gratification prior to seizing the moment. Her need was as urgent as his own, as evidenced by her rapid removal of his shirt and jeans. After tugging her sweater over her head, he made quick work of the rest of her clothing. The search for a condom took more time than it did to put it on, although he was surprised to find that his hands were steadier this time.

As he sank into her soft warmth, the urgency dissipated. He didn't care if dinnertime came and went without them. Cleona was a delight to be savored not something to be used quickly and discarded. He wanted to be by her side for the rest of his life.

She was beautiful, yes, although beauty wasn't everything. He not only admired her for her courage and dedication, he *liked* her. Everything about her resonated with him. They fit together in a way that was as remarkable as it was natural. When he was with her, he felt...fortunate. As though all the trials he'd endured throughout his life were now being rewarded simply by allowing him the opportunity to love her.

She reached up to cup his face in her hands. "What did I ever do to deserve you? To survive and find you when I should've died?"

Turning his head, he kissed her palm. "I could say the same thing."

Her caress of his scarred cheek was as delicate and caring as the first time she'd touched him. His heart swelled at the memory.

"Do you think there's another plan for us?" she asked. "Something beyond deciphering Emhart's formula?"

"Such as?"

"I don't know... Perhaps our child will become a great leader or invent a way to end all disease and suffering." Her eyes clouded. "There's so much of that in the world."

"And we've all had our share." The mention of a child made Kevan wish he'd dispensed with the condom. The time wasn't right for that, though. Not yet. Not when so much remained for them to do. Even taking the time to make love seemed a bit selfish. But then, there should be perks to every calling.

He picked up the pace, delighting in the lazy smile that curved her lips.

"Not suffering anymore. Not now." She slid a leg sensuously along one side of his hip—a move Kevan felt somewhere else entirely. "Not when every single part of you feels this fabulous."

He grinned. "You keep taking the words right out of my mouth."

"That's because we're soul mates," she whispered. "I don't even have to be with you to feel that way. We're part of each other."

"There, now. You did it again." He kissed the tip of her nose. "Said exactly what I was thinking. Are you *sure* you can't read my mind?"

"Wouldn't want to. I like surprises—nice ones anyway. And you—" She paused, giving him a squeeze with her slick, internal muscles that nearly sent him over the edge. "You were the nicest surprise of all."

"I'm very glad you think so." Kevan gazed down at her lovely face as myriad sensations bombarded his body.

Cleona...

Her delicate scent, the softness of her skin, the warmth of her smile... All those things conspired to enchant him like no one else ever had. Like no one else ever *could...*

Wrapping her legs around his lower back, she pulled him in deeper, driving him on until she convulsed around him, her head falling back as she let out a cry of sheer, jubilant ecstasy. In the next instant, the bottom fell out of the sky and scooped him up, sending him hurtling into oblivion.

In a world that had begun to lose meaning, Kevan had finally found purpose—and love—in the glorious depths of Cleona Mahoney's eyes.

Chapter 17

THIS TIME, NO VISIONS OR DREAMS INTERRUPTED THE QUIET JOY IN the aftermath of Cleona's second round of lovemaking with Kevan. Only the annoying, persistent ringing of her cell phone.

"Probably Ita or Sinead," Cleona muttered as she rose from the sofa to rummage through her purse. Upon checking the caller ID, she shook her head. "Nope. It's Jillian. What do you want to bet she's calling to tell us Emhart's middle name?"

"If we pretend we haven't already found it, maybe she'll understand why we haven't deciphered the entire formula yet."

Kevan's sly smile proved what she already assumed, which was that they could have easily done just that if they hadn't gotten "distracted."

So much for polar ice caps melting as we speak.

Jillian was bubbling with excitement when Cleona took the call. "Ranjiv had an idea. He's going to interview the three of us—assuming Susan is willing—and write it up in an article for *The London Times*. All you need to do is figure out how to explain your knowledge of Emhart's formula without mentioning the supernatural aspect."

Cleona cleared her throat. "That might take some doing, but I'll see what I can come up with."

"I had to be less than truthful when explaining certain things to the police," Jillian admitted. "It's tough to get people to believe you when they're already convinced you've lost your marbles. Think maybe Emhart could have told you the code as the plane was going down?"

"I doubt it," Cleona replied. "As you know, things were a bit chaotic at the time. I mean, he only handed me his life jacket because he couldn't use it himself. Don't think he'd have had time to say more, and I doubt his formula is something he would've shared in casual conversation."

"Mmm, yes, although you could say you heard him talking in his sleep. You sat beside him for hours on that plane. He could've muttered anything—his name or something about his book or even his formula."

"The key to it, maybe. Not sure I could've remembered the actual formula, which is still mostly Greek to me." While that wasn't completely true, Jacob hadn't seen fit to pass along the full scope of his knowledge when he joined the Array. Not that she minded. She much preferred being able to play the piano to being on the cutting edge of solar energy research. "Kevan and I have been discussing how to make the formula public without putting ourselves at risk. Publishing it in a newspaper would fit the bill quite nicely. No one would come after me to make sure it never saw the light of day if it was already printed in a major newspaper."

"True," Jillian said. "Although spreading it around in other places might ensure the right people see it."

"We were thinking about Facebook, Twitter, and other social media. Seems like *The London Times* would be better, though, especially if the story got picked up by other news sources."

"Okay, then," Jillian said. "Be thinking about how to tell your story. In the meantime, Emhart's middle name is David."

Cleona giggled. "We know." After noting the time, she switched off the phone and turned to Kevan. "Ita is gonna kill us."

"Oh, I doubt that." He pulled his sweater on over his head and shook out his hair, causing Cleona to choke back a gasp. As stunningly handsome as he was, the scarring on his cheek only made her want to strangle whoever set off that bomb. "Especially if we take her some lamb chops."

Recovering quickly, she managed to quip, "Resorting to bribery now, are we?"

He shrugged. "I've seen it work before. After all, Sinead used you to get me to come to dinner."

Her jaw dropped. "Seriously? You only came because of me?" She cleared her throat, wishing her sentence hadn't ended on a squeak.

With a smile that warmed her heart, he ran a fingertip down the bridge of her nose before tapping the tip. "I should've thought that was perfectly obvious."

His presence certainly had *her* running to the dinner table.

She frowned as she recalled something that could throw a monkey wrench into her fabricated story. "Jillian wants me to come up with a way to explain how I knew the key to Emhart's formula without the Array angle. Not sure I can do that now. Not after what I told Sinead about only remembering his name subconsciously. She's not gonna buy any story about him muttering in his sleep."

"I dunno…looking through his book might've helped you make sense of something you heard him say—something that would lead you to crack the code to the formula."

She stared at him, open-mouthed once more. "Damn, you're good."

"A natural co-conspirator." His wink was followed by a swift, downward glance that served as a reminder that while he'd been getting dressed, she'd been talking on the phone and had yet to so much as put on her undies. "Better get dressed before I prove how good I am…again."

"That would make it three times in one day, wouldn't it?" In her experience, that was two more than she could've expected in a week from her only other sexual partner, whose name was rapidly fading from her memory.

"If you were spending the night with me, I could probably go again a few more times. Been saving it up for quite a while, you know."

His cheeky grin should've provoked her to smack him rather than filling her with the desire to make him prove it. Too bad they didn't have the time.

"So have I," she said. "But I doubt you have that many condoms."

"You might be surprised. You're not the only one who believes in being prepared."

"Glad to hear it." With a wry smile, she began gathering up her clothes, which had wound up in the most peculiar places, some of them far enough from the couch to suggest they'd been tossed.

If nothing else, sex with Kevan was proving to be quite an adventure.

* * * *

They arrived at the Mahoney farm in record time—even before Sinead and Fergus put in an appearance.

"Be right back," Cleona said to her aunt as she breezed through the kitchen. "Just need to run upstairs real quick."

Kevan was glad she didn't elaborate on her "need," especially since he'd been the one to rip her panties.

Gotta be more careful. After all, her wardrobe *was* somewhat limited.

Ita waved her on by "No worries, pet. Take your time."

"Sorry we're late, Ita." Kevan held up two packages of frozen lamb chops. "Figured I ought to contribute to the dinner table since I've been spending so much time at it."

"Well, now, that's very kind of you, Kevan. And you're not late at all. The bread needed to proof a bit longer. It's just now out of the oven."

"Good timing, then." He went over to the refrigerator. "Want these to thaw or stay frozen?"

"Better let them thaw, luv. We'll have them tomorrow." She set the pot of stew on the table. "Unless you and Cleona have other plans?" Her question was as innocent as her tone, but her knowing smile gave him pause—and also the perfect opening.

"We do, actually," he replied. "I need to run over to Cahersiveen, and since Cleona didn't get to see much of the town when she and Sinead passed through there before, she asked to come along. We should be back in time for dinner." He stowed the chops in the fridge and closed the door. "Can I lend a hand with anything?"

"You can set the table, if you like," she replied. "Nice of you to keep Cleona entertained—as long as it's not any trouble."

Kevan wasn't quite sure how to answer that. "No trouble at all. She's a—" One look at Ita's barely suppressed grin convinced him it was time to come clean. "Dash it all, she's a sweet, lovely, intelligent woman, and I'm falling in love with her as we speak." He didn't add the part about her being a bit of a firebrand, mainly because he couldn't adequately explain it without spilling the beans about their "mission."

"So soon?"

He threw up his hands. "Something clicked, Ita. I can't explain it any better than that."

"Nothing wrong with falling in love, Kevan. I'm thrilled, of course, but do be careful. I wouldn't want either of you to get hurt."

"Hurt?" he echoed in disbelief. "How could I possibly be more hurt than I already am? I'm done with being careful, reclusive, or whatever it is that I've been. I want to jump in with both feet and devil take the consequences." Although Kevan had yet to say it aloud, this was precisely the way he felt, and if he wasn't mistaken, the Array agreed with him. He reminded himself once again that the Array was only comprised of random passengers aboard a jumbo jet. Perhaps their "opinion" wasn't as valuable as it seemed.

But were they entirely random? Or had only the necessary souls wound up in the lifeboat that was Cleona Mahoney? Necessary for

Earth's survival. For mankind's survival. Or were they only required to save *her*? What if—

"I can understand that," Ita said, interrupting his thoughts. "Just don't forget that's my niece you're talking about. I wouldn't want her to be one of the 'consequences' if it doesn't work out."

"I'll do my best not to hurt her, Ita. You have my word on it." Such a promise really wasn't necessary. Any pain he caused Cleona would be multiplied in himself tenfold.

"I can't ask for more than that."

Deeming the discussion closed, Kevan began setting dishes and cutlery on the table while his mind worked furiously. What if part of the Array had transferred to him to help him keep Cleona safe—recruiting him as an ally or a bodyguard? Did he know something he hadn't known before? Had he acquired some new talent the way Cleona had suddenly become an accomplished pianist? Whatever it was—if anything—he had an idea it wouldn't surface until it was needed. Cleona hadn't known she could play the piano until her fingers touched the keys. He wasn't sure how piano playing could help them save the world, although stranger things had happened. Case in point, almost everything that had occurred since Cleona boarded the plane to Ireland.

Why hadn't that greater power intervened before the crash claimed so many innocent lives? Emhart could've gone on to the energy summit and shared his formula with the world. Any others representing safe, alternative energy could've done the same. Was their martyrdom so necessary?

Perhaps it was. Perhaps such a heinous crime was needed to shed light on the larger problem. From that standpoint, protecting Cleona became exponentially more important.

The last thing he wanted was for her to become a martyr herself.

A fork slipped through his fingers and clattered on the table as the possibility of her death shook him to the core. Lose her now? He'd rather die.

It may come to that.

Was he willing to give his life to save hers? To allow her to carry on with her work, her destiny? Although that scenario had yet to manifest itself, no one could predict the outcome or ensure against every contingency. Bombs and bullets were random, merciless killers. They didn't care who their targets were.

As Cleona entered the kitchen, the mere sight of her triggered a sickening lurch in Kevan's chest as though his stomach had attempted to swap places with his heart.

He would do it. He truly would risk his life to save her.

His fingers trembled as he raked them through his hair, and the smile he gave her was no less tremulous.

A tiny frown wrinkled her brow then deepened as if she'd read his thoughts. She didn't want him to risk his life; he could see the unspoken protest in her eyes. Didn't she realize she was so much more important than he?

Of all the times to have an audience.

Their audience grew as Fergus and Sinead came in from the scullery, her father's mutterings drawing a shout of laughter from Sinead.

Sinead's eyes shone with warmth as they met Kevan's gaze. "Would you look at that? Kevan's setting the table. Will wonders never cease?"

Kevan wasn't fooled. The only "wonder" was that he was actually in the house. The now-familiar pang of regret knifed through his gut, reminding him of all the years of joyous friendship that his solitude had wasted.

"Don't you be teasing him, now," Ita admonished her daughter. "He might take back the lamb chops he brought over."

"Now, Ita," Kevan said with a smile. "You know I'd never do anything of the kind."

Ita pressed a hand to her chest and heaved a dramatic sigh. "There you go flashin' that wicked pirate's grin at me." She darted a glance at Cleona. "Never does that unless he's up to something. Best to stay on your toes."

"Don't worry, I will," Cleona said. "Although he hasn't been any trouble so far."

The sly look she aimed at him caused a fair amount of trouble, mainly due to its having nearly stopped his heart. "Give me time. You've only known me for a couple of days."

And a couple of *times*, if one cared to use the word in its Biblical sense.

"True." Cleona rounded the table and sat down, brushing the seat of Kevan's trousers as she passed behind him. "I'll probably be wishing to be rid of you by the end of the week."

A tingle of awareness slid from the point of contact to a far more sensitive region. "Oh, I hope not."

"No chance of that," Ita said, her smile having grown a bit misty. "He may be up to no good, but he always was an adorable little chap. He'll grow on you."

After his earlier declaration, Kevan wouldn't have been surprised if she'd gone a step further and told Cleona to start thinking about engagement rings and wedding dresses. If there'd been a matchmaking plot afoot before, it was sure to escalate now. As it was, Cleona appeared to have succumbed to a fit of the giggles.

"Oh, Ita," she said between spurts of laughter. "I was only kidding. I already like him. A lot."

"I'm pleased to hear it," Ita said. "Now, if everyone will sit down, we'll get started.'

Fergus surveyed the feast as he took his seat at the head of the table. "You've outdone yourself, Ita. Not sure any of us will have any room left for the pudding."

Although already famished, Kevan suspected the scent of the stew combined with freshly baked bread would be enough to whet anyone's appetite, and Ita's sticky toffee pudding was the stuff of dreams. "Might have to hang around long enough to get hungry again."

Picking up a ladle, Ita gave the stew a stir. "You'd get no arguments from me if you wanted to stay all night."

Beside him, Cleona seemed to have frozen solid. Even her breathing had gone shallow, while his had all but stopped.

Kevan nearly choked when he finally sucked in a breath. "I might stay a bit late, but I do need to tend my sheep."

Ita nodded. "Aye, I suppose you do."

Kevan was still trying to decide whether he'd detected a trace of regret in her voice when she cleared her throat and held out a hand.

"Now, if everyone will pass me their bowls, I'll dish out the stew."

Chapter 18

KEVAN SPENT A QUIET EVENING WITH CLEONA AND HER FAMILY before saying goodnight in a much less romantic manner than they had the night before. He longed for the time when he could spend an entire night with her instead of stealing kisses in Ita's garden. Although the way they'd been spending their afternoons wasn't bad.

No. Not bad at all.

When he ventured out the next morning, the sight that met his eyes both surprised and shocked him: a healthy, active ewe with the Ballycarbery symbol spray-painted on her side.

He wasted no time capturing the animal and putting her in a pen near the barn. What to do with her after that was something of a dilemma. Keeping her close might be enough to protect her, but what if it wasn't? Notifying the Garda was his next thought, one that he did act upon, but what then?

After calling the proper authorities, he rang up Cleona to tell her the news.

"I'll be over in a bit," she said. "I'd like to hear what the police have to say."

"Same here. Just wish we could tell them the rest of the story." He hesitated. "Looks like this will delay our start to the castle."

"No worries," she said. "Finding out what's going on with your sheep may turn out to be even more important than communing with the Ballycarbery ghost."

Discussing the matter with a human would certainly be more straightforward than deciphering the peculiar methods the ghost had been using. "I hope you're right."

* * * *

Garda Sergeant Jack Halloran arrived at Kevan's farm in a surprisingly short time, looking as tough and capable as he had on his initial visit. Unfortunately, he was still as mystified as anyone by the sheep killings. When shown to the pen, he fixed his discerning gaze on the ewe.

"Aye, that's the same symbol, all right." He wiped a hand across his chin, drawing Kevan's attention to the jagged scar that ran from the left side of his lower lip to the opposite side of his chin. How had he acquired that scar? A knife fight, perhaps? If so, that fight had nearly cost him half of his lower lip. "Still no thoughts as to who would do such a thing or why?"

"No." Despite having all sorts of theories, there were none he could share with anyone aside from Cleona or Jillian. "But this is the first marked ewe I've found alive, and I'd like her to stay that way. I'd like to quarantine her somehow. Perhaps even boarding her at another farm."

Halloran appeared to consider Kevan's suggestion for a moment before shaking his head. "While that would probably keep her safe, it wouldn't help us catch whoever killed the others. One thing this does prove is that painting the fleece and butchering the sheep are two separate actions, mostly likely done by different people. And if the symbol targets a specific ewe—"

"You mean as some sort of animal sacrifice?"

"Maybe," Halloran replied. "I've never heard of anything to compare with what's been happening with your sheep. Some new cult—or even a very old one—might be responsible, although you'd think they'd take her off somewhere else to carry out their ritual."

Kevan dredged up the memory of the grisly manner in which his sheep had been killed—their abdomens slit open with a Y-shaped incision, exposing their internal organs.

"The way the sheep are cut open reminds me of the sort of incision used in an autopsy—that is, if you can believe what you see on the telly. Like someone was trying to determine a cause of death or find a tumor or—" The next link in the chain leaped into Kevan's mind with the force of an epiphany. "What if something was forced down the ewe's throat—something our butcher wanted and wasn't keen on waiting for her to pass?"

"Surgical removal?" Halloran nodded slowly. "Aye. That makes as much sense as anything. My first guess would be drugs, of course—although using sheep as the go-between is a bit bizarre."

Ordinarily, Kevan would have reached same conclusion, but Ballycarbery Castle's ghost hadn't sent him a vision for nothing. He'd have bet the farm that if they were patient, they would find a message similar to the one hidden in the castle wall in the ewe's droppings.

"True," Kevan said. "Although if she *has* been made to swallow something, I for one am perfectly willing to wait for it. I'm sure

Fergus Mahoney would agree to keep her in his barn."

"Good plan." Halloran peered up the hillside toward the road. "I've been wondering... This pasture isn't fully visible from the road. Unless the sheep were up there near the fence, no one would see them. Seems like there'd be another signal of some kind—one that someone driving past might notice."

A moment later, Kevan's attention was diverted by something highly remarkable, as well as quite lovely, albeit coming from a slightly different direction. Clad in jeans and a sweater that accentuated her curvy feminine form, Cleona was making her way down the rock-studded slope from the Mahoney's house.

Although the stile over the fence between the two properties was still intact, there had once been a well-beaten path from Kevan's home to theirs. Too bad the sheep hadn't seen fit to maintain it.

"Wait there, Cleona," he called. "We're coming up."

Anxious to see Cleona again, he quickly climbed the hill leaving the sergeant to follow in his wake. However, the moment they reached her, Kevan wished he'd told her to stay home. Halloran was above-average height with a strong build and a handsome face, despite his scarred chin. And he was in uniform.

Jealousy shouldn't have entered into the equation, and yet it did. Well...not jealousy perhaps, but certainly an awareness that Halloran's scar was far less disfiguring than his own.

He shook off the notion as quickly as it surfaced. Cleona wasn't that shallow, nor was she the type to dump him for a handsome guard. Especially not after all they'd been through together.

Kevan made the introductions, somehow managing to avoid grimacing when the two shook hands, although Cleona's expression when his eyes met hers dispelled any fears he might have had. Judging from her demeanor, she considered Halloran more of an incidental character than a leading man. Her constancy wasn't in doubt. The fault was his own lack of self confidence.

"Any new ideas about what's happening with the sheep?" she asked.

"A few," Kevan replied. He related the gist of his conversation with Halloran, adding, "We were just going to check if there are any obvious signals along the road that would alert the killer to a new target."

She pressed a fingertip to her chin, drawing attention to its charming cleft. "This is the only farm where sheep have been killed, right?"

"Aye," Halloran replied. "No others have reported anything of the sort."

"Then the 'signal' doesn't have to be here, does it?" Her gaze darted from Kevan's face to the guard's. "I mean, it could be anything—a mark on a billboard along the highway or even a phone message."

Kevan and Halloran exchanged wry grins.

"She's smarter than we are," Halloran acknowledged. "Although I still believe it's worth a look. After all, our perpetrators may be none too smart either."

Considering the havoc he suspected those perpetrators of causing, Kevan had his doubts about their lack of intelligence. However, he kept those doubts to himself as they climbed over the weather-beaten stile onto the Mahoney's drive and followed it out to the road before turning to walk the perimeter of the pasture fence.

They hadn't gone far when Cleona stopped short. "I think I may have been wrong about the signal being somewhere else."

"How so?" Halloran asked.

She pointed toward a bit of gorse growing along the edge of the road. "There."

Kevan followed the gesture with his eyes, then shook his head. "I don't see anything."

Parting the branches of the thorny shrub, Halloran pointed toward a yellow rag concealed within the foliage. "If this is the signal, chances are the intended recipient didn't see it either, which may be why that ewe of yours is still alive."

Kevan nodded. "And with the cloth being the same color as the blooms, most people driving by wouldn't pay any attention to it."

"But someone on the lookout might." Cleona shuddered. "Do you think they'll come for her tonight?"

"Wouldn't be a bit surprised." Halloran released the branches and straightened to his full height. "Ordinarily, I'd say we let the sheep run loose and try to catch our criminal in the act. Although I can understand why you wouldn't want to do that."

"We could still keep a watch," Kevan suggested. "Just imagine the bloke's frustration when he sees the signal and can't find the right ewe."

Halloran grinned. "I like the way you think." Reaching through the branches once more, he gave the cloth a tug to make it more visible. "That should do it. We'll set a watch tonight. In the meantime, let's move that ewe to a safe place and keep an eye on her for a few days. If you're right, something quite interesting should eventually come to pass." He paused, tipping up his cap. "You might consider shearing off the painted fleece. If our man spots the signal and can't find a sheep that's been marked, he may decide to search the nearby farms."

"I'll do that." Kevan smiled at Cleona. "Care to learn how to shear a sheep, Cleona?"

"I'm game," she replied. "Anything to keep that creep from cutting her open."

* * * *

Although Cleona had never have handled a sheep or a pair of clippers, when she finished with the ewe, all traces of the paint were gone, and she'd managed to blend the edges to make it less obvious that part of the wool had been clipped.

"Nice job," Kevan said as he inspected her work. "Not a full fleece, of course—that takes a bit more practice—but for our purposes, she looks perfect."

Cleona rubbed her palms together. "My hands are really greasy, though. I forgot about the lanolin thing."

"They say no one has softer hands than a man who shears sheep." With a brogue as broad as his grin was wicked, he added, "Haven't you noticed how soft me hands are?"

"I believe I have." Though to be honest, they were more gentle than soft, and judging from the length of the wool on his sheep, it had been a while since any of them had been sheared.

She wiped her hands on the towel Kevan offered. This was the sort of thing she'd envisioned doing during her visit to Ireland. Simple, everyday activities that didn't involve butchered sheep, ghostly messages, or removing death marks from hapless ewes.

Nearly dying in a plane crash was enough excitement for one lifetime. Now she was faced with attempting to unravel more sinister plots than Agatha Christie's Miss Marple. Well, maybe not *that* many, but certainly mysteries with more far-reaching effects.

After a call to Ita and Fergus, who agreed to harbor the sheep, Cleona helped Kevan load the ewe into a small trailer he'd hitched to his car.

While Kevan tied the sheep in the trailer, Cleona stepped back to gaze up the drive toward the road. The hills beyond were similar to Kevan's own land—rocky sheep pastures with boulders large enough to provide excellent hiding places. Anyone could be up there watching and they would never know.

Fortunately, there were no obvious signs of an intruder; the sheep grazed undisturbed, while birds came and went without any evidence of fear.

As Kevan climbed down from the trailer, she gestured toward the hill. "Ever see anyone up there?"

"No one who doesn't belong there," he replied. "The land belongs to Owen Driscoll, although I seldom see him in the field. These days his son Brian does most of the work with the sheep."

"Think they could be the ones killing your sheep?"

"You mean an attempt to drive me off my land?" He closed the tailgate and secured the latch. "No. I don't see that at all. Totally out of character."

She shook her head slowly. "I still don't get why anyone would target *your* sheep and no one else's, especially if there's a connection between the university bombing and everything that's happening now. Seems like too much of a coincidence."

"I agree, although it may be intentional."

"I don't get that either."

"Could be a warning of some sort. Or there may be no connection at all." The wind lifted his dusky curls, tossing them gently as the full force of his brooding gaze connected with her own. She would have expected her weak-kneed reaction to those eyes to dampen with time. Clearly, it hadn't happened yet. "We could be completely wrong about *all* of this."

If only…

She exhaled sharply, stiffening her resolve to remain upright. "You don't believe that any more than I do."

"No, I don't. Although the possibility does exist." He nodded toward the car. "We'd best get going. We'll leave the trailer at Fergus's barn for now. I'll pick it up on the way back."

With a reluctance she wanted to kick herself for feeling, she climbed into the passenger seat. The thrill of the chase was gone. She was so much better at puzzling things out within the confines of her office, tapping at her computer's keyboard with all the information in the world at her fingertips. She was no field agent, and she had no desire to confront terrorists anywhere, let alone Ballycarbery Castle. Even now, the memory of the place brought on a shiver. Despite the houses and farms in the surrounding area, the castle had still seemed isolated, cut off from the present day, locked in another time.

Perhaps the presence of its ghost was what had her spooked.

Ha, ha...

Despite her inward laughter, she was afraid—not for herself, but for others. Even though Kevan may have been right about the two of them being protected in some way, other people could get hurt. Innocent bystanders, with no inner Array to steer them in the right direction, might get caught in the crossfire.

Crossfire, hell. Neither she nor Kevan was armed. They were going up against guys with guns and bombs and had nothing apart from their wits to protect them.

Somehow, she didn't see Mother Earth providing them with helmets and bulletproof vests.

"You've gotten awfully quiet," Kevan said as they drove into the Mahoney's barnyard.

"Just a little nervous about what we might find at the castle."

He shrugged. "Might be nothing at all."

"I know. But if the vibes I'm getting are any indication, something is going to happen. I can feel it."

"The chances of anyone involved showing up while we're there are pretty slim, don't you think?"

"Yes, but I still feel sort of creeped out." With a shudder, she added, "I can't seem to shake it."

"Have any strange dreams last night?"

"None that I can recall. You'd think I would have, though. Did you?"

"Not strange ones. My dreams were actually quite nice." He leaned over and kissed her before hopping out of the car, the warm press of his lips leaving her body humming with anticipation. As distractions went, his kisses were astonishingly effective.

Fergus came out and helped Kevan unload the ewe and lead her into the barn.

"She'll be safe enough in here," Fergus said. "Anyone who dares to come looking for her will have to get past the goats first."

While Kevan laughed in response, Cleona felt another inner chill. Goats would be no match for whoever had been killing Kevan's sheep. Not when they were armed with razor-sharp knives. She still couldn't understand why Kevan would be so upbeat.

Then it struck her that this was one sheep they'd managed to save.

Maybe things were looking up after all.

Chapter 19

"YOU'RE SURE WE WON'T GET INTO ANY TROUBLE AT THE CASTLE?" Cleona asked as they exited the N70 at Cahersiveen.

Kevan hadn't missed the change in Cleona's attitude or the way her fidgeting had increased as they drew nearer to their destination.

"For all anyone else knows, we're only sightseers. You're my American sweetheart and I'm your Irish lover. No one has any reason to suspect us of anything beyond that."

That at least drew a giggle from her, although it was rather short-lived. "Until we break the law by climbing the fence."

"There is that," he admitted. "We'll have to wait until any other tourists have gone. Perhaps this will be a slow day."

Given the weather, that was quite possible. Although the morning had been clear and dry, clouds were rolling in, darkening the sky and threatening rain.

As they pulled into the car park below the castle, the rain made good on its threat, coming down in thick sheets tossed about by fitful gusts. The two lone visitors to the castle were already running toward their car.

"If it wasn't for the rain, I'd say the ghost scared them off," Cleona remarked as the couple reached their vehicle and jumped inside it, slamming the doors against the downpour.

Kevan cleared the fog from the window with his sleeve. "What makes you think the ghost didn't bring on the rain?"

"Yeah. Right. Silly me. I keep forgetting about the Mother Earth connection, although it isn't as though she talks to me a lot. After that first little speech, I haven't heard squat."

"Disappointed?"

"A little. That whole 'all in good time' crap has me bugged. If we're on the same side, seems like sharing information would be a better strategy. But then, I'm not the one making the rules."

"I'll not argue with that." Kevan watched the other car in his rearview mirror until it disappeared beyond the surrounding hills. "If Mother Earth wants us to find what we came here for, I'm guessing the rain should stop right about...*now*."

Cleona turned toward him, open-mouthed as the rain came to an abrupt halt, as though someone had shut off a faucet in the clouds. "Oh, you have *got* to be kidding me."

"Well, you did say we were on the same side." He unfastened his seatbelt and got out of the car. "Looks like it's going to hold off for a bit."

Cleona followed suit, despite peering up at the cloudy sky as though she didn't trust it for a second. "Freaky."

He shrugged. "It is what it is. Now, if we're lucky, the gate will be unlocked and the ghost will have our suspect neatly trussed up in the rear of the castle."

Cleona held his hand as they started toward the gate. "Don't think I'd count on that. Remember that 'sweat of human endeavor' business? We'll probably have to climb the fence. Then we'll get caught in a storm and the local cops will arrest us and lock us up in the looney bin when we tell them what we're doing here. Hope you have Halloran on speed dial."

Although Kevan knew she was joking, he wasn't exactly brimming with confidence himself. He hated to admit it, but the weather's behavior had him a bit spooked too. Opting for a show of bravado he was far from feeling, he flung his free arm wide. "I don't see any guards around, do you? Can't imagine they patrol this area very much. Besides, I'm guessing the main reason the castle is fenced off is to keep the morons from climbing up on the battlements and falling to their deaths. We only need to check the back side for secret messages. No climbing necessary."

"Good. Didn't think to bring along my castle-climbing gear."

"Me either. Guess we'll have to count on the ghost to provide the view from the top."

She peered up at him through narrowed lids. "You say that like you almost mean it."

"Why wouldn't I? I mean, if we can't explain any of this in a rational manner, we might as well embrace the madness."

"There's some sort of twisted logic there," she said, although the slow wag of her head suggested otherwise. "I'll let you know when I figure it out."

Kevan released her hand and jiggled the gate. "Well, now... Would you look at that? The lock is secure, but the hinges are broken. Some ghostly presence must be looking out for us."

"Yer killin' me, MacFinnin," she quipped. "I, on the other hand, believe that if Mother Earth is responsible for the weather, then she's the one who made the hinges rust away."

"That's a bit nitpicky, wouldn't you say?" He pulled the gate open with ease. "This is only a guess, mind you, but it would seem that this gate is used fairly often."

"What? You mean because most tourists can't read signs?"

"No," he replied. "Because our suspect comes here at least once a week."

"How would you know that?"

Unsure of the source himself, Kevan shrugged. "The ghost told me?"

"The weird thing is, I'm pretty sure you're telling the truth." She shook her head, grumbling as she passed through the open gate. "And to think, I was perfectly sane when I left home. Don't suppose the ghost mentioned whether he'd already been here this week."

Kevan pulled the gate shut behind him. "No, although I'm guessing he hasn't. The signal is still up."

Stopping in her tracks, she spun around to face him. "What signal?"

He pointed at the castle wall. "*That* signal."

Her gaze followed his gesture, her eyes flicking back and forth as she scanned the ivy-covered structure. "I'm not seeing it."

"Focus on the bigger picture. What do you see that shouldn't be there?"

She continued to stare at the crumbling pile of stone. "Sky, stone, ivy—" With a swift inhale, she stopped. "Hold on a sec."

"See it now?" he asked. "Something shiny on the lower portion of the wall?"

"A soda can? Seriously?"

"Well, it *is* green. Blends in rather nicely, don't you think? I mean, it took you a while to spot it."

She nodded slowly. "True. It doesn't belong there, even though you see them everywhere else."

Kevan slid an arm around her waist. "Let's check our hiding place, shall we? I lost a eve the day you arrived. If I'm right, there'll be a message hidden in the wall around back."

They circled the castle to where adjoining pointed arches fashioned from hundreds of stacked stones formed two chambers that were open on the southern side. Although he'd never explored the castle himself, he'd seen close-up photos of this section, presumably taken by someone who had been granted access to the grounds. Anyone obeying the signs could only see this side from across the bay.

Without the vision to aid him, Kevan never would have found the right stone in a million years. Heart pounding, he removed the stone only to discover that the recess behind it was empty.

"Damn." His mouth twisted into a grimace and he nearly threw the stone down in disgust. "I was so sure there would be something here."

"Maybe the soda can was the all clear signal," Cleona suggested.

"Possibly. There's also a chance we could be completely wrong about all of this."

"We've been through that before," she countered. "I still believe we're on the right track."

Kevan stared at the empty niche as if he could conjure up a missive through sheer stubbornness of will. He'd been convinced they would find a package of some kind. If all went well, his ewe would provide something else to put there. But how to signal the pickup? Someone had to deliver the message—presumably the person responsible for butchering his sheep—for the other man to find.

A vision of that would be useful right about now.

But of course, the ghost wasn't talking. Or haunting or whatever it was ghosts actually did.

He would never be able to explain any of this to the guards. He could easily imagine Halloran's incredulous expression and scoffing tone when he informed him that a ghost had told him where to look. Then again, the symbol painted on his sheep was this very castle. He hadn't told the guard they'd figured out what the symbol was meant to depict, nor had he mentioned where he and Cleona had planned to go that day. Even now, he wasn't convinced he should have.

"As a landmark, Ballycarbery Castle is probably known to every tourist ever to set foot in County Kerry. Halloran, on the other hand, was originally from Dublin. He might not recognize the shape. We only put it together recently ourselves."

"We could say we saw a man coming back from the castle and went to investigate," she suggested.

"Aye, that would be suspicious activity in itself. We can certainly give an accurate description of the man."

"Remember what Jillian said about having to be less than truthful when dealing with the police? All we have to do is make sure our stories match and that they're believable. No one could disprove it anyway."

"Wait. I've got it," he exclaimed. "We can say that seeing the castle today made us realize what the symbol is meant to depict."

She appeared to consider this, tugging her lower lip with her teeth. "That works. And if you catch anyone skulking around in your pasture tonight, maybe he'll talk."

Kevan had his doubts about that. Then again, if their hit man hunch was correct, money rather than ideology was the motivating factor. A religious zealot might not talk—might even sacrifice his life for the cause—whereas someone in it for the cash could be manipulated or bought. "Guess we've no choice but to wait, then." He scratched his head. "Although I might dose the ewe with mineral oil to hurry the process along a bit."

She made a face. "You just had to say that, didn't you?"

"Not as gross as some other things I could name." Despite his disappointment, he managed a smile. "I guess we're finished here. We can stop in Cahersiveen for lunch and have a look at some of the shops, which is what your family expects us to do."

"That's one lie we won't have to tell." She took his proffered arm and they started toward the gate. "And to think, I've always been such an honest, upstanding citizen."

"Same here, although ignoring the NO TRESPASSING sign is the only illegal thing we've done so far. Too bad we don't have anything to show for it."

Leaning closer, she gave his arm a squeeze. "Yes, we do. We found an empty hidey hole and a can of soda."

"Aye, but I was hoping for more."

They had almost reached the gate when a gust of wind blew past them from across the inlet, followed by a tinkling sound and what he could have sworn was a tap on his shoulder.

He turned around, half expecting the ghost to be hovering behind him. No specters met his gaze, although the source of the sound he'd heard was immediately evident. The can had fallen from the wall.

Frowning, he stood for a moment, weighing the possibilities. That breeze hadn't been strong enough to knock over anything that wasn't essentially weightless. A more important signal would have to be one that was unaffected by the elements.

"What if the pickup signal is a *full* can of lemonade, and the all clear is an empty?"

"Works for me," she replied. "How'd you figure that out?"

"I didn't." He nodded toward the castle. "If I'm not mistaken, the ghost just gave me a hint."

* * * *

Sitting across the table from Kevan in a cozy Cahersiveen pub, Cleona finally voiced a suspicion that had been bugging her ever since they left the castle. "If we'd come here yesterday instead of going to the Black Valley, we may have found something."

He took a sip of his tea before replying. "No, going to the valley was important. I'm sure of that. And we discovered at least two things that will help us. We know where the hiding place is, and we're pretty sure we know the signals. If we catch someone in my sheep pasture tonight, we'll have taken out at least one link in the chain."

"And now we know how to lure the next one in. At least, we think we do." Giving her soup a stir, Cleona hesitated before mentioning the other factor that had been bugging her. "Most of this is so subtle... Honestly, if it weren't for the way your sheep have been butchered, I'd have said they were a pretty smart bunch."

He nodded. "Something tells me our butcher is the weak link—someone impatient enough to draw attention to the scheme."

"Yeah. If they'd quarantined the sheep and waited, spraying the castle symbol on the fleece would've looked like a harmless prank."

"They didn't even need to use paint." With a derisive snort, he added, "We use chalk all the time. Each ram has his own color and he leaves his mark on the ewe when they mate. That's how we tell which ram fathered the lambs. Some farmers even dust their sheep in different colors to amuse the tourists. Using paint and killing the sheep is—"

"Stupid?"

"Aye. Although we should be thankful that at least one of the people involved is a bit of a dimwit. Otherwise we never would've known there was a darker plot at the heart of it."

"We don't even know that yet," she reminded him. "Right now, we only have conjecture."

"The details are still a bit murky, I'll grant you, but we're gaining ground every day." His eyes squeezed shut, and he bit his lip as though momentarily stricken by intense pain. In the next instant, he seemed to have regained control, although the agony was clearly visible in the depths of his eyes. "Tell me again... How much longer were you planning to stay in Ireland?"

While her original itinerary had her returning to Dallas at the end of the month, she truly didn't want to go home again. The fear of flying wasn't the issue. Even her determination to solve the mystery that had been thrust upon them couldn't have chained her to Ireland forever. If that were the only factor, she would stay on until Mother Earth's master plan was revealed and implemented. The tie that was Kevan MacFinnin was far stronger, eternally binding her to Ireland's green pastures, desolate mountains, and rugged shores.

"Until the end of the month," she finally replied. "Although I'd much rather stay forever. I know we've joked about it, but is remaining in Ireland really feasible?"

His gaze shifted from her face to an indefinable point somewhere in the space that separated them. Blood pounded in her ears as she waited for his response.

"Getting cold feet?"

"No. It isn't that. I have…responsibilities back home. A job, friends, family—my boss would have a fit if I didn't come back."

"Cleona," he said gently, "you came very close to not getting *here*."

"What?" She stared at him, momentarily bewildered. "Oh, right… I see what you mean. There would be no question of going home if I'd died in the crash."

And if I had, I wouldn't be the Carrier of Life's Preservation.

That fact alone changed everything. But even if she did manage to save the world from mankind, what then? The future was as murky as it had ever been. What to do. Where to go. Whom to trust. Deciphering Emhart's formula was only part of the puzzle. After all, he could have shared his knowledge with the world far more effectively himself if he'd been the one to survive. An investigative reporter—Ranjiv, perhaps—could have been the one to expose the alleged plot to keep the world dependent on oil production.

Unfortunately, neither of those people could give Kevan MacFinnin the love he so desperately deserved.

At the moment, that particular destiny seemed to outweigh the rest.

She reached across the table and grasped his hand. "Guess they'll just have to muddle through without me."

Chapter 20

CLEONA WAS STRUCK WITH A TWINGE OF GUILT WHILE SPENDING THE afternoon scouring the shops of Cahersiveen like any ordinary tourist, although the majority of her shopping did go toward replenishing her scanty wardrobe rather than accumulating trinkets. When she'd gone shopping with Sinead, she'd had no desire to buy much beyond the bare necessities. Perhaps some of the shock had worn off. If nothing else, the annoying buzz in her head was gone. Or perhaps simply being with Kevan made her feel more normal. His reminder that unlike nearly everyone else aboard Flight 2324, she did, in fact, *have* a future had helped to sharpen her perspective. In the days immediately following the disaster, she'd been detached, adrift in a sea of uncertainty, and although she wasn't completely anchored now, having hope and purpose made a huge difference.

For the moment, however, she was content to let Jillian and Ranjiv do the legwork. As a reporter, Ranjiv was bound to be better at that sort of thing than most people, and, having spent some time with Jillian, Cleona had no reason to suspect that her fellow survivor was lacking in intelligence or common sense. In the immediate aftermath of the crash, both Jillian and Susan had coped far better than she had, although the babble of voices from the Array was undoubtedly responsible for Cleona's prolonged mental fog.

The Array had been essentially silent for some time. With no headaches to mark their departure, Cleona suspected that the remaining souls were only there to help her solve the mystery surrounding the deaths of Kevan's sheep and the possible connection to acts of terrorism.

With the exception of the pianist, that is. Beyond an inherent love of music, Cleona had never given the theories behind it a second thought, nor did she ponder the current musical trends and styles. Now, she caught herself doing that more and more. Birdsong was no longer simply beautiful. Not only could she identify the notes, she also remembered their sequence. How that would help her save the planet was a mystery in itself. Or perhaps that particular member of the Array simply refused to leave.

On their return trip to Kenmare, she even asked Kevan to turn on the radio in the hope that a healthy dose of Irish pop music would divert her near-obsessive thoughts about the evils they faced.

Kevan obviously wasn't fooled by her ploy. "Can't blame you for that," he said as he selected a station. "Could stand a bit of a break, myself."

"Yeah. We've pretty much talked it to death. Too bad we're no closer to a solution."

"Seems like we've mostly been killing time until tonight," he said. "Come to think of it, I should probably get back home and take a nap so I'll be awake and alert when we catch our culprit."

His air of confidence and cheeky grin surprised her. Somehow Cleona doubted that apprehending a suspect would be as simple as keeping an eye on his flock. "You say that like it's a done deal."

Kevan shook his head. "More like using the power of positive thinking. I've not had a chance to do much in this case beyond waiting until I find another carcass. We're closer to predicting the next attempt than we've ever been."

That much, she couldn't deny.

He turned up the volume a tad, leaving Cleona to assume the discussion was closed. Song after song played while neither of them spoke and the car ate up the distance between Cahersiveen and Kenmare.

The rain, which had held off for most of their excursion, chose to put in another appearance. Raindrops splattered the windshield and made tiny streaks on the side windows as they drove through Sneem. Frequent rain was another aspect of life in Ireland to which she would have to become accustomed, although the pattering raindrops she'd experienced thus far paled in comparison with a Texas thunderstorm. Still, she wouldn't miss the threat of tornados, nor would she regret leaving the blistering heat behind.

Thankful that her mind had somehow managed to drift on to less turbulent topics, she glanced at Kevan just as he waved at an oncoming car.

The lurch of her stomach as she spotted the black sedan was more than enough to confirm that she hadn't entirely suppressed her underlying fears. "Who was that?" she gasped, her blurted question sounding more like a demand.

"That was my neighbor, Brian Driscoll. I doubt he gets down this way any more than I do." He peered in the rearview mirror.

"Now, where do you suppose he's headed?"

She hoped her sigh of relief wasn't as obvious as her gasp of dismay had been. "No telling. Although I'd be willing to bet he isn't on his way to Ballycarbery Castle."

"Probably not." He slanted a speaking glance at her. "You might as well admit it, Cleona. You've been on the lookout for black Beemers, haven't you?"

"Of course I have," she replied, slightly miffed that he'd noticed. "Although I doubt we'd pass the right guy coming from that direction, especially since he's the one who retrieves the messages as opposed to delivering them."

"Doesn't matter. If we happened across him, I'd turn around and follow anyway. Anything we could learn about him would be useful."

"True." She reached over and gave his arm a squeeze. "Sorry if I sounded snappish. I was trying so hard not to think about it, but I guess this cloak-and-dagger stuff has me more on edge than I'd care to admit."

"Not exactly your cup of tea, is it?"

"No. And I suspect it isn't yours either." Her wry smile became a moue of distaste. "What hope do a couple of amateurs have against a ring of terrorists and spies?"

"Oh, so they're spies now?" A quick chuckle canceled any sting his words might have contained. "Are you forgetting our allies?"

"No. Although I almost wish I could." She stared out the window for a long moment as the view of Sneem was gradually replaced with open countryside. "Do you suppose Mother Earth will only speak to me in the Black Valley?"

"Possibly," he replied. "The valley road is a bit out of our way, but if you'd like to drive through there again, now's the time to ask."

"No," she said. "I don't feel the need to do the 'becoming a tree' thing again. All I want is a little more information." Where to find that information was anyone's guess, although Kevan's farm seemed as good a place as any to commune with Earth's spirit. "We'd best be getting back anyway."

"Aye. I've a dose of mineral oil to administer."

She giggled. "I'll let you handle that. Something tells me the ewe won't be very cooperative."

"Easier than getting her to swallow a plastic bag," he said with a shrug. "Sure hope it comes through all right. I don't like the idea of losing another ewe. Goats will chew on odd things and occasionally swallow something they shouldn't, but I've never had that problem with my sheep. They're a bit more selective."

"Think it's worth calling the vet?"

"I'll give him a call if she gets into any distress, but I doubt he'd tell me to do anything different—especially since we aren't absolutely sure she swallowed anything."

"You're right," she said. "I keep forgetting that. All of this stuff we think we know, when we really don't know anything. It's...bizarre."

"Aye, but they're good guesses—logical anyway. That is, if you accept the existence of ghosts and souls of the departed and such. Oh, and that Earth is actually conscious."

"All of which is a pretty tough pill to swallow."

"True, but it's the only pill we have."

Cleona nodded her agreement, then stared out the window again. There were no trees to speak of, only grass and patches of gorse, their bright yellow blossoms adding color to an otherwise green landscape. According to Sinead, County Kerry had once been covered in forests, but the woodlands had been exploited to the point that they never grew back. Killarney National Park had the only significant number of trees left in the county—certainly the oldest—and even they had most likely been planted. The native forests were all gone. Perhaps the voice that had spoken to her in the Black Valley had been the collective souls of the lost trees, although recalling those barren, rocky peaks, she had a hard time imagining that vegetation of any kind had ever grown there.

Great. Now the freakin' *trees* had souls. She'd definitely lost her marbles this time.

"Don't be silly. You haven't lost your mind. You've expanded it."

Despite being momentarily startled, she soon realized those words couldn't have come from her own thoughts—not when she was convinced that the opposite was true. Nor had they come from Kevan.

Honest to God, just when I start getting used to not hearing from you people...

"Easy now, Cleona... Don't worry. You're doing fine."

Silently thanking the Array for the reminder that they were more than post-traumatic-stress delusions, she settled back in her seat, pondering the ironically calming effect of having a team of ghostly cohorts at her back.

After all, ghosts weren't killing Kevan's sheep, detonating bombs, or crashing airplanes. Real live criminals were responsible for that.

For once, the ghosts were the good guys.

* * * *

They arrived at Kevan's farm without mishap, and after watching him dose the ewe with mineral oil, Cleona couldn't imagine anyone stuffing a plastic bag down a sheep's throat without knowing their way around animals, and sheep in particular.

"Seems like something a veterinarian should do," she remarked.

"Anyone who raises livestock has to be able to doctor them now and then," Kevan said. "Otherwise you'd be spending all your profits on vet bills and the vet would be run off his feet more than he is already." He gave the ewe a pat on the head. "A job like this only takes a bit of know-how and the proper equipment."

"Well, I certainly couldn't have done that, although I'm guessing catching the sheep would be the hardest part."

"That's why we have dogs." He stepped out of the pen and stripped off his coveralls. "I've been giving some thought to the plastic bag idea. If I needed to do something like that, I'd use one of these." He held up the device he'd used to administer the mineral oil, which looked like a cross between a syringe and a squirt gun with a long metal tube on the end. "It's called a drenching gun. Delivers a set volume of whatever liquid you need to give them. Wormers, antibiotics—that sort of thing. You could fold the bag over the tip like an umbrella, put it in the sheep's mouth, pull the trigger, and let the fluid force it down. You could also use a stick or a long metal rod, but you'd be ramming the bag down the gullet instead of using water pressure to make the ewe swallow it. Although the gun would be safer—less risk of perforating the esophagus—either way would be relatively portable."

She threw up her hands. "Okay. I'm convinced. So, basically, what you're saying is that anyone who's ever worked with sheep would be able to do it?"

"Aye. They might even have their own dog to help out."

She cast a wary eye at Mac, who sat quietly panting nearby. "And *your* dog wouldn't object to that?"

Kevan drew in a slow, deliberate breath. "Probably not, which is why I'm beginning to suspect one of my neighbors. Someone with a dog Mac knows." Having dropped that little bomb, he caught her eye for a long moment as the implication sank in.

She gasped as the puzzle pieces clicked into place. "The man we passed on the road today? Didn't you say any involvement in this mystery would be out of character for him?"

"It is." Kevan's expression darkened to a scowl. "But with the right sort of leverage, you can get people to do all sorts of things they would ordinarily never dream of doing."

An icy chill slid through her heart like a sword. "You blackmail them by threatening their family."

He nodded. "I have no family to threaten, so I'm no use in that way, which is probably why my sheep are the carriers. But Brian... Both of his parents are still living, and he has three younger sisters, plus a wife and son."

"And we know just how ruthless these people are." If terrorist acts like the university bombing and the plane crash were any indication, the responsible parties considered human life to be an expendable commodity. "Think we could get him to talk?"

"No idea. That's a pretty tough barrier to crack." He hesitated then shook his head. "No. We'll have to catch the one who's been killing the sheep first. I can't imagine Brian would be doing that. Passing the message along perhaps, but not killing my sheep. In fact, I'd be willing to bet that whoever's been doing the butchering isn't supposed to do that."

"Yeah. Talk about a way to draw attention to their scheme." She groaned as another possibility struck her. "You don't suppose word has gotten out about what's been happening to your sheep and the butcher has been replaced with someone more discreet?"

"Someone willing to wait for the message to pass? Aye, that would complicate matters quite a bit. Might even mean this sheep has already passed the message along to the next link in the chain."

"Let's hope not. Otherwise, there's no way we could convince Halloran that there's a connection between your sheep and the castle."

"You're forgetting the symbol, which is an excellent clue all by itself. That is, if we can convince him that it actually refers to that particular castle. Without our inside information, we'd have had a hard time realizing what it was ourselves."

"Wish that castle wasn't so far away," she said with a rueful grimace. "We'd have a tough time keeping it under surveillance. Setting a watch on your sheep will be hard enough as it is. You do realize that whatever we find, Halloran will want to keep as evidence?"

"That's why we need to find it before he does and make a copy."

She nodded. "Then we could take it to the castle, put it in the niche, and set up the soda can." She huffed out a mirthless laugh. "Then all we'd have to do is figure out how to catch the guy who picks it up." Try as she might, she couldn't imagine how they could get the police to believe a word of their theory, especially since so much of their information had come from the Array and other spiritual entities.

"I was hoping to get a bit of help from the ghost on that." If his facial expression was any indication, he wasn't joking.

"While you're at it, try asking the ghost how to explain all this to the police."

This time, he smiled. "You know as well as I do it doesn't always work that way. Sure would be helpful, though."

"No kidding." She stared at the innocent ewe, which was now standing quietly in the stall, nibbling at a pile of hay. "How long before the mineral oil takes effect?"

"We'll check her again after dinner. If she hasn't passed it by then, I'll give her another dose. We need to know what she's carrying, and we need to know it soon." He stepped into Cleona's line of sight and lifted her face to his with a knuckle beneath her chin. "Nothing to worry about until we do. No one knows we know what we know, so we can't be suspected—or targeted."

"Yet." She shivered. "This stuff is giving me a worse case of the willies than the Array did when they first started talking to me."

Kevan slid his arms around her. "Need a hot-blooded Irishman to keep you warm?"

The heat emanating from him stopped her shivers instantly. "Yeah. Although I wouldn't say no to a nice hot cup of tea."

He grinned. "What a blessing that I can provide you with both." After giving her a hug that created tingles of an entirely different sort, he bent his head and proceeded to kiss away her fears.

Kevan was so solid and dependable. So...real, and so much a part of the planet she wondered why he hadn't been the one to grow roots and branches and commune with Earth's spirit instead of her— although perhaps he didn't need to. Cleona had been a city-dweller all her life, separated from the elements by walls of stone and steel. In recent years, walking across the university campus had given her glimpses of nature's beauty, but Kevan's heartbeat already meshed perfectly with the rhythm of the seasons, keeping him grounded and in complete harmony w th his surroundings.

Closing her eyes, she twined her arms around his neck, drawing comfort from his kisses and courage from the deep well of his inner strength.

That which does not kill us makes us stronger.

Nietzsche's famous quote popped unbidden into her mind—or possibly the Array had spoken again, believing she needed additional encouragement. She sighed against Kevan's lips before deepening the kiss. If Nietzsche's words were true, the two of them together should have been invincible. Perhaps they were.

In times like these, invincible was a good thing to be.

Chapter 21

"MERCIFUL HEAVENS, THAT SMELLS GOOD," KEVAN EXCLAIMED AS he and Cleona entered the Mahoney's kitchen—although he couldn't recall a time when Ita's kitchen *wasn't* filled with heavenly aromas. The chocolate potato cake cooling on the bakers rack wasn't the only thing he smelled either.

Chuckling, Ita never glanced up from the cutting board where she was chopping fresh herbs. "Would that be a testament to my cooking or the quality of your sheep?"

"What? Oh…right. The lamb chops. Forgot about that."

Cleona leaned over the stove and sniffed. "With mint sauce?"

"Of course." Ita scooped up the herbs and tossed them into a pan with melted butter. "Wouldn't be the same without the mint."

"I've wanted to try that for ages," Cleona said. "But then, lamb is incredibly expensive back home."

"So I've heard." Ita shook her head, frowning. "Never could understand why."

Cleona shrugged. "Could be a carryover from the days when the cattle and sheep ranchers fought range wars over grazing rights."

Taking up a pot of steaming potatoes, Ita poured the contents into a colander in the sink. "I take it the cattlemen won, then."

"I believe they did—particularly in Texas. Although considering the price of lamb these days, raising sheep might be the more lucrative business."

In that moment, Kevan realized he didn't know one bloody thing about American history beyond what he'd seen in the movies and the high points any school kid would've picked up in a world history class. Clearly, he had a lot to learn, although he was certain that Cleona could make even the driest of subjects seem fascinating. Helping to familiarize her with Irish history and culture was a task Kevan was more than willing to undertake.

Might take years and years.

Ita nodded at the shopping bags Kevan held, bringing his pleasant musings to an end. "I see you did some shopping."

"Sure did," Cleona replied. "Speaking of which, I'd better run these up to my room.' She darted a glowering glance at Kevan before taking the bags from him and starting toward the stairs. "I was running out of underwear, among other things."

"Did Kevan help you pick them out?" Ita called after her.

Cleona stopped in her tracks. "What? The underwear?"

"Oh, not that necessarily," Ita replied, although her knowing smile suggested otherwise. "Perhaps a new dress? One he thought looked pretty on you?"

Kevan thought it best to intervene. He hadn't told Cleona what he'd said to Ita the previous evening, nor had he mentioned to Ita that his feelings for Cleona were returned.

We really need to have that conversation.

"She chose everything herself, Ita," he insisted. "All I did was carry the bags."

"Sure you did, Kevan." Judging from her tone, Ita obviously had no intention of dropping the inquisition. "Never ventured an opinion? Never said which color you liked best?"

"I may have," he admitted. "What does it matter?"

Ita ran her hands under the tap then dried them on her apron. "Well, if you're sweet on a woman, you do things of that sort, don't you?"

Apparently the time for that "conversation" had come.

"Aye, you do," Kevan conceded. "But there's no need to tell her that. She knows."

"I'm sweet on him too, so it's all good." Cleona held up the bags. "Can I take this stuff upstairs now?"

"Sure. Go on with you, then," Ita said with a flap of her hands. "Dinner will be ready shortly."

Cleona ran up the stairs while Ita went on with her preparations, dumping the drained potatoes into a dish before dousing them with butter and herbs.

Kevan thought he was in the clear until Ita gave him a look that nearly pinned him to the wall. "Did you find out anything on your jaunt to the castle?"

For a moment, his only response was a blank stare. When he finally spoke all he could say was, "Castle?"

"Aye. Ballycarbery, if I'm not mistaken."

"How did you—"

"'Twas fairly obvious, having seen that ewe you brought over."

He eyed his neighbor with a twinge of suspicion. "We sheared off the paint before you came out of the house."

"I was looking out the window and saw you when you found her this morning," Ita explained. "You know, if you'd showed me the fleece of one of the others that'd been killed, I could've told you what the symbol meant. You may have grown up in Kenmare, but I was born in Cahersiveen. I'd know the outline of that castle anywhere."

"Why didn't you say something?"

She arched a brow. "Didn't need to once you said where you were going this morning. You'd obviously made the connection—or you would have after you'd visited the castle with Cleona."

Kevan gave it one last shot, although when it came to verbal sparring, there was little doubt as to which of them would win. "Sinead already took her there last week."

"That explains the secrecy, then." With a sniff and a nod, Ita confirmed her triumph. "Really, Kevan. You can share this mystery with us, you know. We won't go blabbing it about."

"I know. But this whole thing…it's dangerous, and there's so much that can't be explained." *Now or never.* He drew in a fortifying breath. "Unless you believe in ghosts."

Ita narrowed her eyes in mock disdain. "And you call yourself an Irishman. Why, half the castles still standing are said to be haunted. There are mystical beliefs and religions dating back to the first people to inhabit this island."

"But do you truly believe all that?" he asked. "Or is it just superstitious nonsense?"

"Who are we to say?" she countered. "There are forces at work that none of us understand completely." Smiling, she added, "One must believe in magic in order to find it."

"Is that a quote?"

She shrugged. "Something my grandma used to say anytime someone said she was crazy for claiming she could talk to spirits."

"There's nothing strange about *talking* to spirits. It's hearing them talk back that makes you completely mental."

Ita's piercing gaze should've seen straight to his soul. "Have they been talking to you, Kevan?"

He took a moment to weigh his options. Whether Cleona chose to tell her family about the Array was entirely up to her; he certainly wouldn't tell anyone. But by the same token, his own confession was his choice. Considering all that had happened to him and his family, it was a wonder he hadn't already been labeled as a looney. Actually admitting his insanity probably wouldn't surprise anyone.

With a slow nod, he said, "Aye, they have. More than one, I believe. But the one that's told me the most is ghost of Ballycarbery Castle."

Ita never batted an eyelash. "And when did this start?"

Another deep breath, drawn in gradually and carefully exhaled heralded his confession. "The first time I kissed Cleona Mahoney."

She nodded as though the timing made perfect sense. "Go on."

"There have been a few actual voices, but I usually see things rather than hear them. Most were in dreams, while others were more like visions. Memories have come back to me. Some of my own. Some that can only belong to someone else. Although it's hard to explain, I believe what's happening with my sheep is connected to other tragic events."

"Like when your parents died?"

"Aye. I never knew any of this, never felt anything similar in my entire life. But then Cleona came… She's the key. She unlocked my own memories and left me open to the memories and visions of others. I believe I know who killed my parents, and I'm very close to figuring out why."

"You mean 'we,' don't you?" Ita prompted. "Cleona is more than a mere key, isn't she?"

He nodded toward the stairs as Cleona came down them. "I'll let her tell you about that."

* * * *

Cleona had blundered into a scene she wasn't sure she was prepared to face. Yet. "Tell you what exactly?"

"You might consider starting with what really happened during the plane crash," Ita replied. "Although all I'd really like to know is what I can do to help."

Cleona barked out a sardonic laugh. "You've already done plenty, and so has Sinead. Keeping me distracted while the dust settled helped enormously. Not to mention introducing me to Kevan. I'm very grateful."

"I told her about the visions," Kevan said to Cleona. "You might as well tell her everything."

"Might want to wait and tell Sinead and Fergus as well," Ita suggested. "They'll be here in a few minutes."

Cleona rolled her eyes. "In for a penny, in for a pound?"

"Something like that," Ita said. "If nothing else, you should have an interesting story to tell over dinner."

"I wish that's *all* it was." Cleona still had a hard time believing everything that had occurred since she left the airport in Newark. "So much bizarre, uncanny stuff has been happening." She glanced at Kevan. "I take it we're talking about the unedited version?"

"Aye," he replied. "But you're right, Ita. We should wait for the others."

Cleona was pleased to know she had time to compose her tale and maybe delete some of the weirdness.

No. Not happening. Oddly enough, the part she'd been the least anxious to tell was also the most normal, which was her relationship with Kevan. However, since they'd already spilled the beans on that score, there was no going back, and the Array story would easily eclipse the details of their budding romance. After all, people fell in love every day. Being dubbed the Carrier of Life's Preservation was far more noteworthy.

Ita went on with her work as though spirits and leprechauns traipsed through her kitchen on a regular basis. Taking a bowl of spinach from the refrigerator, she added sliced mushrooms, chopped boiled eggs, crumbled bacon, and croutons before topping it with a dressing fresh from the blender.

"Don't suppose you put any Irish whiskey in that, did you?" Cleona asked. "I'm feeling the need for spirits."

"I can add some if you like," Ita replied. "But right now, it's naught but the usual oil and vinegar with onions and spices."

Cleona sighed. "Never mind. I'm supposed to avoid alcohol." Even the doctor's words echoing through her memory didn't alter the need, although if she was going to tell a coherent story, she needed her wits about her. Perhaps even some help from the Array.

Or Mother Earth.

C'mon, Mom. Give me a little help here. Please?

Perhaps later during the retelling would be best. Turning into a tree again would certainly wow her audience, although because that transformation had been mental rather than physical, making everyone privy to her thoughts would be tough. The running commentary alone would provide sufficient grounds for a straightjacket.

She took the bowl of potatoes from Ita and set it on the table. One glance at the empty cups and she stepped back, hands on hips. "Why is the tea gone? Why is the tea *always* gone?"

This time even Kevan stared at her like she'd lost her marbles. "What on earth are you talking about?"

"Nothing," she mumbled. "Just a random thought." *Not likely.* More like the Array deciding to actually use her mouth to speak. Considering what she'd just said, they seemed to be trying to get her to lighten up.

Easier said than done.

Ita took the entire exchange in stride. "No worries, pet. The kettle's just now on the boil." She tossed several teabags into a large pot sitting on the corner of the table before pouring in the boiling water.

Cleona plopped down in the nearest chair and stared at the swirling steam as it rose from the open pot. The mere sight of it soothed her nerves and quieted the growing buzz in her ears. "Where would the world be without tea?"

"Drinking coffee?" Kevan suggested.

Cocking her head, she regarded the steam as it feathered into the air and disappeared. "Without tea, we'd be like that steam. Rising up only to fade into nothingness."

"Are you saying that *tea* is the answer to the world's ills?" The incredulity in Kevan's expression had finally found its way into his voice.

She nodded. "Seems that way, doesn't it? A cup of tea with the world and we'd all calm down enough to figure things out."

"You're placing quite a burden on one cup of tea."

"I know it sounds crazy, but after the plane crashed, the guys on the boat that picked us up gave us each a cup of tea. It was the best thing I'd ever tasted in my life." She leaned closer and inhaled the aroma. "I mean, smell that. It's clean, refreshing. Wipes out any other thoughts entirely—like aromatherapy for the entire world."

After taking another sniff, she leaned back in her chair and closed her eyes, letting her spirit drift on a rippling sea of tea.

Moments later, her eyes popped open and she leaped to her feet. "We need to check on that ewe. Now."

* * * *

Leaving an astonished Ita standing in the kitchen holding a pan of lamb chops, Cleona and Kevan dashed out of the house and raced to the barn. After donning a pair of latex exam gloves from a box on a shelf beside the stall, Kevan retrieved the plastic bag from a pile of manure.

"That mineral oil worked much faster than I thought it would." He opened the bag and held it out to her. "Put on a pair of gloves and pull out that paper, will you? We don't want to get any of our fingerprints on it."

Cleona followed his instructions then unfolded the single sheet of paper, gasping in dismay as she stared at curves and squiggles she couldn't even begin to understand. "We probably should have guessed it wouldn't be written in English. I don't even know what language that is."

"I do." Kevan stripped off his soiled gloves and tossed them into a nearby bin. After putting on a clean pair, he took the paper from her. "It's Persian—which only proves that whoever wrote this knows that language."

"The intended recipient must understand it too. I can't see taking it to a translator. God only knows what it says." A moment's reflection provided at least one piece of the puzzle. "Persian... That's an Iranian language, isn't it?"

"Aye. And to the best of my recollection, it isn't one I've ever learned. But I can read this."

"You mean someone in the Array is from Iran?"

"Apparently, which would explain why I can read the message. I'm guessing the delivery boys probably can't."

"That makes sense. I mean if someone knew they were sending instructions to a hit man or a terrorist, they'd probably freak out and burn it. I'm almost afraid to ask what it says."

"*Target: Geoffrey Taggart. Location: Municipal Courthouse, County Cork. Date and Time: 1 June 10:00 am,*" he read. "Pretty much confirms our hit man theory, wouldn't you say?"

Cleona's heart took a dive like a bungee jump off a thousand-foot cliff. "That's less than a week from now."

He nodded. "If we deliver this message, Geoffrey Taggart will probably die along with anyone else in the vicinity."

"Are you suggesting we *don't* deliver it?"

"Would you?" He shook his head. "Up until now, we only had a theory, which this message confirms. We can't pass it on or—"

"Wait. If you can read Persian, does that mean you can write it?"

"Send a false message, you mean?" He paused, frowning. "I could try, but we still need to show this to Halloran. Be interesting to see what he'll make of it."

Cleona nodded. "Think we should put it back the way we found it first?"

"Right. Don't want to be accused of tampering with the first solid piece of evidence we've found." Picking up the manure-stained plastic bag, he held it while Cleona reinserted the paper then closed the seal. He nodded toward the shelf. "Hand me one of those paper towels, will you?" After she did as he asked, he wrapped the bag in the towel and hid it under a box of tools. "It should be safe there for now."

"About Halloran," she began as they removed their gloves and dropped them into the waste bin. "This strikes me as something that needs action from someone higher up."

"Aye, but what if they're part of the conspiracy or on the take? Halloran might be the only impartial official around."

"We don't even know that." So much was happening that Cleona hadn't a clue how to deal with. They needed someone with more expertise. "Too bad Sherlock Holmes isn't in the Array."

"Be useful, wouldn't he? Not likely though."

"Hey, if Earth can call on anyone it wants, with the possible exception of fictional characters, we ought to be able to at least get a decent detective on board."

He laughed, shaking his head. "I believe that's us. Otherwise, someone else would've been chosen for this job."

"Is that what we are? Chosen? Seems so strange to think of it that way. The Chosen Ones… Certainly not the most likely pair."

"Sometimes it's the least likely that works for the best." He dropped an arm around her shoulders and pulled her close. "After all, who would suspect us of being detectives and knowing what we know?" The kiss he pressed to her cheek was as sweet as it was natural. "I think we can trust Halloran, though. He has a reputation for being a bit of a loner. Good at solving crimes, of course, but if I had to describe his character, I'd say he was incorruptible."

"Incorruptible is good, but can we tell him about the Array? Can we trust him that much?"

"Possibly. He might even believe us."

"Or lock us up." With a groan, she snuggled closer, resting her head on his chest. "Too bad he doesn't have an Array of his own. The only reason Jillian believed me is because she'd had a similar experience, and the same is true of you. What are the odds that Halloran has collected his own assortment of spirits?"

"Pretty slim, I'd say." He drew in a deep breath. "Still, in order to convince him, we may have to tell him everything."

"I hope not. I kinda like the idea of keeping this to ourselves. Once we start telling people outside of the family what we know, we could be setting ourselves up as targets."

"That's a risk we'll have to take at some point."

"Yeah. You're right. Our own personal safety is nothing when compared with saving the planet." Cleona reminded herself that she and Kevan were supposedly invincible.

Too bad that wasn't how she felt.

Chapter 22

HAVING FINALLY FOUND A TANGIBLE PIECE OF EVIDENCE, TELLING her family about the Array was far easier than Cleona ever expected. They even bought Kevan's part of the story.

"I *knew* there was something strange going on with you," Sinead exclaimed when they'd finished recounting their tale. "First finding that book in the bookstore—which seems even more amazing now than it did then—and when you and Kevan clicked the way you did. It was…uncanny."

"Uncanny is right,' Ita said. "But you weren't the only one to have suspicions, Sinead." She smiled at her niece. "You have a touch of magic about you, Cleona. I felt it the moment I laid eyes on you."

Cleona gave her aunt's hand a squeeze. "I'm guessing you're a bit magical yourself. Otherwise, you wouldn't have noticed it."

"Perhaps," Ita conceded. "Although I can't say that I've ever seen a ghost."

"That makes two of us," Cleona said. "The Array doesn't ever show itself. The communication is all mental." She paused, tapping her temple. "I feel it here whenever any of them leave." She glanced at Kevan. "You haven't lost any more of yours, have you?"

"Not for a while," he replied. "I'm thinking we're down to the most essential personnel."

Fergus hadn't said a word since Cleona and Kevan began their story. Interestingly enough, he didn't start off with a discussion about the existence of ghosts. "You say Sergeant Halloran is coming tonight? Have you told him any of this?"

Kevan shook his head. "I'm not that daft. If he hadn't already known about the deaths of my sheep, I doubt I would've spoken to him at all." His eyes narrowed. "That being said, we may need him."

"Aye. Terrorists and murderers and such." Ita shuddered. "I'd never have guessed any of this."

"Which is a good thing, in my opinion," Fergus said. "Far as anyone knows, you don't know anything. Nor could you have read that letter you found." He shook his head, gazing at Kevan in wonder. "You being able to read it is the strangest part of all, and one we should count as another point in our favor. Obviously none of the criminals think any of us in these parts can read Persian or they'd have chosen a different language."

Sinead nodded her agreement. "Seems pretty bizarre to be using sheep that way, though."

"Halloran thought so too," Kevan said. "His take on the matter was that this was simply drug traffickers trying out a new method."

A really crazy method, in Cleona's opinion. "It's all pretty weird, but you have to admit, without what we know from the Array, their trail would be nearly impossible to follow."

"I'm not sure it isn't impossible now," Fergus said. "Do you really think any of our neighbors are involved? For that matter, how do you know it isn't one of us?"

"To be honest, we don't," Kevan said. "But if you *had* been a part of this, I doubt you would've let me be the one to find that message."

"True," Fergus agreed. "We aren't part of the scheme, of course. But you see what I'm saying, don't you? You can't trust anyone."

"Not even Halloran?"

Fergus hesitated as though giving careful thought to the matter. "I'd trust him more than many I could name. He's a good man. But then, I'd have said the same of Brian Driscoll."

"Do you think it would be worth talking to Brian?" Cleona asked. "Would he even confess?" If Brian was only in it for the money, he might talk. She couldn't imagine anyone spilling their guts when their families' lives were at stake.

Kevan shrugged. "I think we'd have to catch him in my pasture before we could justify an interrogation of that nature, which is the main reason for including Halloran. Besides, if I suspect Brian of anything, it's putting the message *in* the sheep rather than taking it out."

"I certainly hope so," Ita said, bristling with indignation. "I can't imagine him butchering your sheep in such a grisly manner." Shaking her head, she huffed out a breath. "Why, you've known Brian all your life. We all have. I'd suspect a stranger long before I'd ever believe it of him."

Cleona hoped complete strangers were involved in each and every phase of the operation. The use of friends and neighbors—perhaps even family—in such a scheme was as horrifying as it was heartbreaking. After that kind of betrayal, trusting anyone would be next to impossible.

"That's why I don't plan on questioning him or even telling Halloran what I suspect." Kevan said. "But you must admit it makes sense. I doubt that anyone is involved by choice."

"When is Halloran coming?" Sinead asked.

Kevan glanced toward the window. "He said he'd be here after sundown. We'll probably watch in shifts, although I can't imagine our 'mule' would be up to no good until after midnight. I closed the gate to the lower field, so we'll only have to concern ourselves with the pasture nearest the road."

"You really should have taken a nap," Cleona said, taking note of the deepening shadows. "Maybe Halloran will volunteer for the first watch." She shuddered to think what might happen if they were to spot someone prowling around. At the very least, their quarry would be carrying a knife, which could spell danger for anyone attempting to catch him in the act. She knew that the majority of the Irish police force didn't routinely carry firearms, although the sergeant was bound to be armed in some fashion. She had no idea what sort of weapon Kevan might use. "Then again, it might be best if you kept watch together."

"I'll let the sergeant decide that," Kevan said. "He knows more about this sort of thing than I do."

"Can't say I care for the idea of you being involved at all," Ita said, echoing Cleona's thoughts. "I'd leave it to the police, myself." She didn't hesitate to add, "But I'm sure you won't be doing that."

Cleona bit back a laugh. If the attacks on his sheep had been more frequent, Kevan probably would have camped out in the field every night.

Would the perpetrator be desperate enough to kill more than sheep? If his motivation was as dire as they suspected, he might be. Even reminding herself that she and Kevan were invincible wasn't much help. There were no guarantees they were right about that, and surely no one was ever completely invincible. Not even with the entire planet to back them up.

"Are you going to tell him what that message says?" Fergus asked. "Jack Halloran may be a competent detective, but I'd be very surprised if he can read Persian."

"Hadn't thought of that," Sinead remarked. "Doesn't seem as though you could translate it for him without telling him the rest of the story."

"We may have to let him show it to someone else," Kevan said.

"I'm thinking the more people who know about this scheme, the better."

"Well, there are five of us now," Ita said. "Do you think it's time you were posting this on the internet?"

Kevan shook his head. "Halloran would have kittens if we did. Plus, we don't want to alert the criminal element. They'd simply find another mode of transmission. This one is weird enough as it is. I hate to think what they'd resort to if this method were ever exposed."

"They can't keep on forever," Cleona said. "I mean, you only have so many sheep."

Kevan nodded. "True. To be honest, I'm surprised they've carried on for this long. It's not as though I didn't realize they were killing my sheep."

Cleona had a new thought. "What if the 'mules' themselves are trying to expose the plot? They might be butchering the sheep to draw attention to the scheme."

Kevan appeared to consider this for a few moments before shaking his head. "The one doing the butchering, perhaps, but not all of them, unless they were in contact with one another. Not a complete impossibility, of course, but highly unlikely. Since we have no way of knowing when the next message will come through, our best bet is capturing the pickup man."

AKA, the Butcher.

"I'm a little worried about the repercussions," Ita said. "What if the poor sod you catch *is* being coerced—his family held hostage or something equally horrific? If he—or she—were to confess, or even tell the police what they suspect, they could be indirectly responsible for the deaths of their loved ones as well as the intended targets, perhaps even themselves."

"There comes a point when one's life becomes a risk worth taking."

Only after silence reigned for several moments did Cleona realize she'd been the one to speak. Or was it the Array? Since they were already dead, the Array could say things like that without risking much of anything.

Except the life of their current host.

Considering the way several had transferred over to Kevan, Cleona figured if she were to die, they'd simply jump ship again.

Which meant she was as expendable as a red-shirted *Star Trek* crewman.

Great. In the course of one day, she'd been downgraded from invincible to cannon fodder.

* * * *

Kevan didn't doubt she meant that for a moment. He, on the other hand, had no intention of allowing Cleona to risk her life unnecessarily. Planet Earth would continue to exist with or without humankind, and the end of that species would be more of a whimper than a Big Bang. In the meantime, his job was to ensure that Cleona lived a long and happy life.

"A noble stance, I'm sure," Ita said. "I just—"

Her remark was cut short by the ringing of Kevan's mobile. "Excuse me," he said after a glance at the caller. "It's Halloran. Better take this one."

"Any results from the ewe?" Halloran asked when Kevan answered.

"Aye. The message isn't written in English, but it's definitely worth a look. I'm at the Mahoney's farm."

"Great. I'll meet you there in about twenty minutes." Without even saying goodbye, he rang off.

"Not much of a talker, is he?" Sinead remarked as Kevan pocketed his phone.

"Can't say that he is " Kevan replied. "Have you met him?"

Sinead shook her head. "I've managed to avoid any run-ins with the guards." She darted a look at her father. "At least, since Sergeant Halloran started at the local station. Conall might know him, though."

Sinead had engaged in her share of teenage escapades, mainly due to the boys she'd dated. None were out-and-out rotters, but some had been a bit dodgy. Kevan wouldn't have put Conall in either category. "And here I thought you were dating a higher caliber of men these days," he teased.

"I am," Sinead said with a defiant lift of her chin. "Conall has never been in any trouble. But he *is* in town more often than you are. He might've met Halloran at the market or the post office."

Kevan deemed it best to drop the subject since Conall's character obviously wasn't something Sinead cared to joke about. "I'm sure you're right."

Ita rose from the table, flapping a hand at her daughter. "Enough of that. You'd best be getting out to the barn, Kevan. Tell the sergeant he's welcome to some cake, or there's a bit of the apple amber and sticky toffee pudding left as well. He might need something to help keep up his strength tonight."

Having downed a substantial serving of the cake, Kevan knew it would provide enough energy to keep a man going long after the sun went down. The trick would be staying awake. "Strong coffee might be a better choice."

"Aye, that it would," Ita said with a nod. "Or it would if we had any."

"Hopefully he'll bring his own," he said, although knowing Ita, she would probably brew up a strong pot of tea and have it ready before Halloran arrived.

* * * *

True to his estimate, Halloran drove up precisely twenty minutes later. After parking his clearly marked and highly conspicuous police vehicle inside the main barn aisle, he followed Kevan to the stall where the ewe was being kept. Thankfully, the note was still safe in its hiding place.

"I looked it up online," Kevan said as he handed over the missive. "It's written in Persian." He was lying, of course, and while Halloran might have his suspicions, the time for a full confession hadn't come yet. "I couldn't tell any more than that. D'you suppose there's anyone around here who can translate it?"

The guard nodded. "There's an Iranian couple running an import grocery in town, but I'm not sure I'd want to show this to just anyone. Might take a while for it to go through the proper channels."

Kevan practically had to bite his tongue to keep from admitting he knew exactly what the strange writing meant. In the end, all he could do was nod.

"Finding this doesn't rule out the need for our stakeout tonight," Halloran went on. "I'm thinking we should keep watch together. We can keep each other awake, and it'll likely take more than one of us to run the man down anyway."

"Run him down?" Kevan echoed. "D'you really think that'll be necessary?"

Halloran actually laughed. "I can identify myself and tell him to stop, but that rarely works. Trust me, they nearly always run." Any residual amusement quickly drained from his expression as he continued, "I must admit I don't like involving you in this. Ordinarily, I'd have brought a constable with me, but we're a bit short-handed, and this isn't the sort of murder investigation that warrants more than one of us."

In Kevan's opinion, what they were dealing with called for the assistance of every guard in Ireland. However, he didn't say so, electing to reply with a simple, "I understand."

"You must also understand the danger. Judging from what we've already seen, this person will most likely be carrying a knife."

Kevan patted the hilt of his own sheathed blade. "We'll be even, then." Which was more than he could say for the guard. As a member of an unarmed police force, Halloran was only allowed pepper spray and a baton.

"Let's hope that's all he'll have on him," Halloran said. "After we've spotted him, I want you to circle around farther down the hill while I head up toward the road. Once he realizes we're onto him, chances are that's the direction he'll run."

Apparently Halloran intended to take the brunt of the danger upon himself. Kevan couldn't argue with the plan, although if he'd been running from the guards, he'd have chosen to run *down* the hill rather than up it. But then, he knew the layout of his farm better than anyone, which might be to their advantage.

Halloran slid the message back under the tool box, after which they left the Mahoney s barn and crossed the stile into Kevan's pasture.

Kevan pointed toward a large outcropping on the hillside just above the barn. "I was thinking we could wait down there. I've been up on this end and couldn't see a sheep standing behind that rock."

"Good idea."

When they reached their hiding place, Kevan's thoughts landed upon another useful item: a shepherd's crook. Catching sheep wasn't the only thing the device was good for, and for increasing a man's reach, it was unsurpassed. Plus, they made good walking sticks. His best one was in the barn, but a perfectly serviceable model hung on the gate to the small pen.

"Here," he said, tossing the crook to Halloran. "You might need this. I've another in the barn."

Halloran held the curved metal tube up to the fading light. "You could break a man's neck with one of these. Careful how you use it."

"I was thinking of using it on his legs rather than his neck," Kevan explained. "Be right back."

Kevan returned with a second crook, and the two men settled in for the long night ahead.

Hours crawled by, and the damp chill of a spring night didn't help. Thanks to a thermos of Ita's hot tea, he wasn't sleepy or particularly cold, but the silence was mind-numbing. The quiet was so complete, he could hear the rustling sounds the sheep made as they grazed, in addition to the flow of water in the creek at the bottom of the hill. Looking up at the sky, he fancied he could hear the stars as they moved across the heavens.

Without warning, Halloran gave him a nudge and nodded toward the road. "Looks like our 'signal' worked."

Where the man had come from was anyone's guess. No cars had driven past for some time, but suddenly, he was there on the hillside, moving toward the sheep.

Dressed all in black with a balaclava covering his face, Kevan could barely see the man and couldn't have identified him to save his life. No knife was visible, although a faint gleam near his waist suggested a sheath.

Halloran motioned for Kevan to go left, away from the road, then mimed heading in the other direction.

The sheep scattered as the man approached the flock, bleating at being disturbed, but not yet fleeing in panic. Despite knowing an obvious predator when they saw one, sheep weren't the smartest of God's creatures, and they allowed him to pass among them despite his having already attacked and killed four of their number.

The man was alone, with no dog to control the flock. Nor could Kevan see that he was carrying a crook or a rope of any kind. Did he normally take down the marked ewes by throwing the knife? If so, this man posed a far greater danger than he'd anticipated.

Crook in hand, Kevan worked his way steadily down the hillside, doing his best to keep his eyes on their quarry without sacrificing stealth. Halloran had all but vanished, his dark uniform blending into the landscape. The culprit, however, was silhouetted against the whiteness of the sheep.

A muted expletive revealed the "butcher's" frustration as he continued to weave his way through the flock. Moments later, his movements became more erratic as his aggravation gave way to desperation.

Now.

Right on cue, Halloran's voice rang out from the darkness. "Looking for something?"

With a sob of panic, the man froze for an instant, and then, just as Halloran had predicted, he turned and ran.

But not toward the road. Darting downhill and away from the flock, he was undoubtedly invisible to the guard, but from Kevan's vantage point, the outline of his body showed clearly against the backdrop of the starlit sky.

Halloran called out again, identifying himself as a Garda sergeant and ordering the man to stop, a directive that was essentially ignored.

Moving directly into the man's path, Kevan crouched down and waited, doing his best to remain both motionless and undetectable.

Too late, the man saw him just as Kevan swung the shepherd's crook, bringing him down with a loud grunt.

Kevan was on him in an instant, using moves and grappling techniques he didn't even know he knew. Seemingly of its own accord, his body responded with knowledge and skill, leveraging the man onto his stomach before ending with a chokehold that rendered him unconscious in seconds. The moment he felt his captive sag in his grasp, Kevan released the pressure.

Halloran came skidding down the hill. "How did you—"

"Don't worry." Scarcely winded, Kevan sat back on his heels. "He's not injured. Just. .sleeping. He'll come to in a minute. You might want to handcuff him."

Detaching the cuffs from his belt, the guard slapped them onto the man's wrists. "When this is all over, remind me to ask how you did that. In the meantime, let's see who we have here."

Rolling their catch onto his side, Halloran pulled off the balaclava and aimed a light at his face. "Recognize him?"

Chapter 23

KEVAN'S HEART TOOK A DIVE THAT MADE HIS HEAD SWIM. "I WISH I didn't."

"So he's a local man, then?"

"A bit too local, actually. That's Conall O'Mara. Sinead Mahoney's boyfriend."

"You're sure about that?"

Not having been born and raised in Kenmare, the fact that Halloran didn't know Conall wasn't too surprising. Still, with the local population at only a little over two thousand, given time, he was bound to run into most of them. Conall must've been keeping a low profile—probably on purpose.

"Yeah. I'm sure. You can check him for identification, but any one of the Mahoneys would tell you the same thing."

Halloran patted Conall's pockets. "Nothing on him but the knife," he said grimly. He shifted the torchlight back to the man's face. "Blond. Caucasian. From the look of him, I'd say he was more likely to be a drug runner than a terrorist."

As surprised as he was to hear Halloran say the word that had been first and foremost in his and Cleona's thoughts, Kevan's echoed "Terrorist?" took a few moments to materialize.

"Aye. What with that letter being written in Persian. Makes you think that, doesn't it?"

With a tiny nudge in the right direction, Halloran might hit on the correct solution without ever hearing any mumbo jumbo about the Array. "D'you think that message could be a plan for a bombing or some other terrorist act?"

"It's possible. Why else go to this much trouble to keep it secret?"

Another nudge. "He sounded a bit panicked when he couldn't find a marked sheep. Almost desperate, I'd say. D'you suppose he's been coerced into doing this? Like he or his family has been threatened in some way?"

"That would make sense," Halloran replied. "More so than a

local man voluntarily joining a terrorist cell. Unless he's been brainwashed into believing in their cause."

"Scary thought."

Brainwashing was a possibility he and Cleona hadn't considered. In many ways that was better than holding someone's family hostage to ensure their cooperation. Bringing them into the fold certainly made the organization's assortment of minions less likely to balk at their plans. The man's reaction was explainable either way.

Doffing his cap, Halloran ran a hand through his hair in a gesture that displayed his frustration along with a touch of futility. "It's *all* scary these days. Seems like the whole world has gone insane, and there doesn't seem to be a blessed thing we can do about it."

A week ago, Kevan might have voiced the same opinion. His outlook had improved since then. He only wished spiritual intervention hadn't been necessary. Perhaps the guard was in need of an Array himself.

"We *are* doing something," Kevan insisted. "We're breaking a link in the chain of…whatever this is."

"But at what cost? Families torn apart or murdered in their beds?" After a slow wag of his head, Halloran replaced his cap as though that act would somehow renew his determination. "Let's see if we can't bring him around. I don't fancy carrying him."

The last thing Kevan wanted was to see Sinead's expression when she heard the news. "Better take him to my house instead of the Mahoneys'. I'd hate for Sinead to have to deal with this tonight."

"She'll have to eventually," Halloran said. "But I agree. Not tonight."

Movement on the hillside above them caught Kevan's eye. For a moment, he thought he'd finally seen a ghost, until with a start, he realized what—or who—it was.

Cleona.

"You caught him, didn't you?" she said as she drew nearer. "I–I couldn't sleep for wondering. Then I…heard something."

Kevan would've bet the farm the "something" she'd heard came to her via the Array. Her timing being what it was, she'd probably awakened from a dream knowing precisely what had happened— possibly even the culprit's name.

"Aye, we did. Don't suppose you brought along any smelling salts, did you?"

Halloran reached into his pocket. "No worries there. I always carry a couple of ammonia ampules, although I usually only need them when delivering bad news."

Kevan suspected one might be required when they told Sinead the truth. But that could wait.

Cleona certainly wouldn't need them.

Halloran broke an ampule beneath Conall's nose with an immediate effect. He awoke, struggling, but his efforts stopped short with the guard's terse, "Save your strength. You're going to need it."

Together, Kevan and the guard hoisted him to his feet. Although he swayed a bit at first, Conall soon became steady enough to stand unaided.

"Right, then," Halloran said. "Let's start walking." He pointed at Kevan's farmhouse. "That way."

* * * *

Kevan never imagined he'd be sitting at his kitchen table across from the man responsible for killing his sheep, or that the culprit would be handcuffed to a chair while the local sergeant grilled him for information. Even less would he have suspected the man would have been Conall O'Mara.

"Let's hear your story," Halloran said, opening his notebook. "And don't bother leaving anything out. We'll discover the truth eventually whether you tell us or not."

"I did it for the money," Conall blurted out. He looked at Kevan without a trace of apology in his voice or expression. "I thought I might get enough to buy your land and give you a reason to want to sell it at the same time. I wanted it for Sinead. Thought she'd like living close to her parents."

"Laudable motives, I'm sure." Halloran was probably going for a neutral tone, but it certainly didn't come across that way. "Now tell us who you're working for."

"I don't know."

The guard was openly skeptical. "Come on, now. Do you really expect us to believe you answered an anonymous ad?"

Conall shook his head. "A bunch of us were in the pub one night going on about how hard it is to get ahead and all. I must've been talking louder than the others because I found a note in my pocket the next morning. No idea how it got there. Said to ring this number for a chance at earning some extra cash." He shrugged. "I figured I had nothing to lose, and it sounded simple enough. The man said all I had to do was wait for instructions and I'd be well paid. He wasn't joking about the money either. Every time I did a job, five thousand euros would be transferred to my account the next day.

"Once I found out all I had to do was collect and deliver a piece of paper hidden in one of your sheep, I didn't see any need to wait for it to pass. Figured I could kill two birds with one stone."

"If you'd been a bit less greedy, you'd have gotten a lot more," Cleona said. "Killing a man's sheep doesn't go unnoticed."

"I'm guessing whoever hired you won't be pleased to know you've been caught." Halloran hesitated. "Were any threats made against you or your family?"

Conall shook his head vigorously. "No. Nothing like that."

The guard responded with a derisive snort. "Call that number again and tell them you want out. I'll bet there'll be threats aplenty."

Conall's already pale complexion turned ashen. "Over a bit of paper?"

"You never took it out and looked at it, did you?" Halloran turned toward Kevan, pinning him with a steely-eyed glare. "Go ahead, Kevan. Tell him what it says."

Kevan threw up his hands in protest. "I don't—"

"Oh, I think you do," Halloran said. "I don't know how you're able to read Persian any more than I know how you were able to take Conall down so neatly, but you can." The guard was either very good at spotting a lie or he had an Array of his own coaching him. Kevan's money was on the former.

"Persian?" Conall stared at Kevan, his mouth agape. "What are you? Some sort of–of Middle Eastern—"

"Terrorist?" Halloran suggested. "I doubt that. Secret agent, perhaps, but not a terrorist."

"No, he isn't a terrorist," Cleona said, filling in the gap in the conversation left by Kevan's astonishment at the mere thought of being a suspected secret agent. He was, actually, although he wasn't working for any particular government, nor was he equipped with any James-Bondian gadgetry. "But we think the people you're working for are." She drew in a breath as her eyes met Kevan's. "Should we tell him now?"

* * * *

"Not yet," Kevan replied. "Not everything anyway. But I *can* tell them what the message says."

Cleona nodded, thankful she didn't have to recount their story again. Once a day was enough.

Kevan cleared his throat. "It says: *Target: Geoffrey Taggart.*

Location: Municipal Courthouse, County Cork. Date and Time: 1 June 10:00 am."

Conall looked as though he was about to have a stroke, but it was Halloran's low whistle that ultimately broke the silence.

"So... It's a hit, then. An assassination?"

Kevan nodded. "That's what we believe. We also believe these murders are linked to climate change. The targets have all been involved in alternative energy research and development in some manner. We don't know who's behind it all, but I'll take a wild guess and say it's the oil producers. And they're paying a bundle of money to keep their energy source as the only game in town. It goes back to the bombing that killed my parents, and possibly further than that."

"Including the plane crash I was involved in," Cleona said. "By the way, Jillian called after you guys left last evening. Among the people killed in the bombing was a climatology professor by the name of Lawrence Gunter."

"That fits." Kevan aimed a glare at Conall. "You're delivering these messages to Ballycarbery Castle, aren't you?"

Conall was really freaking out now. His blue eyes were as big as silver dollars and he jerked on the handcuff hard enough to bloody his wrist. "How could you possibly—"

"Never mind how I know," Kevan said. "It's true. Isn't it?"

Conall nodded. "But I have no idea who picks them up or what happens next. I–I'm no murderer." He gazed beseechingly at Halloran. "You've got to believe me. I don't know anything!"

"Be that as it may," Halloran said with a shrug, "you've killed four of this man's sheep, and you may have been instrumental in the deaths of any number of innocent people. That makes you an accessory to murder." He shook his head slowly. "I'd say you were in pretty deep. Can't even claim you were brainwashed, can you?"

With any semblance of self-assurance stripped away, Conall had all the markings of an innocent dupe. If he'd been brainwashed, either the effect had worn off or he was one hell of an actor. Desperation oozed from him like the beads of sweat on his upper lip and forehead. He'd been pale enough before. Now he was turning green and his hands trembled uncontrollably. Cleona almost felt sorry for him.

The Array, on the other hand, was already gearing up inside her, their righteous anger threatening to spill over into actual speech and actions.

Take it easy, gang.

She felt remarkably calm herself. Perhaps that was her role in all of this. One level head among the storm of emotions. Kevan was working the secret agent angle like a pro—giving out just enough information to be intriguing without ever admitting his source.

Cleona couldn't claim that distinction. Her knowledge had once again come to her in a dream. The vision of Kevan capturing Conall had been as vivid as a high-definition video, and the best she could tell, she'd seen it in real time. Either Mother Nature was filming scenes for a documentary or one member of the Array was working through both Cleona and Kevan.

Could a spirit actually divide itself between two hosts?

She had an idea that the ordinary rules, if indeed there were any, had been suspended for the duration of this venture. Earth might have been every bit as desperate as Conall, but it was far more determined, not to mention resourceful.

"What do you want me to do?" Conall wailed. "Either way, I'm a dead man."

"Not necessarily." Halloran seemed as calm and unruffled as lake water. "Dunno how far claiming ignorance will get you, but the more you help us now, the better off you'll be."

Conall huffed out a breath. "Aye. I suppose I'll get my reward in heaven."

"That's up to you," the guard went on. "Tell us everything you know, starting with how they got your account information. Did you give it to them over the phone or email it?"

"I told the guy on the phone." Conall's smile was grim and his short laugh contained no amusement whatsoever. "That was stupid of me, wasn't it? He could just as easily have cleaned out my account as put money in it. Not that there was much there to steal."

"That's no help," Halloran said. "I'd imagine the phone number was one of those untraceable pay-as-you-go mobiles. Tracing a call certainly isn't as useful as it was in the past." He leaned forward, resting his elbow on the table while he stroked the scar on his chin in a contemplative manner. "We'll think on it a bit. The one thing we don't want to do is tip off anyone else in the loop. I'm thinking it might be best to stake out the castle and see who comes poking around looking for the message."

A swift inhalation heralded Kevan's comment. "We already know who does that. Not a name, of course. But we have a description."

Halloran aimed a blank stare at him. "I suppose you're not going to tell us how you know that either."

"Um, no," Kevan replied. "Suffice it to say he's the same man I saw at the university bombing. Just took me a few years to remember seeing him there." He hesitated as though considering whether to say more. "Cleona helped me with that," he said after a few moments. "She's been the key to all of this."

"You think the plane crash and these other events are related?" Halloran asked.

Kevan didn't mince words. "I'm sure of it. The same group is responsible for all of this. There were several scientists aboard that plane, every one of them headed for the energy summit in Paris. They perished in the crash, but one of them was sitting next to Cleona and passed on the key to his formula before he died. It's our job to stop this terrorist ring and expose those responsible and make his formula available to everyone."

Halloran leaned back in his chair, eyeing Kevan with increased respect, but also with a trace of skepticism. "And how do you propose to do that?"

"We already have people working on getting the formula made public. Once it's out there and the right people see it, this world of ours will undergo a dramatic change for the better." He glanced at Conall. "Considering the large sums of cash involved, I'd say this is a political war based on greed rather than ideology, and the people behind it have enough money to fund any schemes they choose. However, revolution is coming, and when it does, retribution will be swift and merciless."

The strange cadence in Kevan's voice was one Cleona recognized from her spiritual experience in the Black Valley. Was the planet speaking through him now? She didn't mind that someone else was doing the talking; she'd felt a little weird about being the only one anyway. Besides, it worked better coming from him. The scars on his face and the fire in his eyes augmented the conviction in his speech.

"Plenty of culprits have already been identified. Some are even self-professed. They don't think anyone is willing to risk bringing them down because there was never a viable alternative to oil and gas. There is now." Kevan nodded toward Cleona. "And she knows what it is."

Without the planet or the Array telling her what to do, Cleona could only repeat what she'd been told, although she adjusted the source a bit. "Jacob Emart was a prominent solar scientist. He was trapped by falling luggage as the plane was going down. He gave me his life jacket and the key to his formula. He told me I had to survive in order to save the planet."

She hadn't even told the Mahoney's this next part, and she was hesitant to say it now.

Perhaps it's time.

"Something helped me get free of the wreckage and pushed me to the surface. It was as if the sea itself rescued me." She paused, pressing her lips together while she debated whether to spill the entire story or keep her mouth shut. In the end, she realized she had no alternative. "Earth is fighting back against what we've done to it, Sergeant Halloran. Kevan and I are among those who've been chosen to help wage the war. I can't explain it any other way."

A slight widening of his eyes was the only indication Halloran had heard her. He turned toward Kevan. "So…you aren't a secret agent?"

"Not by a long shot," Kevan replied. "She's the Carrier of Life's Preservation. I'm only her protector."

"I think you're a couple of nutters," Conall declared. "But I'll do whatever you say." His voice dropped to a mumble. "Not that I have much of a choice."

Kevan aimed his compelling gaze at Halloran. "What do you say, Sergeant? Are you still with us?"

Chapter 24

"I THINK IT'S TIME YOU WERE CALLING ME JACK," HALLORAN SAID. "And yes, I'm still with you. I don't know where you're getting your information, and between us, I don't care. Because wherever it's coming from would appear to be a reliable source. One thing I'd like to be clear on, though. The real message *cannot* be delivered. We don't know how close we are to the implementation stage. We can't risk having it fall into an assassin's hands."

"Agreed." Kevan had no problem agreeing with those terms, mainly because he was almost one hundred percent sure the next step *was* the assassin. "If necessary, I can write something else. Even nonsense would suffice."

"Or you could have it say something like 'We're onto you' just in case he slips through our net," Cleona suggested.

"That's another thing we can't let happen," Jack said. "Having stopped the flow of letters, this will be our only chance."

Cleona grimaced. "Too bad we don't know enough to stop it at the source."

Kevan had an idea that Mother Nature/Planet Earth probably knew precisely who was responsible. He and Cleona simply weren't the ones destined to make that discovery. Would Susan be the one to do that? Or would all three of the crash survivors have to join forces to bring the instigators to justice?

"I doubt a single individual is behind it," Jack said. "More likely an organization of some kind."

"We don't have to look hard to figure that one out," Cleona snapped. "It *has* to be the oil producers. Most politicians don't give a damn whether our energy comes from the sun or an oil well unless they've been paid off." She bit her lip, clearly doing her best to keep her anger in check. "The corruption in politics is downright frightening. Too bad the guys building solar collectors aren't as well-heeled as the oil companies. I really wish a single person or company was behind it all, but I can't help believing this conspiracy is huge."

"I agree," Kevan said. It would have to be big to finally get the planet itself to sit up and take notice. "The sad thing is we may never expose them all." He glanced at Conall. "Not only that, the cell you're involved with may only be one branch of a larger terrorist organization."

Conall gulped and seemed to shrink in size, his shoulders sagging even further than before.

"Like a starfish..." Cleona mused. "Cut off one arm and it simply grows another.' She was silent for a moment, a frown knitting her brow. "The same man has been active for at least ten years, possibly more, which would indicate that they're either secretive to the point of allowing someone else to claim responsibility or they're very well protected." Her eyes met Kevan's. "The man you saw at the bombing... He wasn't alone, was he?"

"No. And if his behavior after the explosion is anything to go by, he didn't seem to have any fears for his own safety." At Jack's curious expression, he added, "He and his buddy high-fived each other."

"Would you recognize the other man?" Jack asked.

"Maybe," Kevan replied. "I'm not sure. Didn't get as good a look at him." He saw no need to explain why that was. The scars on his body were reason enough. He was a little surprised that Jack accepted the idea that Cleona had helped him to remember the one man he did recall, especially since he was quite certain that memory was a scene Professor Gunter witnessed immediately after his death. That part of the story would never appear on a statement to the police. Jack Halloran would never hear it either. Not even off the record.

"Just a question," Jack said with a shrug. He turned to Conall. "Now, Conall. Tell us what you're supposed to do with the messages you receive."

Conall perked up slightly, perhaps hoping his minimal involvement would be enough to prevent him from being accused of anything other than killing sheep. His rundown of the procedure was precisely what Kevan and Cleona had already envisioned or deduced—right down to the can of soda.

"Does that fit with what you know?" Jack asked Kevan.

"Perfectly," Kevan replied, giving the Ballycarbery ghost a mental pat on the back for accuracy.

"We'll go ahead and do that, then," Jack said. "All I need is for you to write a bit of Persian gibberish to pass on to our mark. Once we arrest him, the rest will be a matter of how much we can get him to admit. You may be able to place him at the scene of the bombing, but beyond that, we can't connect him to any other incidents." He rubbed a knuckle over his chin as though that gesture might help him think more clearly. With a short nod, he continued, "This group being responsible for killing your sheep justifies questioning you in the matter. Once you've seen the man, you can make the other accusation. With any luck, more witnesses will come forward to corroborate your story or place him at the scene of another assassination." Jack leaned back in his chair. "There isn't much left to do tonight except to take our prisoner back to the station." He glanced toward the window then added, "Or should I say this morning?"

Kevan nodded, noting the faint glow of dawn outlining the eastern hills. "Assuming you don't want to leave your prisoner unattended, how about I take Cleona home and then drive back down in your car?" Arching a brow, he aimed a pointed look at Conall. "I'm also going to assume you'd rather not face Sinead."

"I doubt she'll ever speak to me again," Conall said with a miserable wag of his head.

Kevan could understand a man wanting enough money and land to provide for a wife and family, but he found it hard to sympathize with someone who'd gone about it the way Conall had. "That's something you should've considered before getting mixed up in this. Although at the moment, I'd say Sinead's reaction was the least of your worries."

* * * *

Sinead's possible involvement rather than her reaction was what concerned Cleona during the short drive to the Mahoney's farm. Anyone less sensible than Jack Halloran might assume she was in on Conall's scheme, from which, if successful, she would certainly benefit. She'd been present when the plans were discussed and could easily have tipped off Conall, although that detail might not matter to a corrupt judge looking for scapegoats.

Not being able to trust anyone was the toughest part of saving the world. There were too many people willing to put their own best interests ahead of what was best for the planet and mankind as a whole. She tried not to think about that. It only made her angry, and an angry mind didn't always focus on the right path.

"What are we going to tell them?" she asked.

"I have no earthly idea," Kevan replied, obviously mulling over the same dilemma. "I hate to say it, but telling the truth might be our best course. Knowing Conall is involved might bring other information to light."

"I see what you mean." Cleona caught herself chewing on her lower lip. "I still don't like it, though. There's something weird about him being the one. I mean, his reasoning made perfect sense, but..." She paused, gazing out at the surrounding hills. Such a quiet, peaceful scene. And yet danger lurked behind every rock and shrub.

"Do you think Sinead knows?"

Her subsequent bark of laughter was devoid of humor. "I see we're having similar thoughts, although I have a hard time believing she's a part of this." Despite having said that, Cleona was forced to admit that Sinead had been relatively scarce since their arrival at the farm. Helping Fergus with the cattle and dating Conall explained a great deal. However, even if she knew what her boyfriend had been up to, she was certainly cutting her losses now. "Conall seemed pretty concerned about her finding out the truth. Maybe that's proof enough."

"Let's hope so." Kevan parked the car and they both got out. "Do you want me to come in with you?"

"No." Feeling suddenly cold, she crossed her arms, rubbing them with her hands. "I can do this alone. You and Jack can come back later. With any luck, everyone will still be asleep and won't even know I've been gone."

He glanced at his watch. "Maybe so. I wouldn't normally be up at this hour myself." The swift kiss he gave her brought her shivers to a screeching halt. "I'll be off then. Be back as soon as I can."

Cleona waited until Kevan drove off in the guard's vehicle then slipped in through the front door, toed off her muddy shoes, and padded into the kitchen.

Cold silence greeted her as she entered, quickly dissipating the heat of Kevan's kiss. She filled the electric kettle with water and switched it on. A hot cup of tea might not solve the world's problems, but it would surely drive the chill from her bones.

Or would it?

The feeling went deeper. Perhaps the Array was trying to tell her something.

Be a little more specific, will ya?

The tea was already steeping by the time muted footsteps drew her attention to the doorway.

Ita entered, tightening the belt of her robe. "My, you're up early."

"Couldn't sleep," Cleona replied with perfect honesty. "I might have to take a nap later to catch up."

"I'm not surprised." Ita took a package of sausages from the fridge. "Don't suppose you've had any word from Kevan or the sergeant?"

"Not yet." Cleona was glad Ita wasn't looking at her or she would have spotted the deception in a heartbeat. As an explanation for her stocking feet occurred to her, she added, "I went out a bit ago. Didn't see anyone."

Ita unwrapped the sausages and dropped them in a skillet as though she had no concerns beyond fixing breakfast. "Ah, well. I expect we'll hear from them soon enough. Sinead and Fergus just went out to feed the stock. Perhaps they'll see something."

"I suppose so."

In all likelihood, the first thing they would notice was that the guard's Isuzu Trooper had been replaced by Kevan's Volvo. While that could be explained without mentioning Cleona's role in the exchange, she hadn't seen Fergus or Sinead when she returned. Hopefully they hadn't spotted her either. In the greater scheme of things, none of that mattered. The problem was that Cleona simply wasn't prepared to tell her cousin about her boyfriend's arrest. What crime would he be charged with? Trespassing, destruction of property, or terrorism?

She had no doubts about Jack's competence. He might never have dealt with a similar crime, but that didn't mean a damn thing. His belief in them was all that really mattered.

A moment's reflection on how easily she and Kevan had convinced others of the paranormal aspect of their knowledge made her realize something. The supernatural was the only way to explain what they knew. Unless they were involved themselves.

They were, of course. Just not in a way anyone would ever expect.

Kevan would be back soon. Perhaps Jack would drop him off on the way to the station, unless he went with them or followed in his own car so he could give his official statement. The wording of that was still something to contemplate. One thing for sure, if they were writing a note to stuff in the back wall of Ballycarbery Castle, she had every intention of being there to wait for the terrorist/assassin to retrieve it.

The more she thought about that, the more real the danger

became. The man was a hardened criminal, accustomed to killing others for money. How hard would he be to catch? What sort of repercussions would follow his capture? Would some of his pals attempt to break him out of jail? Or would they see to it that he was dead before he could ever be brought to trial?

Purely to get herself out of her own head, Cleona asked Ita to teach her how to make scones. While measuring out the ingredients, she found herself humming.

"What's that tune, pet?" Ita asked after a bit. "Sounds vaguely familiar."

"Umm… Beethoven's Piano Concerto No. 5."

Not the sort of thing I normally hum.

"I thought as much," Ita said. "Or at least something along those lines. Amazing you suddenly being able to play piano like that. Perhaps the most amazing thing of all."

"Maybe." One thing for sure, after everything else she'd been through, the strange dreams and weird voices, the piano playing ability was the one thing that could be considered a perk.

Ita went on with her cooking instructions, letting the matter drop, but Cleona suspected the tune in her head was more than the typical earworm. Was the pianist trying to tell her something? Was this information pertinent to their mission or was it simply the general background musings of the Array? How could she tell the difference?

For the first time, she considered the dreams to be the most useful means of communication. This one, she would have to figure out. Somehow.

Number five… Was there significance to that number?

When the opening notes of Beethoven's Symphony No. 5 started ringing through her head, any doubts evaporated.

Counting the one that lived, five sheep had been used.

This was the last one. The ring of assassins wouldn't utilize this route again. How the pianist knew was another of life's great mysteries, but Cleona didn't doubt it was true. Jack was right. This was their last chance. In the future, another method would be used—most likely one involving entirely different people and locations. Even using the same chain five times was pushing their luck. But then, assassinations didn't happen every day. Kevan had said they'd been happening roughly once a month until this last one.

Why the sudden rush?

With a frown, she began kneading the dough with more vigor

than was strictly necessary.

"Don't work the dough too hard or the scones will be tough," Ita cautioned.

Nodding, Cleona pressed the dough out on the board then used the cutter to shape the biscuit-like dough.

Like the scones, a light touch was what their mission required. Something as subtle as the wisps of dreams that were guiding her fate.

"Smile, Cleona. This is going to work."

So the Array hadn't forgotten how to speak.

Thanks. I needed that. Again.

Why couldn't the planet simply revolt? Refuse to allow the exploitation to continue? Natural disasters seemed to be doing that on their own. Too bad they weren't targeted at the true culprits instead of randomly taking the lives of innocent people.

But are any of us truly innocent? People drove their cars everywhere and expected the lights to come on with the flip of a switch. The dependence on power was as frightening as it was crippling. Cleona drew the line at electric toothbrushes and can openers, and though she certainly wasn't alone in that, there were others who never gave their power consumption a second thought. Not even when they paid their utility bills.

In making life easier, we've signed our own death warrants.

She'd always assumed science and technology would save the planet. She never dreamed Earth would have to save itself, although, ultimately, the planet would survive regardless of what happened to its inhabitants. Civilization might undergo radical change, but Planet Earth would continue to orbit the sun.

"There, now," Ita said. "We'll just pop those in the oven and get on with the rest of breakfast."

With a jolt, Cleona realized the scones had been cut out and placed on the pan seemingly by themselves. She certainly couldn't remember doing it.

This time, her lack of attentiveness was noticed by someone who understood what it meant.

Ita arched a brow as Cleona slid the scones into the oven. "The Array talking to you again, pet?"

"Um…yeah. A pep talk, actually. Seems like I need those more and more all the time."

"A bit of optimism couldn't hurt," Ita said with a shrug. "Although preparing for the worst will certainly keep you on your toes."

"I can't argue with that." Nor could she argue with the old adage that honesty was nearly always the best policy. Sinead was out with Fergus. Keeping the truth from Ita was pointless.

She drew in a deep breath and exhaled slowly. "Okay, Ita. I might as well tell you now. I know exactly what happened last night. I was there when Kevan and Jack caught Sinead's boyfriend in with the sheep. He admitted to everything. Said he was killing the sheep instead of taking them and waiting for the messages to pass. He wanted to put the money toward buying Kevan's farm and give Kevan a reason to sell at the same time."

Ita's gaze never wavered. "That comes as no surprise. I've always thought there was something strange about that boy."

Cleona couldn't believe it. Ita hadn't said a thing when Sinead claimed Conall had never been in trouble. Not one word. "Don't tell me you suspected him."

"I did," she said with a firm nod. "Oh, not his motivation, perhaps. The timing was what made me wonder. Conall always seemed to stop by to see Sinead the night before one of Kevan's sheep turned up dead. Those weren't the only times he visited, of course. And not before that fourth one, mind you; Sinead was with you in Sneem then. But all those before and since…"

"Wait a minute. You're saying he was here last night?"

"Aye. After you went up to bed. He didn't stay long. Said he was in the neighborhood."

"Wow. He's even dumber than I thought."

Ita chuckled. "Struck you as being a bit dim, did he?"

Cleona smiled. *Finally.* "Maybe not when I first met him. But last night? Absolutely. Fortunately, he's being cooperative. Too bad he doesn't seem to know much about what's coming next. We probably know more than he does. Kevan and Jack can fill you in on that—they may have found out more by now. But even if we hadn't caught Conall in the act, this is our last chance to catch the next link in the chain. Conall's boss won't be contacting him again."

"You seem pretty sure about that."

"I am." She hesitated, combing mental fingers through the clues. *Beethoven's fifth piano concerto. His fifth symphony.* "The fifth time was the last. Just wish I knew who told me."

"Hmm… Considering that concerto you were humming, I'd say it was the pianist," Ita said. "Or perhaps Beethoven himself?"

"As cool as that would be, I don't see how Beethoven could

possibly be in the Array."

Ita shrugged. "If our civilization dies, so does his music."

"You have a point."

Thanks, Ludwig.

Chapter 25

KEVAN DIDN'T EXACTLY DAWDLE OVER HIS MORNING CHORES. Nevertheless, it was mid-morning by the time he returned to the Mahoney farm to break the news to Sinead.

Cleona sat on the sofa with her aunt and cousin while he related the events of the previous night.

When he'd finished, Sinead blew out a long, resigned sigh. "I guess that explains how Conall could afford the expensive restaurants he's been taking me to over the past few months." With a shrug, she added, "I should have known it was too good to be true, but he said he'd found this terrific new job. He even paid for my share of the hotel in Sneem."

Kevan's first thought was that Conall had only footed the bill to keep Sinead out of the way, but he immediately dismissed the idea. With respect to Conall's "job," Sinead's presence or absence was irrelevant. Speed, however, was essential. If the other four notes were anything like the one they'd intercepted, they were time-sensitive.

"You couldn't possibly have known what he was up to," Ita said. "It wasn't until this last time that I made the connection myself."

Cleona leaned over and gave her cousin a hug. "He probably didn't know it, but this would've been his last drop. The money would've dried up in a hurry."

"That wouldn't have mattered as long as they didn't kill him when they were done with him." Sinead shuddered. "He said he hadn't been threatened, right?"

"He was only being paid, not coerced." Kevan hated the thought of being even remotely connected with such a scheme, no matter how the "mules" were motivated—although win or lose, at least he was on the right side. "Conall also said he normally goes straight to the castle after retrieving a message in order to have it in place before noon. Jack thought it best to wait until tomorrow morning to make a run to the castle. Since we'll be delivering a bogus message, the timing isn't critical. Besides, I'm not sure we could've made it by noon today even if we hadn't been up all night." The adrenaline high he'd been on a few hours before had already worn off and the look on Sinead's face when he broke the news sapped his energy even further.

"I'm so glad you aren't going there today," Cleona said, sounding greatly relieved. "Now would *not* be the time to botch this job by having one of you fall asleep at the wheel."

Kevan smiled. "We could've let you be our driver."

"Yeah, right," Cleona drawled. "I can really see Jack letting me drive the police car."

"He could've called for backup," Kevan mused. "Although I doubt he'd be willing to hand this case off to another officer."

"I'm not too keen on that idea myself," Cleona said.

Neither was Kevan—and probably for the same reason. Halloran believed their story. Convincing someone else might not be as easy.

"In the meantime, you'd best be getting some sleep," Ita suggested. "You'll have a long day of it tomorrow."

Sinead fretted her lower lip with her teeth. "I've been thinking Cleona and I should take a run over to Garnish Island." She heaved another sigh. "Guess we might as well do it today. God knows there isn't any reason to stick around here."

"There now, that sounds lovely, doesn't it?" Ita patted her daughter's hand then rose from the sofa. "I'll pack a lunch for you, and after you've toured the island, you could go on to Bantry. There's a spectacular view from the pier. Lots of nice shops and pubs too."

Even though he'd wanted to be the one to show those sights to Cleona, Kevan urged them to go. Sinead could use some time alone with her cousin, and he didn't want to inhibit the man-bashing conversation that was bound to ensue. Not that he blamed her. In her place, he'd have been tempted to include a bit of physical bashing along with the verbal variety.

* * * *

Later that morning, Cleona gazed out across the bay toward Garnish Island while she and Sinead waited for the ferry. "If the view Ita was talking about is half as good as what we've already seen, I'll be very impressed."

"You haven't seen anything yet," Sinead said. "The bay is quite pretty, I'll grant you, but Garnish Island is one of the most beautiful places in Ireland. The entire island is one huge botanical garden. You won't believe the size of the rhododendrons, and there are all sorts of rare plants from around the world."

Sinead's enthusiasm was in sharp contrast to the relative silence that had prevailed during the drive to Glengarriff, although her emotions had been easy enough to guess. Anger. Frustration. Betrayal. All of those things and more on top of the heartbreak of discovering the true nature of a man she thought she knew.

Cleona had attempted to banish her own disturbing thoughts by focusing on the passing scenery as they followed the N71 from Kenmare into County Cork. Although initially hemmed in by trees clipped as neatly as a hedge by passing vehicles, the road eventually wound its way into open, mountainous country, sometimes skirting the sides of the mountains and, more than once, actually tunneling through them.

Nevertheless, the need to have her feet firmly on the ground grew more overwhelming by the second. She needed to reconnect with the planet. Needed to draw strength and knowledge from the world's vast size and history. Apparently Mother Earth—or did she prefer to be called Gaia?—couldn't commune with her spokesperson within the confines of a car.

Gaia. Why hadn't the name occurred to her before?

Maybe she had to be here, in this particular place, for any of this to happen. Ireland possessed an ancient magic that set it apart from every other place on Earth. Perhaps it was the nearness of the sea; the way life clung to every surface like the seals lounging on the smooth rocks that dotted the bay, or how plants sprouted from every niche, like the tiny rose-shaped succulents thriving amid the rocks on the edge of the quay. Others might argue that they could commune with nature from wherever they called home, or even a favorite vacation spot. Cleona's Gaelic roots might be responsible for the affinity she felt with Ireland. But whatever the reason, the communication barrier seemed thinner here, allowing Gaia's voice to be heard above the din of modern society.

Having paid their fare, they boarded the *Harbor Queen II* and began the voyage to the island. Safe and dry on a seat in the enclosed ferry, Cleona recalled a different boat, one whose crew had plucked her and her fellow survivors from a life raft, if not actually from the sea. Had that incident changed those men as much as it had altered the women they'd rescued? Cleona couldn't imagine anyone being untouched by such an experience. Susan had to have been affected as well. Differently from Jillian and Cleona, perhaps, but changed nonetheless.

"You've gone awfully quiet," Sinead remarked. An instant later, her hand flew to her lips. "Oh, my. I hadn't thought—"

"About?" Cleona prompted.

"The sea. You nearly drowned in it. You're bound to be nervous in a boat."

Cleona schooled her features into what she hoped was a reassuring smile. "It's not like that. The sea was my rescuer, not my killer. I'm okay. Really."

"I hope you mean that. I'm sorry I didn't think of it before. I've been a bit…preoccupied."

"We both have a lot on our minds. That's why we came here, isn't it?"

Sinead blew out a breath, visibly relaxing. "You're right. We're supposed to go wild over all the beautiful plants, take hundreds of pictures, and then go have a drink. I know a pub in Bantry you're sure to love. Very historic."

Cleona's laughter wasn't nearly as forced as her smile had been. "Aren't they all?"

Sinead shrugged. "Some more than others, I suppose. But you're right. We're just used to all the history around here."

They must be used to the magic as well. Cleona certainly wasn't. She was itchy and restless. Hopefully, Sinead would continue to attribute her mood to other causes because Cleona hadn't a clue as to the source. She only knew the feeling was there, a prickling sensation in the very marrow of her bones.

"Speaking of pubs," Cleona began, giving voice to the first thought that popped into her head. "Back home, everyone eats corned beef and cabbage on St. Patrick's Day, but I've yet to see it on a single menu in Ireland. Why is that?"

"Because the corned beef and cabbage combination isn't Irish," Sinead replied, apparently finding nothing peculiar in Cleona's question. "From what I've heard, it was created by Irish immigrants in New York who got their meat from Jewish delis. We don't eat that much beef here. It's too expensive. Pork and lamb are more common." She stared at her cousin, her expression curious. "Your father could've told you that."

"Hmm… I suppose he could have. Never really thought about it before. Maybe if we lived in New York instead of Texas, it might have come up sooner."

Her explanation was reasonable enough, although she was fairly certain the question had its origins in the Array. A moment later, a sharp pang at her temple confirmed it. Someone had actually stuck around hoping to get authentic corned beef and cabbage in Ireland.

What a letdown that must have been.

Had she been an Array member herself, she'd have stayed long enough to sample all of Ita's specialties. But then, tastes differed.

She wiped the condensation from the window and gazed out across the waves, her mind drifting with the rhythm of the sea, the hum of the engine, and the wash of the wake. Her thoughts settled on Susan. Where was she? Had she gone back to work as though nothing had happened? Her lack of communication seemed wrong somehow. Cleona reminded herself that she had reached out to Jillian only after realizing that the Array was responsible for the buzz in her head. Perhaps Susan's reaction was even more delayed.

She was still mulling over possible explanations when the ferry docked at the island. As soon as they disembarked, Cleona's breath caught in her throat. Following the paths through the foliage did nothing to dim her astonishment.

Towering rhododendrons grew in profusion, their branches laden with clouds of blossoms ranging from snowy white to vibrant red and every hue in between. Despite the northern latitude, tropical plants and trees thrived there, reaching amazing heights. Tree-sized ferns and what looked like giant rhubarb plants flanked a rocky creek bed. Fuchsias grew like weeds, hundreds of flowers bobbing from every branch. Wisteria hung in long, lavender clusters from gnarled vines clinging to the walls of a Chinese-style building. Paths of dirt, brick, or gravel led from one breathtaking planting to another. Stone steps—some broad and some narrow—led from one tier of the island to the next.

The effect was staggering. Never having seen so much beauty in one place, Cleona should've been communing with Gaia from the moment she set foot on such an enchanted isle. She longed to linger over each marvelous plant, but beyond pausing to take a few pictures, she kept moving, driven onward by an unseen force.

"Slow down a bit," Sinead urged after a brief pause to photograph a salmon-colored azalea. "You're missing some really beautiful stuff."

"I know. I just.. " She couldn't explain the need, but somewhere there was a place… A place she had to find.

Like an echo from the ancient past, an eerie medieval chant

reached Cleona's ears. "Do you hear that?" she whispered.

Sinead came to a stop beside her. "Hear what?"

"That singing. Sounds like a Gregorian chant."

"I don't hear anything."

"Why am I not surprised?" Cleona muttered. If this was indeed the place she'd been searching for, it stood to reason that her cousin wouldn't have heard a single note. "There's something important here, Sinead. Something I have to find…" The music drew her gaze upward to a cylindrical stone tower rising from the brush-covered hill above them. "That's it."

"You mean the sentry tower? It's been there for ages."

"I don't doubt it." Not as ancient as the standing stones that had spoken to Jillian at Stonehenge, perhaps, but certainly older than any other structure on the island. "You're sure they never play music from the tower?"

"Not that I know of. I've been here several times. Never heard any music. Still don't." The quaver in Sinead's voice was impossible to ignore. "Is it the Array?"

"Maybe," Cleona replied. "I'm not sure." On any other day, she'd have dismissed it as a group of talented tourists taking advantage of the tower's acoustics.

But not today.

Especially since she seemed to be the only one who could hear it.

Gravel crunched beneath her shoes as she hurried along the path to a flight of broad, stone steps. After climbing the rough stair, she continued along a dark, twisting trail through the woods until a sharp bend in the path sent her toward an arched opening in a high stone wall.

The music continued, louder than before, luring her on.

Beyond the archway, the tower stood alone on a flat, graveled space, flanked by a pair of rough stone walls. Ivy grew in the niches between the rocks, along with clusters of purple wildflowers. A sturdy, if somewhat incongruous, metal stair led up to the tower's entrance.

Grasping the handrail, Cleona put one foot on the lowest step. The moment she did so, the music ceased. Not even an echo remained.

"Are you sure you should go up there?" Sinead sounded anxious, worried.

Cleona gazed up at yet another arched doorway located about

halfway up the tower. "I'm okay, Sinead. Haven't gone bonkers. At least, not any more than I was before."

She ran lightly up the steps and passed through the doorway, noting that the tower's interior seemed much smaller than its outer circumference would suggest. A narrow spiral stair led her to a high-walled, unroofed chamber with a band of worn stone blocks lining the inner perimeter. Stepping up onto the blocks raised her to shoulder height with the wall's upper edge and provided her with a breathtaking, panoramic view of the bay and the surrounding mountains. From that vantage point, the thickness of the wall was also clearly evident; Cleona couldn't have reached the outer edge unless she wriggled across the slab of stone and mortar on her belly.

She stared out at the bay and the rocky headland beyond, imagining ships filled with marauding invaders sailing up the channel to wreak havoc on the countryside. Suddenly, her mind went blank, allowing other images to creep in.

Fishing boats. In a town called Liscannor...

Closing her eyes, she turned toward the north and a vision of Susan standing on a cliff overlooking the sea slowly came into focus. Not the Fogher Cliffs that Cleona and Sinead had visited on Valentia Island, but a place further up the coast near the crash site.

"The Cliffs of Moher." The name popped into her head as though one of the Array had supplied the information, if not the actual vision. A stone lookout tower, a bit more recent in design than the one on Garnish Island, lay to the north of Susan's location. Cleona recalled having seen it from the life raft, but its name escaped her.

"O'Brien's Tower."

No doubt the Array had been the source of both of those tidbits. Cleona was pleased to think they were still with her, but did Susan have her own Array? She stood perilously close to the edge, staring down at the crashing waves below. Unlike the area near the tower, no stone walls bordered the rim to protect the careless from falling to their deaths.

Had survivor's guilt driven her to the brink? Was she contemplating joining the others who had died in the crash? Or was she trying to summon their spirits?

"Susan!" What had been intended as a mental shout became a verbal one, and Cleona went on, speaking not only for herself, but also for Jillian. "We have a mission to complete. A quest to fulfill. We need you."

Susan's head snapped up and swung northward as though the nearby tower had been the source of Cleona's voice. Stepping back from the cliff's edge, she turned and began walking briskly in that direction, passing a number of sightseers on the path. One woman put out a hand as if to stop her—possibly recognizing Susan from newspaper accounts of the disaster—but whatever her purpose, she drew back, allowing Susan to pass unhindered. No doubt Susan's expression reflected the strangeness of the episode, shocking the woman to silence.

The two towers had to be connected. Not by sight, of course; too many miles lay between them. But if dirt was the planet's flesh, stone was both its skeleton and its nervous system, providing structure while allowing spiritual currents to flow through seams of living rock. The Earth spirit had used conduits of this nature before—the rocky crags of the Black Valley for Cleona and the great trilithons of Stonehenge for Jillian—seeming to prefer stone to any other medium. The link made sense, and considering where she was heading, Susan's portal was O'Brien's Tower.

Cleona watched Susan's progress through her fellow survivor's eyes. Upon reaching the tower, Susan passed over the two-euro admission fee and climbed the spiral stair to the viewing platform. When she finally reached the top, she turned southward, her eyes meeting Cleona's as though they stood face-to-face.

"Are you still there?" Susan's voice sounded tentative and wary.

"Yes," Cleona replied. "I saw you on the cliff's edge. I–I was afraid you were going to jump."

"I should have," Susan snapped. "Everything that matters to me went down with that jet."

Cleona hadn't thought about it at the time, but unlike Jillian and herself, Susan must have actually known some of the people on the plane. Other crewmembers and perhaps even some of the passengers.

"I'm sorry for your loss." Cleona's response was automatic and, like most condolences, totally inadequate. "But as I said before, we *need* you."

Susan seemed oblivious to the strands of hair blowing across her face, only brushing it aside after a few moments in an absent, distracted manner. "I've already done what I had to do. I helped to save you and Jillian. My job here is finished." She drew in a breath. "If I can stomach another transatlantic flight, I'm going home. There's nothing here for me now."

That attitude was the exact opposite of the grim determination Susan had displayed in the wake of the crash. She'd seemed more angry than sad back then. What had changed?

"I'd say there was quite a lot for you here," Cleona countered. "In case you haven't realized it, you aren't exactly talking to me on a cell phone."

"I noticed that," Susan drawled. The corners of her mouth lifted in a faint glimmer of a smile. "I probably look like a lunatic standing here talking to the wind. I certainly feel like one."

"Maybe. Although most people would assume you're using a Bluetooth connection." Fishing her phone from her pocket, Cleona checked the signal icon. NO SERVICE. "But enough about that. You need to go to Liscannor and charter a boat."

Surprisingly, Susan didn't ask why. "The same boat that picked us up?"

"I think that would be best," Cleona replied, recalling how taken one of the fishermen had been with Susan and her red hair. Jillian and Cleona had teamed up with Ranjiv and Kevan. Susan deserved a sidekick of her own, and a guy with a boat could prove to be a definite asset. "I have no idea what will come of it. I only know it's important. Can you do that?"

"I might as well." Susan's tone was as bleak as her shrug was forlorn. "God knows I don't have anything better to do."

Cleona grinned. "Chin up, Susan. You'll have plenty to do from now on. We're about to save the world."

Chapter 26

"Now, *that* was weird."

Cleona turned to find her cousin standing a few feet away, her eyes open a bit wider than usual. Sinead might have heard about the other strange occurrences, but this was one of the few she'd witnessed firsthand. She obviously hadn't reached the point where she considered them commonplace.

"Um... This tower and the one at the Cliffs of Moher appear to be connected." With a shrug, Cleona held up her phone. "Better reception than I'm getting on this thing."

Sinead giggled. "I take it you were talking to one of your fellow survivors?"

"Yeah. Susan Maxwell." Frowning, Cleona shook her head, still puzzled by Susan's bleak attitude. "She said everything that mattered to her went down with that plane, and I honestly think she was about to jump off the cliff. She seemed so heartbroken and hopeless. I'll admit I never even thought about her knowing the rest of the crew."

"She must've lost some good friends."

"I suppose so. Although I can't help thinking there was more to it than friendship. I probably should've called her sooner, but she wasn't like that before. I was a total wreck after the crash. She was the strong one who took charge."

"Delayed reaction?" Sinead suggested.

"Possibly." The connection now broken, no visions altered the view as Cleona gazed out at the peaceful sea. What had happened since the crash that could explain Susan's current frame of mind? Had her own version of the Array driven her mad? Or was grief the lone cause of her misery? "We went our separate ways afterward; each of us at least attempting to get back to normal. I dunno... Maybe we should've stuck together longer—formed a support group or something."

"You're doing that now, aren't you?"

Cleona huffed out a laugh. "More like occupational therapy. Being chosen to save the world forces you to focus on the important stuff." Her own mood had certainly benefitted. Evidently Kevan's and Jillian's outlook had also improved.

Susan, it seemed, was a different kettle of fish. "As a flight attendant, Susan must've known or interacted with dozens of the passengers and crew. Jillian and I only met a few people on that plane. Susan suffered a far greater loss than either of us."

"Either that or she's the type who's a tower of strength in a crisis only to fall apart when it's all over."

"Makes sense." Nodding absently, Cleona began taking pictures. She needed to remember this place. Every angle, every nuance, every detail. The color of the trees, the sea, and the distant mountains. Realizing she hadn't taken so much as a selfie since her arrival in Ireland, she held out her phone. "Here. Take one of me, will you? I need evidence to prove I was actually here."

If her cousin saw anything strange in the request, she kept it to herself. After snapping the photo, she returned the phone to Cleona. "See how you like that one."

Cleona tapped the screen, then inhaled so sharply, she nearly choked on her own spit. "Holy cow. I can see the Array."

"Oh, you can*not*," Sinead protested. Snatching back the phone, she gasped, "I'll swear they weren't there when I took it."

"They are now," Cleona said grimly. Enlarging the picture, she pointed at the man standing beside her. "That's Jacob Emhart. These others, though… No idea who they are." She certainly couldn't pick Beethoven out of the crowd.

Damn.

And there *was* a crowd. More than she ever would've guessed, which made her wonder how many of them had actually been on the plane versus those she'd picked up along the way. "Kinda makes me want to take a picture of Susan and see who's following her around. When we get done with our piece of this puzzle, we need to meet up with her somewhere."

"You think we *will* get done? Successfully, I mean."

"By that I assume you mean without anyone else getting killed—Kevan's sheep, included." Poor Sinead. In solving the sheep-killing mystery, she'd lost a boyfriend—a boyfriend who still might end up as a target for making the mistake of getting caught. Cleona opted for a degree of optimism she wasn't sure was justified. "Oh, yeah. That much is in the bag. It's what happens afterward that has me bugged, although that may turn out to be Susan's problem."

Drawing in a deep breath, she pocketed her phone. "What do

you say we finish our tour and head for that pub in Bantry? I don't
know about you, but a pint o' Guinness would go down pretty well
about now."

"It would at that," Sinead replied. "Might as well make the most
of the day. Something tells me tomorrow won't be quite as
enjoyable."

"You got that right." Cleona gestured toward the stair. "Lead
on."

* * * *

The rest of the day passed without any major events, spiritual or
otherwise. The pub was cozy and the view from the pier as fabulous
as Ita had promised, but Cleona was anxious to see Susan again, and
just as anxious to get this business over with. Restlessness continued
to plague her throughout the drive back to the Mahoney farm.

There was another possible explanation for her mood, one that
could easily be remedied. "Think anyone would mind if I spent the
night at Kevan's place?"

"Not really." Sinead's eyes slid toward her cousin. "I'm
surprised you haven't already moved in with him."

"Seemed kinda tacky. After all, I came to Ireland to see you and
your family."

"A trip that didn't turn out entirely the way we planned."

"No joke." She blew out a sigh. "I may do that, then. At least for
tonight. We'll want to get an early start to the castle, and I don't
want to give them the chance to run out on me. I'm as much a part of
this as they are, perhaps even more so."

"If they did try to talk you out of going—and I'm not saying
they will—it would only be for your own protection."

Cleona snorted. "Funny thing about protection. Surviving the
un-survivable kinda skews your attitude toward dangerous
situations."

"You figure you're invincible?"

"Yeah. So does Kevan, which could either result in some truly
heroic acts or lull us into believing we can survive anything short of
a bullet to the brain. We actually discussed the idea that Earth might
be protecting us—keeping us alive so we can complete our mission.
Unfortunately, a successful mission doesn't necessarily guarantee
we'll still be alive at the end."

"True." Sinead gnawed at her lip then glanced toward her
rearview mirror before continuing. "I can't stop you from doing as
you see fit, but there's no need to do anything foolish."

"I don't plan to. By the same token, I doubt our terrorist friend goes about prepared to shoot anything that moves."

"I wouldn't put it past him," Sinead said. "He obviously doesn't object to killing. At least, not on moral grounds."

"Financial, maybe," Cleona mused. "He wouldn't get paid for killing any of us, although self-preservation is a pretty powerful motivator. But enough about that. We can't do a damn thing until tomorrow morning anyway. Let's talk about something else."

"Like whether you'll actually be sleeping with Kevan tonight?" Sinead drawled. "That's a great diversion."

Cleona laughed. "Oh, come on, Sinead. I shouldn't have to tell you that. I should've thought it was perfectly obvious."

"Maybe. Although going over the details would certainly take our minds off saving the world."

For about three seconds tops. "Okay. Let's just say I wouldn't mind doing it again."

"For the rest of your life?"

At the moment, Cleona truly couldn't vouch for how long her life might be, but either way, the answer was the same. "Absolutely."

"Eat, drink, and be merry, for tomorrow we die."

Sinead had only replied with a nod and a smile, which meant that tiny pearl of wisdom had come from the Array.

Oh, hush up, you guys. Like I really needed to hear that.

"Sorry. Gallows humor."

Totally inappropriate.

Cleona gave herself a mental pat on the back for not reacting aloud. Fortunately, she didn't have to hide her interactions with the Array from her cousin anymore. Not that blabbing about it was strictly necessary. Some conversations were best kept private.

As were some aspects of her life, specifically her relationship with Kevan. The thought that there might be voyeurs observing such things almost made her wish the two of them had waited until after the entire Array had moved on to do the deed.

No. They'd both had too many important visions in the aftermath for celibacy to be an advantage.

Then again, while they might be observing, at least the gang hadn't been critical.

"Respectful silence."

Mmm... I see. Don't suppose you could close your eyes, could you?

"That would be tough. We're just sort of...here."
Never mind. I'll get over it.

Thus far, Kevan had done a fine job of making her forget about the Array—at the crucial moments anyway. Hopefully, that trend would continue.

* * * *

Hours later, as she lay in his arms, he proved it once again.

An older, thick-walled Irish cottage, Kevan's house was nearly silent; not a sound reached her ears, save for the occasional hum from the refrigerator and the ticking of the clock in the hall. Her Dallas apartment was never that quiet. The constant din of traffic, sirens, and the electrical vibrations of every appliance known to man were always buzzing in the background.

She lay beneath sheets of cotton and blankets of wool, surrounded with natural, earthy warmth and the pleasing, woodsy scent that was so uniquely Kevan's own. Inhaling the fragrance of his passionate desire, she let it flood her senses as it coursed through her lungs to mingle with her own essence. His kisses drove out her worrisome thoughts before replacing them with tenderness and love. The cloudy sky above diffused the moonlight to a soft glow, enabling her to see shapes and shadows, as well as the occasional liquid gleam of his eyes.

Cleona didn't need the Array or Mother Nature or Gaia or anyone else to tell her he was her one-and-only true love. The sheer and utter rightness of their joining stirred her soul, sending it swirling forth to envelop him in color and light, as though their auras had combined along with their bodies. As he moved inside her, the ambient temperature rose, driven upward by his steady climb to the peak of ecstasy, rendering her incapable of any thought that didn't include him. Her only regret was the barrier between them. She longed for them to truly be melded into one, nothing separating them but a whisper of breath in the night.

The urgency escalated so slowly, she was aware of each degree of increasing joy until at last, the summit was reached. Her spirit took flight, ascending into the dark sky like the wings of an eagle. Upon reaching the droplets of moisture held captive in the clouds, she shook them loose, allowing them to fall in a barely audible rhythm on the shingled roof.

I can make rain.

Had her soul become one with Earth and sky? Perhaps. But right now, loving Kevan was her only need, her only purpose.

Even so, she was flying, soaring over mountains and hills, swooping down into bays and lochs before at last circling the castle on the hillock by the sea to observe the drama playing out below. The tide was in, the waves lapping the shore as Kevan stood beside the gate, triumph and sadness both clearly evident in his expression as he faced the man who had nearly destroyed him so many years ago. The total lack of regret emanating from those cold, soulless eyes wasn't surprising. Not one shred of remorse tainted the pride in having succeeded in his evil endeavors.

The shock of sadness filled her before giving way to anger, followed by disgust and disdain. The man deserved no mercy. No reprieve. Death awaited him, as surely as it awaited every soul on Earth. He would be absorbed into the fiber of the planet's matrix, the matter comprising his existence neither created nor destroyed, merely transformed.

Earth would win in the end. Mankind, no matter how corrupt or malevolent, couldn't triumph over a supremacy that dwarfed any power they could possibly envision. The planet couldn't be destroyed by man, but the reverse could happen quite easily. That was the cataclysmic event they sought to prevent.

In the end, no cloud of dust or billowing smoke marked the demise of the old era and the birth of the next. Only the dawning of a new day.

* * * *

As soon as Cleona opened her eyes, Kevan knew they had shared yet another vision.

"We're going to win this one, aren't we?" she whispered.

He rose up on one elbow to gaze down at her. Tracing the line of her brow with a fingertip, he went on to thread his fingers through her dark, silky hair, combing it back from her face while marveling at her beauty and how very much at home she seemed in his bed. "If you believe that was a premonition. I'm not so sure myself."

"Maybe Mother Earth is using the power of positive thinking to help us along. You know what they say… Picturing your goals helps you achieve them."

"Aye, but we only saw the outcome. Seeing the actual method would have been a lot more helpful."

"I can't argue with that." A frown flitted over her brow as she trapped her lower lip between her teeth in an adorable manner that was peculiarly her own. "Maybe it means we'll be successful no matter what happens."

Kevan shook his head. "It couldn't be that easy."

Sighing, she snuggled closer. "Probably not. Nothing ever is."

"We should get up and get going," he advised, although he felt no enthusiasm whatsoever. He longed for the time when they could lie late abed and—

Who am I kidding? There would always be livestock that required care and feeding. And possibly children as well. *Something else to look forward to.*

He glanced at the clock. "Jack and Conall will be here soon."

She flung back the covers and sat up. "How about I fix breakfast while you do whatever it is you have to do for your critters in the mornings? Ita gave me a lesson in scone-making yesterday. I want to see how well I can manage on my own."

"Sounds great," he replied, once again struck by the ease with which she had become a part of his life, and a vital one at that. Leaning closer, a single kiss nearly became twenty, but he forced himself to keep moving. There would be other mornings when he would be free to linger over the soft warmth of her lips and the satin smoothness of her skin.

He rose from the bed and pulled on his clothes while she did the same. She displayed no embarrassment, not bothering to hurry or attempt to hide herself from him. Then he realized he was the one who should have been overcome by shyness. He hadn't even considered the need until it was too late.

Except that there *was* no need. When her gaze landed on his scars, she didn't mention them or even flinch. Most people seemed shocked whenever they looked at him, quickly averting their gaze to something less disturbing. Not Cleona. Her quiet acceptance of his disfigurement warmed his heart.

They went out to the kitchen together. After pointing out the location of a few items he thought she might need, Kevan left her to it. Ita's coaching and her own common sense would take care of the rest.

Memories of the previous night crowded his thoughts as he closed the door and whistled for Mac. The long vigil, the quick tussle with Conall that had seemed so effortless at the time, but when viewed in retrospect, had been rather astonishing. Jack had certainly seemed impressed by the ease of Conall's capture. Would today go the same way? For that matter, would the assassin even make an appearance? This might be the first of several visits to Ballycarbery, days of seemingly endless boredom while they waited for him to take the bait.

Kevan could have relied on the ghost for further information if he hadn't already been given all the facts he needed. Conall's instructions to deliver the message before noon, plus the position of the sun in the original vision were quite enough. No shadows had stretched across the lawn in any direction.

High noon. "Simple as that." A soft bark drew his attention to Mac. The dog stood nearby, alert and waiting for the next command. "Who knew being haunted could be so useful?"

He signaled for the collie to bring in the sheep while he poured feed into the trough. The first ewe to arrive received a pat on the back as she began nibbling the grain, and Kevan grinned as the rest of the flock scampered down the hill.

Having spent the night with Cleona was reason enough for his jovial mood, but the imminent completion of their mission was also a factor. With a light heart and a spring in his step, he fed the hens, then gathered the eggs and carried them into the scullery. Mac followed close behind, knowing that Kevan would feed him before washing the fresh eggs. This was their normal, daily routine.

But today was different. Kevan wouldn't be fixing his own breakfast, nor would he be eating it alone. Cleona might even have the meal ready by the time he finished with the chores. Breakfast or no, the mere thought that she would be there when he returned was enough to have his heart pounding madly.

In all the years since his parents died, he'd lived alone; no one—certainly no woman—had ever been there in his house, anticipating his arrival. The experience was totally unique, a milestone of sorts, and one he'd never dreamed of achieving.

Although he couldn't say he hadn't been prepared, when he opened the scullery door and went into the kitchen, the impact nearly knocked him flat. The aroma of freshly baked scones, mixed with that of frying sausages and buttered eggs assailed his senses, filling his heart with joy and his eyes with tears as he beheld the most welcome sight in recent memory. Cleona, standing there in his kitchen as though she'd lived there all her life. She was even wearing his mother's apron.

Obviously noting his tears, Cleona gazed at him, her brow knit with concern. "What is it?"

"You." He swept her into his arms, wanting nothing more than to hold her forever, never to be parted from her again. "Just you."

Chapter 27

CLEONA AND KEVAN WERE ALMOST FINISHED WASHING UP THE breakfast dishes when Jack Halloran's white Isuzu Trooper with its distinctive yellow stripe and blue lettering pulled into the drive.

Cleona handed him the last plate. "Seems like he should be driving something a bit less conspicuous today."

"I'm surprised he didn't bring Conall's car," Kevan said as he dried the dish. "Although if it comes to a car chase, I'm sure he'll be pleased to have one with a siren."

"I suppose so. But what if someone is already there to watch Conall make the drop? They might see the police and warn the other guy off."

Kevan took a moment to consider the idea before shaking his head. "That'd be a bit much, wouldn't you say?"

"Probably." After a sharp exhale, she added, "Especially since no one gave Conall a nudge when he missed the last signal."

"I've been thinking about that. These assassinations may be time-sensitive, but they could easily give this one another go if they botch the job the first time—especially since it involves a local official as opposed to someone who's only in the country for a short time."

"Scary, isn't it? We might thwart this attempt only to have another group go after him."

"That's something the Garda will have to deal with—giving him increased protection or something of that nature. Then again, this hit may be in regard to an upcoming vote. Once the votes are cast, there'd be no reason to try again."

"Until another environmentally significant issue is on the ballot." She grimaced. "We should've done some research on that guy."

"Actually, I did." Kevan hadn't slept the entire time Cleona spent with her cousin; he only wished he'd mentioned it to her sooner. And he would have, except that when she'd come knocking on his door the previous evening, any thoughts of politicians and murder suspects had been banished by her arrival. After all, she was the Carrier of Life's Preservation. Such things didn't belong in the same world as Cleona, much less the same thought. "As we could have guessed, he's one of the more staunch environmentalists in local government, although I'm not sure why they would target him, specifically. Could be a matter of convenience—someone knowing his whereabouts in advance—or perhaps he's been more vocal than others about the need for reform."

Her frown faded into an expression of thoughtful serenity. "When it comes to saving a life, the why doesn't matter, though, does it?"

"I don't suppose it does. Jack would certainly see it that way."

She nodded as a knock sounded at the door. "I'll be glad to get this day over with so we can get back to normal, whatever that is."

Kevan thought she might be overly optimistic, but he shared the same hope as he ushered Conall and Jack into the house.

Normal. No dead sheep. No terrorist attacks. No assassinations. He was okay with that, as long as normal life included Cleona.

Like the previous meeting, their planning session took place at the kitchen table, although minus the handcuffs. Neither man had made any comment about Cleona's presence. *Yet.*

"We need to make this drop look as normal as possible," Jack began. "Conall, I want you to deliver the message as usual, and we'll take it from there. There'll be an unmarked car at the turnoff to the castle, plus lookouts stationed at the Cahergall fort and the opposite side of the bay. A shallow inlet borders the castle grounds on the west and south. To the north and east are pastures, with a scattering of houses further up the slope. There's very little in the way of cover beyond a bit of gorse, so we should have no difficulty spotting him, even if he goes in on foot."

"He won't," Kevan said. "I've seen him. He drives right into the car park in a black BMW X6." On this point, Kevan knew no one could dispute his word, unless it was the castle's ghost. "Do you think he'll show up today?"

"He'd have to check every day, wouldn't he?" Cleona said. "Or at least every other day. Once a week wouldn't be nearly enough."

She aimed a questioning gaze at Conall, who threw up his hands in protest. "Don't look at me. I don't stick around to see who comes for them. I just deliver the bloody letters."

Jack snorted with disgust. "A delivery that's already two days late. I hope we haven't missed the cut-off point—if there is one."

"This is the weirdest form of communication I've ever heard of," Cleona remarked. "Email would be so much easier."

"Aye, but emails can be hacked," Jack said. "These guys are smarter than that. A string of paid operatives who don't know a damn thing about what they're involved in, and all of it done offline. Nothing traceable unless you follow the money, and I'd be willing to bet it comes from a numbered account." He glanced at Conall. "Am I right?"

Conall nodded grimly. "No doubt I've seen my last paycheck." A night in jail must've given him plenty of time to reflect on the consequences of his actions. Hollow-eyed and slump-shouldered, he looked even more miserable than when he'd been handcuffed to the table.

"Let's hope you haven't seen your last sunrise," Jack said, giving voice to a fear Conall was probably too scared to even think about.

"Kevan and I will pose as tourists," Cleona said. "Once your man across the bay spots the guy, you can drive down from the road above and be waiting for him when he comes back to his car."

"Actually, he won't be one of *my* men," Jack said. "Ballycarbery is out of my jurisdiction, but I've been in touch with the local guards. They'll be providing backup, so we'll have more than enough manpower for the job." He cleared his throat in a manner that hinted at his next question. "That being said, since Kevan can identify the suspect, why do you need to be there?"

"Dunno," she replied, clearly unperturbed. "I just have to, that's all."

The guard's eyes narrowed with suspicion. "You aren't telling me everything, are you?"

"You wouldn't believe me if I did," Cleona declared. "Trust me. My orders come from a higher source."

"Dunno why you're arguing with her, mate," Kevan said. "I may know a lot about what's going on, but this is her gig. The rest of us are only here for support."

"Protecting innocent citizens is *my* gig," Jack countered. "The man we're after is a dangerous criminal. You might be taken hostage or killed, Cleona. I can't let that happen."

Cleona nodded. "I understand that. But I have a level of protection you can't possibly match. Really. Trust me."

"Aw, let her come with us, you prat," Conall said wearily. "All we need to do is catch that bloke before he kills anyone else." He looked at Cleona. "For what it's worth, I believe you."

Jack's disdainful glance demonstrated how little he valued Conall's opinion. Nevertheless, after only a moment's hesitation, he nodded, albeit somewhat reluctantly. "Right, then. You can be there, but not on the castle grounds. I insist that you stay outside the fence."

She shrugged. "I have no problem with that. Just as long as you understand that for this operation to work, it has to play out a certain way."

Kevan knew why, of course, although he had no intention of admitting he and Cleona both had the same dream.

At least he thought they had. *His* dream had only hinted at the outcome. Had hers revealed more than she let on? Possibly. On the other hand, she could easily have had another vision while they sat there talking.

What hadn't she told him?

Hopefully, it wasn't something he needed to know.

* * * *

The drive to the castle reminded Cleona of the trip from Connemara to Galway. Granted, her only fears at the time involved the tests she would have to undergo at the hospital, but the residual anxiety from the crash, plus the buzzing in her ears, had made it almost as uncomfortable as this journey. She reminded herself that their goal was in sight. All they had to do was avoid mucking it up in the homestretch.

Having traveled that particular route several times now, she was beginning to recognize landmarks along the way, although the scenery still captured her imagination with its narrow roads, treeless slopes, and rugged coastline. The smooth green grass carpeting the fields and hills still seemed strange to her, no doubt the result of thousands of years of sheep grazing—something few places in the States could claim.

"Jack should've let Conall drive his own car," she said suddenly. "He wanted everything to be normal. I can't help thinking someone else will be watching the castle."

Kevan replied with a sardonic snort. "Can you really see him turning Conall loose on the road? We'd never see him again."

"Maybe not. He's probably too scared to run, although I can't blame him for wanting to disappear."

"Oh, he'll disappear, all right. Into jail—at least for a while."

"But will that stop anyone from trying to shut him up

permanently? These people are ruthless."

"True enough, although he's a fairly minor player. I doubt they'd bother with him."

To be perfectly honest, Cleona was a little surprised no one had bothered to come after her or her fellow survivors. Silencing Susan might turn out to be the most important factor, especially after what she'd said about everything that mattered to her going down with the plane. The very idea made her dangerous, a crusader who'd been positive the crash wasn't an accident, even in the immediate aftermath. Plus, if she hadn't been there to deploy that raft, Jillian and Cleona might have drowned before the fishing boat could pick them up, despite their life jackets. The sea hadn't been particularly rough at the time, but a life jacket couldn't protect them from the numbing cold.

That boat was significant too. Cleona didn't know why she thought so, especially since the boat had a perfectly good reason for being on hand at that particular time and place. Sunrise over the Cliffs of Moher was probably almost as cool as sunrise over Stonehenge. If it hadn't been for the tourist angle, the boat's proximity and prompt arrival would have seemed too fortuitous to have been the result of mere chance.

"Not everything is a miracle, Cleona."

Yeah. I keep forgetting that. Some things are just plain luck— good or bad.

Her own conscience might have been responsible for that bit of wisdom, although she preferred to believe it came via the Array.

They seemed to be chiming in more in the past day or so.

"We truly are nearing the end, aren't we?"

"Aye, that we are. At least, I *hope* we are."

Kevan's reply startled her slightly. She hadn't realized she'd spoken aloud. "Has your Array been talking to you?"

"A bit," he replied. "Enough to know that our suspect, as Jack calls him, will show up around noon."

"Makes sense, I suppose." She grinned. "Did the ghost tell you that?"

"More like I interpreted the vision that way." He returned her grin with a wry smile of his own. "No shadows around the castle."

"That works for me. By the way, did I tell you Beethoven popped into my Array?"

His shout of genuine amusement warmed her heart. This was what she wanted their life together to be like. Happy and fun without the grim dramas they'd endured in recent days. No doubt his past was more depressing than hers, but she'd been so busy with work, she'd never noticed her own lack of gaiety.

"You're bamming me, right?" he said.

She held up a three-fingered salute. "Scouts honor. Someone was playing songs—Beethoven's Fifth Symphony and Fifth Piano Concerto—trying to let me know this was the fifth and final time the terrorist ring would use Conall and the others."

He arched a brow. "Sure it wasn't the pianist?"

"That was Ita's first suggestion. Beethoven was the second. I'll admit the pianist is the most likely source, but bringing Beethoven on board would be quite a coup, don't you think?"

"I do indeed."

Recalling one other pertinent detail, she pursed her lips in disappointment. "Didn't see him in the picture, though."

"What picture?"

"The one Sinead took of me on Garnish Island. The Array can be seen standing all around me. I couldn't spot Beethoven, but that doesn't mean he wasn't there."

Kevan turned to gape at her for a long moment before finally returning his attention to the road ahead. "You know something? We need to work on our communication. Case in point, that vision we both had... It only showed the outcome, right?"

"Um... Sort of."

Gripping the steering wheel, he clenched his teeth in apparent anger, frustration, or both. "Jack thought you were holding back information. That makes two of us. Spill it, Cleona. What else haven't you told me?"

"Nothing big, I promise. I'm just afraid if everyone knows what's *supposed* to happen, it'll affect the result."

"So... Only you need to know?"

She nodded. "Only me."

Me, the Array, and Ballycarbery's ghost.

* * * *

The drop went as planned, except for Cleona's insistence that Conall drive Kevan's Volvo to the site alone. She claimed the make of the vehicle was insignificant, as long as it didn't have GARDA emblazoned on all four sides in bright blue letters. No one could argue with her logic, and Conall swore on his life, Sinead's, and everyone else's that he could be trusted. Fortunately, he did exactly as he promised, returning to the rendezvous point at the pull-off that served as a car park for the Cahergall stone fort, which was less than a mile from the castle by road and considerably less as the crow flies.

The fort was about a quarter of a mile off the main road and had to be approached on foot. Any guards stationed there would have a clear view of the castle from atop the southern wall, but whether they could make it back to their vehicle in time to intercept a fleeing suspect remained to be seen. How a car chase would turn out was anyone's guess, although Kevan doubted the local constabulary drove anything that could catch a BMW.

"We'll stay here," Kevan told Jack as Conall took Cleona's place in the front seat of the guard's SUV. "It's as good a place as any to watch the road."

"Right," said Jack. "There's a driveway a bit closer to the castle that's surrounded by enough shrubbery to hide us from anyone traveling the main road. I'll wait there. Call me if you see anything."

"Will do." Kevan got into the Volvo with Cleona, who was already fidgeting in her seat. By the time he'd turned the car around to face the road, she was drumming her fingers on the armrest. He'd have told her not to fret, but doubted it would help any. His own anxiety had nearly reached the downing-a-shot-of-Jameson level as it was.

An hour later, despite his attempts to engage her in conversation, Cleona was jumpier than ever, gasping whenever a vehicle approached, then glaring at it as it went by.

"I certainly don't envy Jack being stuck with Conall," she said after a Fiat—the third black car they'd seen—drove past. "By the time this is over, his brain will probably be mush, especially after that all-nighter you guys pulled. Honestly, I don't see how police officers stand this surveillance crap. Without you to talk to, I'd be a raving lunatic by now."

Kevan suspected she hadn't far to go to reach that stage. He was halfway there himself. "I'm sure they talk to each other, just like we're doing. It isn't as though anyone can hear us."

"True, although I'm still not convinced no one is watching. Maybe that guy knows we're here and won't come until we leave. It's taking so long...maybe this isn't his regular day to visit the castle."

Plenty of other people had decided it was a good day for sightseeing. A fairly steady stream of tourists had visited the fort— sometimes by the busload—and a good many of them had headed down the road to the castle afterward.

She hitched in her seat and snatched her purse from the floorboards with a white-knuckled grip. "At what point do we decide he isn't coming?" She didn't give him a chance to reply before adding, "And what if he's driving a different car?"

"The guard watching from across the bay would see him. There's absolutely no cover between his position and the rear of the castle where the message is stashed."

With a sigh, she reached over and grasped his hand. "I'm sorry to be such a pain, but I'm about to jump out of my skin."

"I'm pretty anxious myself," he said. "Although the Array may be what's making us feel like that."

"Yeah." She hesitated, briefly capturing her lower lip with her teeth before continuing. "There's so much riding on this. Jack isn't the only one we have to answer to this time. Makes me wonder what he told those other cops. The way he talked, there are several of them here."

"There's enough concrete evidence to justify their involvement, especially given what the original message suggests. And then there's Conall's story. I don't think—"

Kevan's mouth snapped shut as yet another black car approached. He didn't need to see the man's face to know who the driver was. The prickling skin on the back of his neck was proof enough.

"That's him."

Chapter 28

STUNNED SPEECHLESS, CLEONA HAD TO GATHER HER WITS BEFORE she spoke. "Think we should follow him?"

"Absolutely, although I'm quite sure Jack would rather we wait until the bloke actually takes the bait." Kevan tossed his phone in Cleona's lap and started the engine. "Better give him a heads up."

Cleona tapped in the number and put the phone on speaker. "We've seen him," she said when Jack answered. "He's driving a black BMW."

"Aye," Jack said. "Higgins just spotted him at the crossroads. According to Dolan, the guard at the fort, there are two cars parked at the castle. I'm guessing our suspect will wait until they leave before he makes his move."

"Makes sense." She blew out a shaky breath. "Call us as soon as he's made the pickup." She had an idea Jack would do no such thing, but she figured it couldn't hurt to ask. Again. "We need to be there," she stressed. "It's important."

"I'll be in touch," Jack said. "Just sit tight and wait for my call."

Cleona switched off the phone. She didn't have to be a mind-reader to know that if Jack had his druthers, she and Kevan wouldn't get within twenty miles of the castle until the suspect was apprehended and behind bars. "Think he'll actually call us?"

"Are you kidding? Of course not. Having us down there probably violates standard police procedure." He arched a brow. "But we *can* go for a better position. There's nobody further out than us unless the guy at the fort decides to join in, and I'm guessing he won't. The observations from his vantage point are too critical."

"What about that driveway that leads down to the inlet? The one that looks like a small boat ramp?"

"Aye. It's just out of sight of the castle. We can wait there until we get the green light from Jack—*if* we get the green light. Barring that, we can block the road in case our man tries to make a break for it."

"We'll have to pass Jack and Higgins to get there," Cleona

warned.

"I know. They aren't gonna like this a bit."

"They can't exactly turn on their sirens and pull us over, though, can they?"

Hooking a hand around her shoulder, Kevan leaned over and planted a noisy kiss on her cheek. "I like the way you think."

She was pleased to have such an agreeable accomplice. That is, until another potential snag occurred to her. "You don't suppose the guy in the Beemer spotted us, do you? I mean would he recognize you?"

He shook his head. 'I can't imagine he'd make the connection between this job and an assassination he pulled off ten years ago. And even if he did notice us sitting here, when we show up at the castle, he'll only assume we're checking out all of the local historic sites. I'm sure most folks who stop at the fort go on to the castle."

"True." Despite Kevan's sound reasoning, as they approached the turnoff, her heart took a plunge. "Looks like that guy decided to move too."

Kevan glanced sideways. "No. He's parked beside that building across the road. Must've figured sitting out in plain sight wasn't such a good idea, even in an unmarked car."

"I almost wish he *had* moved in closer," Cleona remarked. "He'll probably tell Jack on us—or follow us."

"That's a risk we'll have to take." With a shrug, he added, "At least we're ahead of him."

"Yeah. He can't take our parking space either. Although he *could* block us in there." She huffed out a breath. "Okay. I'll shut up."

Kevan smiled. "Wel...maybe you *are* thinking too much."

"Lifelong character flaw," she said absently, her attention focused on the road ahead. "I can't even blame it on the Array." Surprisingly, her spiritual companions were silent. Anticipating the end of their existence, perhaps? Or were they gearing up for the final battle?

Her body was certainly revving up for the climax, and having to sit still during a massive adrenaline surge made matters even worse. Her heart was racing and her hands trembled. Even her teeth were chattering.

"I'll be so glad when this is over," she whispered. "Don't know how much more I can take."

As if on cue, Kevan's phone rang. "It's Jack," she said as she answered it. "Hey, Jack. Don't worry. We aren't going all the way to the castle, and we'll be out of his line of sight. Just looking for a better position."

"Never mind that," Jack said, brusquely ignoring her explanation. "The other sightseers are getting in their cars. They should be coming your way soon. As soon as they've passed by you, keep going, but pull off on the ramp to the inlet."

She managed to stifle a giggle and the great-minds-think-alike comment that was poised at the tip of her tongue. "That's our plan."

"Right," Jack said. "I'm putting you on speaker so you'll hear GC Byrne's radio report from across the bay."

He actually trusts me. Clearly, she'd underestimated the sergeant. "Thanks."

An eternity seemed to drag by, but at last they passed the two oncoming vehicles.

Kevan nodded toward a tree-lined drive. "We're driving by your position now, Jack."

The ramp to the inlet lay roughly two hundred yards ahead. If Cleona's adrenaline level had been high before, it was positively soaring now. She bit back a scream as the squawk from Jack's radio sounded from the phone.

"He's taken the package," Byrne reported. "Heading back around the castle now."

"My, that was quick," Jack remarked. "Don't bother stopping at the ramp, Kevan. Go on to the castle. I'll give you two minutes before I follow. Carry your phone and keep the line open. Talk to the man if it seems appropriate."

"Will do."

Kevan's own injuries aside, Cleona couldn't imagine what he would say to his parents' killer. *"How much does an assassination go for these days? Making more per murder than you did ten years ago?"*

No. He would never say such a thing. A comment on the weather or a simple greeting would suffice, although in Kevan's place, she would've been hard pressed to speak to the man at all, preferring to throttle the life out of him instead.

They drove by the ramp and covered the remaining distance in an edgy silence, despite the rippling beauty of the inlet at high tide. The castle loomed dark and forbidding on its grassy hill, presiding over the bay as it had for over five hundred years. Masses of swirling gray clouds lit the crumbling walls from behind, turning the windows and doors into sinister eyes and gaping, screaming mouths. Cleona's grip on the phone was so tight she wouldn't have been surprised if it snapped in two. Kevan's own expression was one of jaw-clenched determination. He was about to confront the man who killed his parents and changed his life forever. What on earth could he be thinking?

"Ha!" Kevan said, breaking the silence at last. "The cursed git is drinking the lemonade."

* * * *

Kevan brought the Volvo to a stop and set the handbrake before killing the engine. After retrieving his phone from Cleona, he got out of the car, a little surprised that his knees were strong enough to support him. How often did a man confront his nemesis? With a nonchalance he was far from feeling, he rounded the vehicle to meet Cleona. He dropped an arm across her shoulders and they moved forward together, gazing up at the castle as any self-respecting tourists would have done.

"Wow," Cleona whispered. "That is one spooky-looking castle. Gotta get some pictures of that!" Whipping out her own phone, she moved a few steps away from him, snapping photos as she went.

By this time, their quarry had replaced the empty soda can on the wall and was strolling down the hill toward the gate. He was dressed much as he had been in Kevan's vision, wearing dark, well-tailored trousers and a crisp, expensive-looking shirt under a light jacket. If he hadn't been on the wrong side of the fence, his unhurried manner would have garnered no attention whatsoever.

Kevan waved, hoping the gesture didn't seem too forced as he summoned up a smile. "See any ghosts up there?"

"Not today, mate. They must be sleeping." Amazingly, the man smiled back. Plus, he spoke with an Irish accent. Kevan hadn't expected that—partly due to the man's Middle Eastern characteristics, but also because none of his victims, or even the ghost, had ever heard him speak. He aimed his smile at Cleona. "If it's all the same to you I'd prefer you deleted those pictures of me up by the castle." With a disarming laugh, he added, "I'd hate to get arrested for trespassing."

"Oh?" Cleona's befuddled frown was the picture of innocence. She gestured toward the fence. "You mean we can't get any closer than this?"

"Not legally," he replied. "Although I'd never be the one rat on you."

The man was smooth as glass and every bit as transparent as the plastic bag sticking out of his breast pocket. His close proximity to Cleona made Kevan's skin crawl. Kevan's only consolation was that he was still on the other side of the fence.

"No problem," she said cheerfully. "I can always take more. I was so awed by the castle, I didn't even realize you were up there." She made a show of tapping her phone as though complying with his request. "You probably got some great pictures, yourself."

He shrugged. "A few. If you follow the path all the way around the fence, you can get some shots of the rear of the castle."

"Thanks, I'll do that."

The man's eyes narrowed slightly. "You're American, aren't you?"

"You bet," she replied. "We've got a lot of neat stuff in Texas, but nothing like this. Ireland is the most beautiful place I've ever seen."

"It does have its charm," he conceded. Just as Kevan and Cleona had done, he pushed open the ostensibly "locked" gate with ease, then closed it behind him, aligning the broken hinges until they appeared to be intact. Smiling, he turned to face Cleona. "Have you been to the stone fort?"

She nodded. "Just came from there. Took tons of pictures, including a few of the castle from the top of the wall." With an expansive wave toward the crumbling ruins, she added, "But nothing as awesome as this." She moved even closer to the man, scrolling through the pictures she'd taken before holding her phone up to his face. "See? Not nearly as creepy as it is from this angle."

Kevan wanted to scream in protest, but there was absolutely nothing he could do short of yanking her away from him. In the next instant, he heard the crunch of tires scattering loose gravel on the verge.

The timing couldn't have been worse. A quick glance revealed Jack getting out of his police vehicle—cap, uniform, and all. Another car pulled up alongside, blocking the only exit. When a second guard emerged from the unmarked vehicle, Cleona's gasp recaptured his attention.

"Nobody move or she dies." Holding Cleona pinned against his chest, the man whipped a knife from his belt and swept it up to her throat, eliminating any doubts they might have had as to this man's profession. He might not receive payment for Cleona's murder, but he obviously had no qualms about using her as a shield to escape.

Amazingly, she didn't stiffen or even attempt to fight her captor. What was even more astonishing was her smile—almost as though he'd fallen neatly into her trap rather than the other way round. Closing her eyes, she exhaled, her entire body seeming to deflate in the process. As though her bones were made of hot jelly, she sagged to the ground.

The assassin's dismay was as obvious as it was comical. He couldn't hold the knife to her throat without going down with her, thus compromising his mobility. In the split second before he lunged sideways, opting to run rather than continue with his threat to slit Cleona's throat, Kevan made his move, throwing his weight forward to hit her assailant square in the belly with his shoulder.

Time slowed to a crawl as the two men crashed to the pavement together. Despite the force of the impact, the assassin retained his grip on the knife. Kevan reached for the weapon, knowing he would have little or no time to react before the knife arced down to take his life. Better him than Cleona. He was her protector, and if this was the sacrifice he had to make to save her, so be it. His statement regarding the university bombing had already been given and recorded. Beyond that testimony and his duty to ensure Cleona's safety, his life meant nothing.

But that didn't mean he had to admit defeat. He managed to block the first murderous stab, but his opponent was strong and quick, canceling out any advantage Kevan might have had by being the first to strike. Every grappling move was countered by another just as savvy as those Kevan had acquired from the Array. One minute he had the upper position only to lose it a second later and be flipped onto his back.

Shouts from the guards had no effect on his adversary. With a venomous snarl, he seized Kevan by the throat with his left hand and raised the other for a killing strike. Ignoring the fierce grip on his throat, Kevan grabbed his opponent's right arm with both hands and forced it back.

The man screamed in agony as his shoulder joint gave way with a sickening pop that was immediately followed by a loud crack as Jack struck the assassin's knife hand with his police baton. The knife flew from nerveless fingers in a tumbling, flashing arc, but it wasn't until Cleona moved in from behind to loop her purse strap around the man's neck and twist it tight that he finally released the crushing pressure on Kevan's throat.

Kevan sucked in a breath, amazed that air would even flow

through his battered airway. As the spots finally began to fade from his vision, he saw Cleona dealing with the assassin in a manner that made Kevan very glad she was on his side.

"You murdering son of a bitch," she snapped, giving her purse another twist. "Like that, do you? Now you know how your victims feel."

"Enough now, Cleona." Jack's voice was gentle yet firm as he attempted pull her back. "We'll take it from here."

"Oh, no," she shouted, elbowing the guard aside. "Not until I hear this bastard confess." She yanked hard on her purse and took a step back, dragging her erstwhile assailant a short distance across the tarmac in a remarkable display of strength. "You kill people for a living, don't you? That university bombing ten years ago. You killed Kevan's parents and nearly killed him. Who's your boss? Who's paying you?"

"Don't know," the man gasped. "Don't know."

"A likely story," she scoffed. "You must have some idea. Your people brought down a 747 two weeks ago. I nearly died in that crash. Tell me you didn't know that was going to happen. Tell me!"

He shook his head, clawing at the strap around his neck. "Don't know anything about that."

Confronted with two menacing guards and an enraged Cleona, either he truly didn't know or he was being paid—perhaps even blackmailed—to keep quiet. Kevan wouldn't have been a bit surprised if he'd had a cyanide capsule built into one of his teeth. Although if he did, he obviously wasn't planning to use it or he would have crunched it by now.

"Let him go, Cleona," Kevan said hoarsely. "He might be doing his employer's dirty work, but he probably doesn't know who's behind the plot any more than Conall did."

"It has to be the oil companies," Cleona insisted, stomping her foot. "Has to."

"Maybe," the man admitted. "Don't know for sure."

"Yeah, *right*." The disgust in her tone as she unwound her purse from the bloke's neck should've been enough to make anyone confess.

It didn't, of course. He merely sat up and rubbed his shoulder, seeming resigned to his fate.

Jack looked downright cheerful as he dangled a pair of handcuffs in front of his newest prisoner's face. "No worries. We've a load of other questions for you to answer, starting with your name."

Upon receiving no response other than a mulish scowl, Jack and the other guard hauled the man to his feet. The subsequent pat-down yielded nothing beyond a wallet, the incriminating message, and a set of keys.

"Hmm… Yassim Haddad," Jack said as he scanned the wallet's contents. "That is, if we can believe your driver's license. Let's get you back to the station. In addition to the questions I mentioned, we have all sorts of charges we can bring against you. Starting with trespassing and ending with murder."

"Don't forget GBH," Kevan said, running a fingertip over his scarred cheek.

"Aye. We'll tack on a bit of grievous bodily harm for good measure." Jack slapped on the handcuffs. "I'm sorry if this hurts your shoulder, Yassim, but it can't be helped."

"What about her?" Haddad asked with a nod toward Cleona.

"Her?" Jack echoed. "Why, she'll probably get a medal for bravery."

"That isn't what I mean," Haddad said. "Look at her."

One glance at Cleona had Kevan scrambling to his feet and rushing toward her, his own injuries forgotten. "Cleona!"

Tears streamed down her cheeks as she pressed the heels of her hands against her temples, her eyes wide with shock.

Kevan took her in his arms, smoothing the hair back from her face. "What is it, love?"

She leaned against his chest, crying in earnest. "The Array," she whispered between sobs. "They're gone."

Chapter 29

THE SENSE OF LOSS WAS OVERWHELMING. "I FEEL LIKE EVERY ONE OF my best friends vanished at the same time." Cleona hadn't realized how much a part of her the Array had become. Even when they were silent, they were always there, just beneath the surface of her consciousness. Her mind echoed with an emptiness she'd never associated with normalcy. But of course, normal was precisely what that emptiness was. As a general rule, no one had a collection of souls ready and waiting to offer advice or encouragement, although, as superpowers went, it was one of the more useful.

"Are you sure?" Kevan asked. "Not just some of them?"

She shook her head. "They're *all* gone. This must have been what they were waiting for." She searched his face for evidence that he'd undergone a similar alteration. "What about you? Are yours still there?"

"Probably not," he admitted. "I felt a bit of a twinge a moment ago. But then, I'm guessing I didn't have as many rattling around in my head as you did."

"We should take pictures of each other to see if they're still there."

"Later," he said, giving her a squeeze. "I'm sure Jack wants us back at the station to make our statements. We need to get going."

She heaved a sigh. "Do you suppose this means it's over?"

"Not completely. This is only the end of a chapter, not the entire story."

"You're right. What with all the excitement, I'd almost forgotten about giving Ranjiv that interview and delivering Emhart's formula to the world. Seems like forever since we talked to him and Jillian." She hesitated, wondering if her next question was too trivial—or too selfish. "Do you suppose I'll still be able to play the piano?"

He grinned. "If not, you can always take lessons."

"True. But having that natural—" She paused as a curlew called to its mate, then smiled as she identified the notes. "Well…at least some of it seems to be there." She glanced up at the castle. The sky had cleared, eliminating some of the structure's sinister nature. Was the ghost hovering nearby? Or had it moved on with the rest of the Array?

The slamming of a car door diverted her attention from the castle and its ghost. Haddad had already been stowed in the back seat of the unmarked car while Conall remained in Jack's Isuzu.

Jack waved and started toward them. "That's one mystery solved. Opened up another can of worms, of course, but we'll see how that plays out. You two can come by the station tomorrow and we'll take your statements and get some photos of your injuries to use as evidence. Not strictly necessary considering the scope of this case, but the assault will give us something to start with. Proving Haddad was involved in the university bombing may take some doing, especially given that the case is pretty much cold." He tipped up his cap. "Right now, if I were you, I'd head for the nearest pub." Arching an eyebrow, he peered at Cleona. "Or should I suggest a visit to a hospital?"

"No," she said firmly. "I'm okay. I probably hurt him more than he hurt me. I'm more concerned about Kevan."

Kevan winced as he rubbed his neck. "I should have some colorful bruises for your photos by tomorrow, but it doesn't feel as though there's any lasting damage."

"We'll be off then." Jack extended a hand. "I don't know how you two managed it, and quite frankly, I'm not sure I want to know. But thank you."

Kevan gave the guard's hand a firm shake. "Thank you for believing in us. Not everyone would have."

"If it weren't for *that*"—Jack inclined his head toward the cars containing his two prisoners—"I might have given up on you. But I certainly can't argue with the results." He held out his hand again. "Cleona, it has truly been a pleasure."

Cleona ignored his offer of a handshake and gave him a hug instead. "Thanks, Jack. You've been great." She took a step back. "Do me one favor? Take a picture of us in front of the castle?"

"I'd be happy to," Jack replied.

Cleona opened the camera app and handed over her phone. "Just tap the little shutter thingy."

Ignoring Kevan's quizzical expression, she wrapped an arm around his waist and leaned closer, smiling for the camera.

After taking a few photos, Jack handed her the phone. "Should be at least one good shot in there."

"Thanks," she said. "See you tomorrow."

With a quick wave in farewell, Jack headed back to his car. Cleona pocketed her phone and watched him go. As soon as the two vehicles rounded the bend in the road, her eyes were drawn to the rough, gorse-covered slope. Beyond the scattering of houses above the pastures, she glimpsed the crest of the fort. A subtle nudge from within fixed her gaze on the stone wall. If there was one thing she'd learned from this adventure, it was to not ignore even the slightest whim.

"Let's take a run up to the fort," she said. "A pub sounds great, but right now, I feel the need to do something touristy."

Kevan laughed. "You can't fool me. You're hoping to commune with Mother Earth again, aren't you?"

"Either her or Susan. I didn't tell you about that, did I?" She rubbed her temple. The sharp pain caused by the Array's departure had gone, but the soreness remained. "Sorry. Having all those extra people in my head must have made me assume everyone is privy to my thoughts." She went on to relate her experience at the sentry tower on Garnish Island, ending with, "Susan was tough as nails during the disaster, but now, she seems…devastated."

"I can't blame her for that," he said. "I know the feeling."

"Yeah. I suppose you do." She smiled up at him, loving the warmth of his smile and the kindness in the depths of his dark eyes—eyes that captivated her regardless of their expression. "I'll have to make a point of keeping you informed. I don't need to hide anything from you or make excuses. I like that."

"So do I." Dipping his head, he pulled her close until their lips met in a kiss filled with love, passion, and the promise of even better things to come.

* * * *

Half an hour later, Cleona stood atop the fort's southern wall, gazing down at the castle as the chilly fingers of the wind off the bay found their way past her jacket. "Do you suppose it really happened the way we remember it?"

"What? You mean with the ghosts and spirits and such? Aye, it did." If anything, Kevan looked more heroic than he had when he'd come charging to her rescue. The wind swept his dusky curls back from his face while the azure sky outlined his commanding profile. His was the kind of face that would grow more beautiful with age—

the sharp planes of his nose and forehead contrasting with the gentler curves of his lips and chin, along with the smile that transformed his brooding visage from forbidding to something far more approachable.

"Unless we're both sharing the same hallucinations."

He shrugged. "I don't think Jack minds if we're a bit bonkers. As long as we don't come across that way in court."

"No kidding." Truth be told, she'd have given a lot for another spiritual event. Why else was she there? The view was as breathtaking as any other she'd encountered in Ireland. Mother Earth should have been talking her ears off. Instead, she only felt a gentle hand on her shoulder, more of a congratulatory pat than a slap of reproach or even a nudge of encouragement. She smiled to herself as she realized she no longer needed voices in her head to tell her she was on the right path. The truth was part of her now, as unshakable and unassailable as the ancient stones upon which she stood.

Was this how Jillian felt after completing her allotted task? A sort of oneness with the planet? Possibly, although Cleona hadn't been able to communicate with Jillian the way she had with Susan. She'd utilized the more traditional methods to talk to her. Location might have been a factor She and Susan had both been standing atop lookout towers at the time. Prior to that, Cleona had been able to see Susan standing on the cliff's edge. It wasn't until she'd climbed to the top of O'Brien's Tower that Susan had been able to talk back. Perhaps the fort didn't rate as a communication tower the way the other structures had, and God only knew where Susan was now. Cleona had told her to go to Liscannor to rent a boat or at least talk to the fishermen there. That was yesterday. Had she gone there yet? If so, she might be out to sea somewhere about now.

Scary thought.

Cleona gazed out across the surrounding hills and distant mountains, gaining strength and comfort from their solid forms until the sparkling sea drew her eye. Perhaps Susan's power would come from the ocean. She'd been a bulwark of strength when they were on the water. Had that subconscious suspicion been what prompted her to send Susan to Liscannor? Hoping she would regain the strength she'd lost?

Cleona still hadn't come to terms with Susan's delayed reaction and her insistence that everything she cared about had gone down with the plane. Logic suggested that only a lover or husband could elicit a bond of that magnitude. But who? Did it matter?

Jillian had broken up with her fiancé before boarding that doomed flight, whereas Cleona had never had one to begin with. They'd both come through okay. What made Susan so different?

"I was in love." Susan's anguished voice came from out of nowhere, but with such clarity, she might have joined the two of them at the fort. "And now he's gone."

Turning toward the north, as if on command, Cleona could see Susan as though she stood a few feet away rather than hundreds of miles. "Don't let his death stop you from bringing the instigators to justice," Cleona urged. "We need to work together on this. I have some ideas, but I'm guessing you'll be the one to crack the case."

Susan's short laugh was devoid of any pleasure. "Not when everyone involved is dead. Dead men don't tell tales, you know."

"But the authorities are diving on the wreck, aren't they? Surely they'll find *something*. Some clue…"

"I don't *need* clues," Susan snapped. "I know who did it. I even know why. Too bad I can't prove it."

"Yet," Cleona amended. "The spirits of the dead have been helping me and Jillian. If you let them, they'll help you too."

"They already have—if you can call that 'help.'" Susan's tone remained harsh and angry. "I know things I wish I didn't know about a bunch of strangers I've never even met. I've dreamed about the crash from at least fifty different perspectives. What they *aren't* telling me is what I can possibly do about it."

Cleona was undeterred. "Trust me, Susan. They're more help than you realize. If you allow them to coach you, they're almost like having an onboard computer. I called mine the Array. They're gone now, but at one time, there must've been dozens of them. And yes, they were strangers; I only knew one guy's name. Jillian was different. She picked up three women who were seated in the same row with her on the plane. She'd actually spoken with them and knew exactly who they were. My best advice is to hang in there and try to work with your group. Once their tasks are fulfilled, they'll move on. By the way, where are you?"

"I'm at the top of the same damn tower I talked to you from the last time. Why the devil can't you use a phone?"

"I suppose I could," Cleona replied, biting back a smile. "But you must admit this…*link* we have is pretty cool." Considering Susan's current frame of mind, it seemed prudent to refrain from using words like "supernatural" or "telepathic" to describe their connection. Susan didn't strike her as the type to believe in such things. "I have to actually use my phone to talk to Jillian." She wondered why. Perhaps it was because Jillian wasn't in Ireland.

Maybe there's not as much magic in England.

"Yeah, well, thirty years ago, cell phones were hot stuff too."

"Not as neat as this,' Cleona insisted. "Like I told my cousin, I get better reception from these ancient stone towers than I do over any transmitter my phone would use."

"You're overlooking the convenience factor. I for one am getting sick and tired of climbing this tower."

Ruffle her feathers too much, and Susan would do as she'd threatened and simply go home. Just where that home was, Cleona didn't know, although she *did* know that a change of topic was in order. "Did you talk to the guys from the boat?"

"Not yet," Susan replied. "I went down to the dock, but they must've been out fishing or whatever it is those guys do all day. Surely they do more than haul tourists around."

"Maybe so. I didn't think to ask. You got the right boat, though, didn't you? The *Branwyr Eostre?*" Cleona was surprised she could recall the name of the boat herself, although she owed that tidbit of information to Jillian, who'd discussed the name as well as its meaning with the elder of the two fishermen. At the time, Cleona had been too rattled to care.

"That's the one I asked about," Susan said. "I'll check back this evening. A guy at the dock told me I'd be more likely to catch them after six."

Cleona didn't bother to ask why Susan hadn't gone back to the dock on the previous evening. Something told her that until this particular exchange, she had no intention of going anywhere near Liscannor ever again. "Listen, Kevan and I just helped the police catch an assassin who's been targeting scientists engaged in alternative energy research, along with some of the more progressive politicians who'd like to see it implemented. Jillian solved a similar case in London. Now it's your turn."

"I can't even find a couple of fishermen," Susan said with a groan. "Catching criminals is out of my league."

"You won't be doing it alone." Cleona glanced at Kevan. "I've had help, and so did Jillian. I'm thinking maybe you should team up with those fishermen." She had one particular man in mind, although given Susan's attitude toward him at the time of their rescue, she probably wouldn't be too anxious to see him again. Perhaps that was why she was dragging her feet.

"Ugh. I hope you aren't referring to the younger one—Sean something or other. All he cared about was that he'd picked up a blonde, a brunette, and a redhead. I can't believe he'd be much help with anything."

"As I recall, his name was Seamus Quinn," Cleona said with a wry smile. "You know...the one who claimed to be partial to fierce, ginger-haired women?"

"Did he now?" Susan's tone indicated that Seamus's sense of humor still hadn't found favor with her. "I'm surprised you remember that. I certainly don't."

Cleona suspected Susan wasn't being entirely honest with her, but let it pass. "I'm sure he'll remind you once you've seen him again."

"*If* I see him again. I still don't get why finding him is so important."

"Don't worry. You will." Susan might have been doubtful, but Cleona was more convinced than ever. Perhaps Mother Earth was nudging her again. Cleona succumbed to a fit of the giggles as the obvious clincher presented itself. "Believe me, Susan. This is how it's supposed to work. Why else would we be able to communicate like this?"

"Are we really communicating?" After a sardonic laugh, she added, "For all I know, you could be a figment of my imagination. I've already decided I've gone berserk. Talking to you like this is just another symptom."

Cleona tapped her chin. "I'm not entirely sure, but I'm guessing most crazy people don't know they're crazy. They think their hallucinations are real and everyone else is nuts."

"Hmm... You may be right about that. Aside from the fact that a phone call wouldn't be quite as convincing."

"Exactly." Cleona frowned as a different aspect of their conversation occurred to her. "You must've been pretty close to that tower. I mean, I only got the idea to come up here a little while ago."

Susan shrugged as a gust of wind swept her auburn hair away from her face. "Great minds and all that nonsense, I guess."

Cleona's eyes narrowed. "You're lying. You were hanging around the Cliffs of Moher again, weren't you?" Hopefully, not about to jump into the sea.

"I can't help it, Cleona. That's the only place I can get any peace."

"Hmm…well, if you ever want a life beyond those cliffs, you're gonna have to get going and solve your part of the mystery."

Susan's relenting sigh was nearly lost on the wind. "Okay. I'll try, but I'm not sure I have the energy."

"That's where Seamus comes in. If he can get you riled up after rescuing you—and giving you the sweater off his back—he might be able to give you the gumption to see this through to the end."

For the first time, Susan's quiet laugh actually held a trace of amusement. "So his job is to annoy the crap out of me, huh?"

"If that's what it takes, yes." Cleona smiled at Kevan. He'd never annoyed her. Not once. Their connection had been a powerful one from the very beginning. Would that rapport continue now that their mission was accomplished? As with any other relationship, only time would tell.

"We'll see," Susan said with a roll of her eyes. "I'm not promising anything."

"You don't have to promise. Believe me, things will start happening and you won't be able to stop until you've figured it all out."

"I hope you're right." Susan consulted her watch. "Guess I'd better head on back to Liscannor and get this over with."

"Good luck."

Within seconds, Susan's image vanished. Not even the echo of her voice remained.

Cleona stared out across the vast stretch of green hills and iron-grey mountains before her, still amazed at the turn of events. The impossible made possible. Could they actually save the world?

A restless movement at her side brought her back to the present. "Don't suppose you heard all of that, did you?"

"I got the gist of it," Kevan replied. "Think you lit a big enough fire under her tail?"

"No telling. I'm not even sure it was necessary. She has plenty of drive. If you'd seen her after the crash… She was awesome."

"You're pretty awesome yourself. I still can't believe you let Haddad capture you like that. I nearly had heart failure when he put that knife to your throat."

She shrugged. "It was all part of the plan. Besides, I knew you could take him."

"That's a hell of a lot more than I knew," Kevan insisted. "It's not every day a shepherd takes on an assassin and comes out alive."

"I was a bit out of my element as well," she reminded him. "Knowing I had backup made a huge difference."

He nodded as though he understood. After all, Cleona wasn't the only one with an Array. "So… What now?"

"I want to plant a garden," she said after a moment's reflection. "A place of beauty and peace. Something to remind us of what happened here and of what the world is still in danger of losing."

"I've the perfect spot for that," he said. "You've only to promise to be here to tend it."

Taking his hand, she laced her fingers with his. "Promising is easy. Helping things grow is much harder."

"Not really. All it takes is a bit of effort and a little love."

"I can do that." She turned toward him, brushing a windblown strand of hair from her eyes. "What about you?"

A tiny smile twitched the corner of his mouth. "I want to start living again. With you."

Cleona rose up on her toes and kissed him. "You'll get no arguments from me, Kevan MacFinnin. I'm with you all the way."

About the Author

A native of Louisville, Kentucky, Cheryl Brooks is a former critical care nurse who resides in rural Indiana with her husband, two sons, two horses, three cats, and one dog. Her **Cat Star Chronicles** series was first published by Sourcebooks Casablanca in 2008, and includes *Slave, Warrior, Rogue, Outcast, Fugitive, Hero, Virgin, Stud, Wildcat*, and *Rebel*. Her **Cowboy Heaven** series, also published by Sourcebooks Casablanca, includes *Cowboy Delight* (a novella), *Cowboy Heaven*, and *Must Love Cowboys*. Look for her new **Cat Star Legacy** series from Sourcebooks beginning in 2018. In addition to the **Soul Survivors** trilogy, *Echoes From the Deep, Dreams From the Deep*, and *Justice From the Deep*, she has one self-published erotic romance, *Sex, Love, and a Purple Bikini*, and two erotic short stories, *Midnight in Reno*, and *Pontoon*. Her **Unlikely Lovers** series includes *Unbridled, Uninhibited, Undeniable*, and *Unrivaled*. She has also published *If You Could Read My Mind* writing as Samantha R. Michaels. As a member of *The Sextet*, she has written several erotic novellas published by Siren/Bookstrand. Her other interests include cooking, gardening, singing, and guitar playing. Cheryl is a member of RWA and IRWA. You can visit her online at www.cherylbrooksonline.com or email her at cheryl.brooks52@yahoo.com